GOD OF MISCHIEF

VIVIENNE SAVAGE

Table of Contents

Chapter 1

Selene ran a comb through her dark hair as she hurried down the carpeted hotel hallway. Late as usual, she blamed an overcomplicated hotel alarm clock for the delayed start to her morning routine.

To make matters worse, awakening had ended the best dream ever. She couldn't remember all of it, only that there had been dragons. Beautiful dragons, and one of them had ebony scales like glossy chips of volcanic glass reflecting sunlight.

"Shelby?" She knocked on her friend's room. "C'mon, we gotta get down there or we'll miss the shuttle."

It shouldn't have surprised her that Shelby was also late to awaken, since they'd stayed out late at a Cinco de Mayo celebration.

A noise erupted from beyond the heavy door, like the hacking sound of an *Alien* facehugger victim. It opened to frame a red-nosed and puffy-eyed Shelby wrapped in a blanket cocoon. Her ginger hair clung to her sweaty brow.

"Girl, I'm too sick to go."

"Oh nooo," Selene breathed. A surge of concern swept away her irritation, and she stepped forward, only for Shelby to ward her off with an outstretched hand.

"I should have known I was coming down with something. My throat itched all yesterday afternoon."

"Do you need me to go get you anything? There's a Walgreens around the corner."

"No, I'll be good here. I don't want to get you sick, and this is your vacation too. Just go on the tour without me."

5

"But—"

"Go on. Have fun. Mingle and meet people. Bring me back some wine." Shelby turned her head and coughed into her elbow, grimacing all the while. "*Lots* of wine."

Half an hour later, Selene sat alone on the shuttle and gazed out the window, focused on the passing scenery. They drove by rows upon rows of grapes on gentle slopes, and if Shelby were there, her wine expert friend would have named each variety. Selene's ignorance on the subject had inspired Shelby's motivation for booking two seats on the wine tour.

At the age of thirty-six, she'd accomplished all her priority goals, at least the ones possible through hard work and perseverance. Now that she owned a bakery, she answered to no boss—except for the tiny, niggling voice in the back of her mind telling her to rise and shine earlier, stay open later, and work harder to fulfill orders.

Business was booming. She'd made a name for herself. She had good friends, reliable employees, and a loving family.

But her romantic life belonged in the toilet and had been circling the drain ever since a messy divorce from her college sweetheart. Selene sighed. Now wasn't the time to think about Carlos and everything he'd done, despite his recent phone calls. She had to remain stalwart in moving on, and she'd begin with a day tour of the best wineries in the San Francisco area.

A serene smile came to her face as she gazed through the window at the cheery California sunshine. Warmth welcomed them as they stepped off at their first stop, and she followed the group inside, unsure of how to join anyone. A bachelorette party of five occupied the table to her immediate left. A pretty blonde wearing a plastic tiara with a short bridal veil was surrounded by laughing friends. She overheard a couple mentioning their

oneymoon to another group on the shuttle and saw a quartet
f sailors in their summer whites.

Then there was the broody cover model, a man who had
een sitting alone in the back of the shuttle, dark hair free around
is shoulders and piercing green eyes focused on some point
eyond the windows. He oozed sex appeal, his lean body clothed
n tailored slacks and a fitted, high-end shirt. She imagined the
nuscles beneath it, and her mouth went dry.

He didn't even notice she existed, or anyone else, for that
natter. She saw a few women from the bridal party checking
im out behind his back, but he remained aloof, failing to
nteract with anyone once their group moved inside the winery.

Who did that? Who went out on a social event to blow off
ther people?

Oh yeah, she did. Selene quickly stuffed her judgment away.
Maybe he'd had plans to attend with a friend too.

After being directed to the long counter, an attendant passed
out sheets listing all the wines available with spaces to jot down
asting notes. Selene took hers and glanced up to see what
veryone else was doing. Her gaze drifted from person to
erson, then stopped on the handsome rock star, startled to see
he was looking back at her from the opposite end of the long
oar.

They made eye contact and he held her gaze. A shot of pure,
unadulterated lust pulsed through her body. Eyes like his should
oe illegal, his come-fuck-me stare an unfair advantage.

"You here alone, darling?" A well-dressed guy with a
opsided smile leaned into her space from the left and jerked her
attention away. He propped himself up against the counter as
though it was the only thing keeping him upright.

"Excuse me?" Irritated by the invasion to her personal space, she shifted her weight back to put an extra inch of space between them.

"Pretty lady like you shouldn't be drinking all alone." He moved in close again. "Give me a reason why I shouldn't buy you a full glass."

No one noticed her discomfort, too wrapped up in their own groups to pay her and her unwanted, tipsy admirer any attention.

"I can give you two good reasons," she began. "One, I don't need a full glass. And two, I'm actually waiting on someone."

The lie made her twitch, but it seemed the best way to go. She hated confrontations.

Unfortunately, her annoying companion didn't seem to take the hint.

***

Loki enjoyed the wine tours as a getaway from the hustle and bustle of his everyday life. Few people struck up conversation during the shuttle rides, and no one ever came alone.

He relished the anonymity, traveling as a stranger among strangers too distracted to recognize his face from the cover of Forbes. He liked that too. Many looked, but no one truly *saw* him. They saw stylish clothes, good looks, and the array of cards in his wallet whenever he unfolded it to pay a bill.

With a low-level charm diverting attention from him, Loki enjoyed the peaceful ambience of the first venue chosen for the tour. He liked the tour company and enjoyed their choices in wineries, especially the hidden gems they often included in ddition to the big vineyards, but he loathed the humans who hared his space. Simpering, pea-brained idiots.

And yet he was drawn to them just the same. The years had ultured a fondness for people-watching, and sometimes he nagined himself among them in the thick of conversation, urrounded by friends who hung eagerly to his every word.

He had that with the Drakenstones now at least and with his ousin Maximilian Emberthorn, the very same cousin who hould have been here drinking wine beside him. Unfortunately, Max's twins were sick with the dragon pox, and while he didn't old it against the old fire wyrm for bowing out of their planned getaway in the city, he mourned the loss of his company.

He would have given anything to trade places with his cousin, envying Max's position with all his soul. Max had it all; a charming, intelligent dragoness for a mate and two stunning cubs. The twins enjoyed crawling over Loki's lap and begging him to show them magic, despite their mother's proclivity for sorcery too.

Dragoness mates were not easy to find, however, and while many would spawn children in contract agreements, they charged large sums of treasure without guaranteed results, which Loki knew all too well. He'd paid the fee twice, tangling with two different dragonesses, and when pregnancy didn't take with either, he'd given up.

It wasn't meant to be. A child was the one thing he couldn't whip into existence with a gesture of his hands, no matter what the old legends claimed. A mate would be even more difficult to obtain. Despite his parentage, he lacked the favorable reputation of the other ancients, known for his trickery, mischief, and troublemaking.

Loki grunted and made a small check beside another win on the list. He liked elderberries, and the inclusion of hone intrigued him.

"Ready for your first pour, sir?"

"Yes. I'll start with Malbec," Loki told the server. When he looked up again, he studied the dark-haired woman at the othe end of the counter. Like him, she had come alone. As if sensing his inspection, she looked up from her paper, her focused gaze staring through his spell.

Now that was interesting.

She looked away first, distracted by a musclebound prick or her left side. Loki's phone beeped. He read his assistant's number in the caller ID window and sighed. "Yes?"

Georgia cleared her throat. "Apologies for troubling you or a day off, but uh, sir, there are complaints that Sif has made unapproved purchases at online stores."

"Define unapproved."

"A customer stated he'd like a new PlayStation 4, and Sif ordered it using his stored credit information."

Loki snorted. "She won't do it unless activated with a 'Hello, Sif' on any standard phone. I know because I've tried it myself on a test model." The program on his personal phone required less, written to suit his specific needs.

"There are multiple complaints—"

"Fix it then," he barked into the phone. "If the virtual assistant is making purchases, require a code on each device. People will complain about the additional level of security then disable it. At that point, it's beyond our control."

"Yes, sir. Of course. Enjoy your vacation."

Loki sighed and ended the call. While he preferred to keep a personal touch over Ragnarok Enterprises, some issues deserved to be delegated to the rest of his senior staff. Upon olving the most recent dilemma, he slipped the phone away and ook the glass of red wine set down in front of him.

The first sip went down smooth, but his attention wandered ack toward the woman. She was looking at him again, ignoring he man beside her.

The guy on her left failed to get the hint.

Asshole, Loki thought. He tried to block it out, but everyone lse seemed willing to do the same thing, or they were too bsorbed in their own parties. Unfortunately, his acute hearing icked up every word.

"Baby, why don't I buy you this bottle of wine, and we can o back to my place and kick it. Just the two of us."

"I really don't—"

"What's stopping you? I don't see anyone here yet," the man persisted. "Name's Ben. I come by once a month to pick up my wine club order."

Not my business, not my business. The human can take care of herself. Loki convinced himself to look away, but then he saw her wildly searching the area, as if hoping someone would speak up. The server was occupied, busy pouring glasses for a group of eight.

Loki growled under his breath and watched the exchange.

"I have a boyfriend."

"Well, I don't see him here."

Is that so?

If there was anything Loki loved, it was the chance to play the part of the mischief-maker, and there were few things more troubling to a man than cockblocking.

And it was safer than conjuring a handful of venomous spiders into the man's pockets.

Abandoning his seat in the corner, Loki dropped the magical veil and crossed the floor in a few smooth steps to reach the girl's side. "My apologies. I didn't mean to keep you waiting—"

He saw her name scrawled across the top of the wine sheet. "—Selene," Loki added pleasantly.

Ben lingered, confused by the appearance of competition.

Selene raised her brows. "No problem," she said in an ever voice, appearing uncertain. "I was telling this *gentleman* a momen ago that I thought my boyfriend would be here soon, and here you are."

Ben sized Loki up.

Loki turned to the failed charmer and stood taller, staking a claim he didn't know he wanted until he came within arm's length of Selene. "Do you have a reason to remain standing there, or were you perhaps hoping my woman would deny you again?"

"Whatever, dude." Defeated and disappointed, Ben backed away and moved to the winery's cashier counter. Loki chuckled after he was gone and turned to find Selene studying him warily.

"Thank you," she said. "He wasn't getting the clue, and I thought I'd have to make a scene."

He waved it off. "Nothing to it." His eyes followed Ben's progress through checkout until he slunk through the door.

"Still, you didn't have to do that, so thanks."

Loki lingered as Selene's body angled toward him and her appraising eyes drank him in, roving from head to toe.

She had to be the most attractive mortal he'd ever seen, and eye contact with her made him uncomfortable in several ways. He couldn't look away from her perfect pink lips or stop admiring her high cheekbones. The smell of her, an intoxicating blend of rose, jasmine, and orange blossom, didn't disguise the subtle traces of magic clinging to her skin and wavy black hair. A witch perhaps. If so, it explained how she'd seen through his spell.

Had she bewitched him? No, he told himself. No mortal could ensorcell Loki the dragon god of mischief. No human had the power.

He realized he was staring and snapped out of it. "As I said, think nothing of it."

"How'd you know my name was Selene?"

"You wrote it on the wine menu."

"Oh." Her gaze dropped to the paper.

He couldn't help the smile that slipped to his face. "Did you believe they'd collect them like a grade school assignment?"

"Well, no," she muttered. "I really don't know the first thing about what I'm doing here to be honest. Everything sounds good by the description, but I know better than to fall for that. The one time I tried a glass of this fancy stuff, it claimed to smell like orange peel and plum, and something about subtle cocoa nuances, but tasted like dirt."

"Then you were given a very poor, and likely cheap, introduction. You'll find these much better, I'm sure."

"Thanks again, mister...?"

"Luka. A pleasure."

A hot blush rose in her cheeks when he took her hand and raised her knuckles to his lips. The gesture may have gone out of style, but he preferred it whether mortal men lost their manners or not.

"Now... where shall we begin? Red wines can be difficult to enjoy when improperly paired. You may find that one to your liking. It's smooth and more fruit forward, lighter on the woody flavors. I own a bottle, in fact, although it was gifted to me by a relative."

Selene eyed the pricey bottle and made a hesitant check beside it. "So you're a wine aficionado then?"

"I don't consider myself an aficionado, but once you've attended enough of these things, you get a taste for what to try and what to avoid."

"There are so many choices, and we only get six. How do you narrow it down?"

"Practice, I suppose. Or just knowing what you prefer. Here, I think you'd enjoy this white as well. The 2014 has a hint of orange blossom." After a pause he added, "Or you can tell me to shut the hell up because you've got this."

"No, please." Her laughter popped the small bubble of tension in the air between them. "I was supposed to be here with my friend, but she woke up sick as all hell. So here I am, lost and alone."

As he marked his own list, he noticed how her body language remained open, matched by his casual lean against the counter. With no signs of her discouraging further contact, he claimed the seat beside her.

"You're certainly not alone now, and if you're feeling brave, I'm willing to share."

"Oh, I couldn't," she protested. "I mean, what if I caught Shelby's germs?"

"Trust me, I'm never sick," he said with a dismissive wave. And if she knew the reason why, he suspected she'd probably be halfway across the parking lot.

Chapter 2

They drank away the morning, tasting a bevy of wines and sharing their samples. With Luka as her companion and friendly guide, Selene discovered several vintages within her budget. She left each of the first two wineries with a bottle for Shelby, and a half case to be shipped home. By the time they reached their third destination, she was starved for the picnic lunch that came as part of the tour.

She and Luka sat together at the end of the long table set up for their group and shared a bottle of chilled, sweet wine with their crackers, cheese, and assorted meats.

Luka exuded sophistication, from his accent to the way he held his glass. So what if he talked like one of those men on the set of *Vikings*? She found his voice fascinating but couldn't pinpoint his country of origin, and she certainly wasn't nosy enough to ask. If anything, she hoped their conversation would last long enough for him to bring it up.

British? No. European for certain, but definitely not a Brit. This man originated from somewhere east of London, and her mind spun with a dozen possibilities. The only immigrant she'd ever met was a Scotsman in college. They'd dated briefly before he went back to Glasgow, but she'd never expected to meet a man with a yummier voice.

Luka startled Selene out of her thoughts with a question. "Do you live in this area?"

"Me? Oh, no, I'm only visiting my friend." She and Shelby had taken a week-long exclusive course with a local pastry chef, an inside connection they'd been offered thanks to their days in a local culinary school. She'd planned it out so she could have a few extra days to enjoy the sights. "I'm from Virginia," she offered. "But I love this area. It's so pretty. You?"

"I've lived in the area for a while now. My cousin was supposed to join me, he actually made all the arrangements for this tour, but he bowed out when his twins fell ill with dr—" He stopped and quietly chuckled. "With chickenpox."

"That's never fun. I hope they get better soon."

"I'll pass along your kind regards, thank you." He smiled, then laughed at himself. "I suppose Max won't believe that I socialized with a human being."

"Sort of a loner, huh?"

Luka shrugged. "So you flew across the country to see a friend?"

"Uh-huh. Well, that and because we both were taking part in a specialty cooking class."

"Oh?" His brows rose. "Are you a chef?"

"Oh gods, no." She laughed, the sound bubbling up with ease. "I tried the whole restaurant kitchen thing, and it's just too frantic. Too stressful."

"Then what *do* you do?"

"I bake. I mean, I *can* cook other stuff, but for work, I bake." She owned a bakery of her own, but a stroke of modesty left her too shy to say more.

"If it doesn't come in a box containing pre-measured ingredients, I find ways to spoil it."

She laughed. "Cooking isn't that hard. Just follow the recipe and don't wander off."

"I must admit, the past few years of my survival are credited to the kindness of others preparing my meals for me. I eat out often or order in." He leaned back in his seat and grinned. "Did the seminar cover baking?"

"I have a few new recipes to test out, but enough about me. What about you? What field are you in?"

"Technology. I, ah…" The good humor faded, transitioning to a guarded expression.

Selene's smile fell away. "Is it top-secret government spy stuff?" she asked, keeping her voice light.

"No. Sorry. It's complicated and rather dull," he explained. "I design electronics programs of varying sorts. Operating systems and software. I live at my computer."

At no detriment to his physical appearance, apparently. When he reached for the wine bottle on their table, his bicep flexed and his shirt sleeve stretched taut over his defined arms. She imagined a lean, strong body beneath the fabric, covered in a healthy, bronzed glow.

A smug, self-satisfied look came over his face, prompting Selene to look away in a hurry.

"All right, folks, we'll be heading out in about twenty minutes, so if you have any purchases to make, now's the time," their shuttle driver called out.

"Shall we?" Luka rose and offered his arm in the manner of a gentleman, the gesture from a time lost long ago.

With each passing moment, an animal sort of attraction developed between them. Raw, unadulterated lust stirred her comatose libido and placed fantasies of undressing her handsome companion. She hadn't experienced desire in a while, not since long before her divorce.

By afternoon, she'd added another four bottles to her already hefty list of wines to be shipped home. She had the start of her own cellar. Tipsy, she giggled.

"What's so funny?" Luka asked.

"Me. The wine newb with, how many did I buy altogether? Ten?"

"More like sixteen." He laughed and finished signing for his final purchase.

"Right. Me, the wine newb with her own collection of wine."

Luka grinned. "It's an addiction."

He was an addiction. Selene had lost count of how many times she let her eyes roam up and down his body, or how often she leaned up against him so she could breathe in his cologne. She had the insatiable urge to run her fingers through his long hair and see if it felt as soft and silky as it looked. Between the black waves that fell to the middle of his back, his thick lashes and full lips, Luka should have appeared feminine. Instead, he was the furthest thing from a girl she could imagine, a masculine Adonis who was way out of her league.

"So… what do you plan to do once this vacation in California ends?" he asked as they stepped out from their last stop into the balmy evening air.

"Go back to real life, you know? Job, house payments—all that fun stuff. Same as you I wager." Though she suspected they led very different lives. She didn't know much about technology, except that it paid well.

They sat together at the rear of the shuttle, their thighs touching as they chatted about the wines they'd tried and which vintages she planned to share with her sick friend. During the ferry ride across the bay, he offered his jacket. It smelled amazing—spice and wood, hints of smoke and musk. She couldn't name the scent or the cologne, but it suited him.

Night had fallen by the time they returned to the city, signaling the end to what had to be one of the better days of her life. She hated for it to end.

"Next up, the Marriott," the shuttle driver announced.

"That's me. I guess we'll be parting ways, huh?" Selene twisted at the waist to meet Luka's eye and let her hand fall to his knee. He stroked his fingers across her knuckles, sweeping them in a back-and-forth motion that made her heart stutter and her pulse quicken. She despised the idea of surrendering his jacket or leaving her seat beside him. "I had an amazing time, Luka. Thank you."

"I'll walk you to the lobby."

"Don't you have your own stop?"

"No. I parked my vehicle around the block. The Marriott is as close as the next hotel."

"You really don't—"

"But I wish to all the same." He raised her hand to his lips and kissed the tip of her index finger. One by one, each digit received the same reverent treatment. "Would that be all right?"

Speechless, she nodded. A familiar satisfied smile spread across Luka's face. He lowered her hand, but he didn't relinquish his hold. Her fingers still tingled.

When the shuttle pulled in front of her hotel, the remaining wine goers called out boisterous and friendly farewells. Everyone had gotten chatty as the day progressed, shared drunkenness bonding them all together.

Luka politely inclined his head, hardly a social butterfly, but friendlier than the standoffish man who avoided them all at the start of the day. Grinning, Selene waved and stepped out into the cool night air.

"Such a gentleman," she teased, linking her arm through his when he offered it. She had Shelby's bottles of wine tucked into a tote she'd purchased in one of the gift shops.

A doorman greeted them and waved them through. Selene beamed at him and breezed through on Luka's arm.

She didn't know if it was the wine still flowing through her system or being on a hottie's arm that made her mood feel so bright and alive. Both, she decided, but the latter most of all. He escorted her through the quiet lobby to the elevator.

"Thank you again." For everything. The company. The flirtations. She'd seen him looking her over more than a few times, and once she'd thought he was going to kiss her in the shuttle, though he'd turned last minute and instead whispered a compliment against her ear. The memory of his words clenched her core with desire and made her crave the sensation of his skin against hers.

"The pleasure was mine, Selene. I…" He paused and met her gaze. "It was an honor to make your acquaintance," he finished in a softer voice.

He stood near enough to kiss her, the scent of cologne clinging to his shirt, surrounding her beneath the jacket. His breath, wine-scented and sweet, tickled her skin when he leaned close and brushed his lips against her cheek.

Behind her, a younger couple stepped off the elevator. An impulsive urge to do something reckless crashed over her after she stepped into the empty box.

Before the doors could shut, she kicked her foot out against one to make them recede. Then she reached out, grabbed him by the front of his shirt, and jerked him inside.

"I'm going to kiss you, and if I've read you completely wrong, I'm apologizing now and you can go back downstairs, no harm, no foul." It was all she managed to babble out before she pushed up against him and slanted her mouth across his.

He met her kiss with searing passion. Her back struck the wall of the elevator, and she discovered, despite his lithe, swimmer's physique, he had the power of a weightlifter. From the moment his tongue swept past her lips, the polite gentleman

ompanion of her evening vanished. A hungry, sexual beast took
is place.

His hips pressed forward, treating her to a hot, hard bulge
entered against her lower abdomen. Trembling, she ran her
ingers over the thick outline and discovered he was huge. His
lick flexed beneath her touch, and he groaned against her mouth
s she tangled her other hand in his dark hair.

Gods, he was impressive, and she hadn't even seen it yet.
Her mind flew to the three condoms tucked in her purse,
pressed on her by an older lady back home. Her kind neighbor
thought she shouldn't spend the years after her divorce alone
and had encouraged her to do what the young kids did these
days.

She'd smiled, accepted Mae's offering, then promptly
forgotten the foil packets after shoving them in the inner pocket
of her handbag.

"Stay the night," she said after she came up for breath, only
to dive right back in. He tasted like wine and sex. As she rubbed
her body against him, she was taken back to the days of being a
horny teen.

"Yes."

The elevator surged upward toward her floor without
making stops between levels, which was fortunate since Selene
savored every second of contact between them. An offer of
more filled her with a thirst too intense for kisses to quench.

Seconds after the elevator stopped and the doors slid open,
a quiet cough brought them back to reality. He separated from
Selene and released her from the wall, the disheveled pair passing
a small family waiting to enter. A young girl giggled at them, and
a teen boy stared enviously.

Without the sense to be embarrassed, she hurried with him
to her room at the end of the hall and fumbled the keycard from

her purse. She slid it three times with a nervous, trembling hand before Luka steadied her grip and did it for her. Inside, it was dark, but she bumped the entry light on, set her purse aside, and attacked his clothes. Unlike the keycard, his belt and buttons presented no opposition.

Luka shrugged off his shirt, introducing her to a masculine torso lined with muscular definition. He found the zipper to her skirt with ease then dragged it off, pulling her panties down at the same time. Her shirt was an unfortunate casualty, buttons scattering when he ripped the silk blouse open.

"You are breathtaking."

The compliment boosted her confidence and gave her the courage to continue. After peeling off her ruined shirt, she handled his pants herself, pushing them down from his hips and verifying her suspicion that he didn't wear undergarments. She made a small sound, a groan of appreciation, then took his dick in her hands. Every inch of him was perfection. Chiseled and lean, the sinewy length of him in her fingers hot and responsive to her touch. She stroked it, gliding her fist from the root to the tip, and he made a growl deep in his chest.

He was a god, as far as she was concerned, hotter than every long-haired Facebook model she'd ever seen. And for tonight at least, all hers.

"I want to see you," he said in a low voice that made her quiver. "All of you."

He fumbled with the clasps of her lace-trimmed bra. Overeager and maybe a little too enthusiastic, he pulled at it and bent all three hooks in the process before he tugged the straps down her arms. Her breasts bounced free of the troublesome thing and into his waiting palms. With only his shoes in the way of being undressed from head to toe, he kicked out of them and stepped from his pants. Bare and shameless.

"Keep the heels on," he murmured against her mouth, before his lips traveled to her ear. He nipped the sensitive shell and bumped his hips forward, fucking her hand.

Keep the heels on. The thought reminded her of pornos and sexy pin-ups. Hell, everything about their evening was like a naughty film. Two practical strangers hooking up.

Seduced by his sensual aura, she crouched and did something equally as bold, taking his length into her mouth while she reached for her purse with one hand. He filled her, stretching her generous lips wide, and she savored the few inches.

Foreign words fell from his mouth, along with pleased grunts and a deep groan of satisfaction that made Selene feel like the most powerful woman in the world. Luka was at her mercy, and she relished every moment. The first salty drops of precum flavored her mouth.

While feeling blindly for her purse, she knocked it from the counter. Its contents, including the object of her search, tumbled onto the floor. Coming off him with a soft, wet pop, she ripped the foil and took the latex ring out. It rolled over him, tight and snug, and she was suddenly grateful sweet neighbor Mae had so much confidence in her that she'd given her magnum condoms. Rising back to her feet, she practically tackled Luka into the bed.

He rolled her beneath him and surged forward, taking her without any preamble, pushing through her tight embrace until he was sheathed full to the hilt. A strong hand grabbed her by the thigh and pulled her leg over his hip, and then he withdrew, only to glide forward in another deliciously long stroke.

"Is this what you desire?" His scruffy jaw dragged across her throat; then his teeth closed around her earlobe.

"Yes."

"Louder."

"Yes!"

His relentless pace was like nothing she'd ever experienced. Unlike Carlos, the passive ex who had been content for her to do all the work, Luka demanded control, and she surrendered it to him, clinging to his muscled shoulders. Every deep-seated stroke made her cry out until she was reduced to breathless pants.

And then he stopped.

"What—"

"Turn over," he growled. His eyes shone bright as emeralds in his tanned face.

Selene complied, excitement and fear intermingled. Carlos had always used the position to get himself whether she came or not.

"Hold the headboard," he ordered in his gruff voice. His hands settled on her hips and he plucked her up, moving her further up the bed with ease, until her fingers grasped the iron rails and curled around them.

Luka slid his hands up and down her kneeling body, around the front to squeeze her breasts then back down again and around to mold against her ass. Kisses tracked their way down her spine as he repeated the pattern twice more, until she trembled and couldn't stand the separation a moment longer.

"Luka, please."

"Please what?" He scraped his teeth over the curve of her hip, nipped the delicate skin, and then suckled the stinging spot.

"Please fuck me," she begged.

"Is that all you want?" His wicked lips traced across her shoulders, and she felt him move in close behind her. His dick pressed into her back until he readjusted, and then the thick length nestled between her cheeks.

"I... I..."

"Tell me, Selene," he whispered. His arms reached around her on either side and his hands settled atop hers on the headboard.

"Make me scream," she blurted. "Make me come so hard I'll never forget it." *Or you.*

"As you desire."

A single thrust reintroduced her to his cock. He was brutal. Passionate. Each crash of their bodies knocked the bed against the wall, creating rhythmic thumps to accompany every moan and pleasured cry.

Heat built up within her body until she felt like she was a blazing inferno. Her muscles tightened, her body going taut, teetering on the precipice of ecstasy.

"I'm so close," she whimpered. "So close."

"Come for me, *skatten min*," he whispered against her ear. "I want to hear you scream my name."

"Luka."

"Louder." He bucked forward, bumping her hips upward.

"Luka!" she cried again. Her fingers tightened around the head rail.

He released one of her hands and molded his palm against her right breast, squeezing the full globe of flesh and flicking his thumb over her stiff nipple.

"I don't hear you, Selene." A slick backstroke nearly parted their bodies completely, and rather than fill her again, he stilled. His hand drifted from her breast down her body until his finger reached her clit. Then he slid forward, inch by torturous inch, while he circled the sensitive pearl with his fingertip. "Say it again. Yell it. Let everyone hear."

He drove forward hard, his cockhead bumping deep, and Selene's fragile composure shattered. His name ripped from her lips on a scream of raw pleasure and then an orgasm took her to exquisite heights with wave after wave of blazing hot bliss. Luka hastened his strokes, hands against her hips as he pounded through her shuddering contractions. Selene's eyes rolled back into her head, and behind her, Luka groaned.

It was a perfect moment. Truly unforgettable.

She sagged back against him, limp arms falling from the headboard. While sweat gleamed on her skin, Luka guided her down to the rumpled comforter and nuzzled her throat. Eyes closed, chest heaving, she tried to catch her breath and slow her racing heart.

"Do not think I am done with you yet."

"Wha—what?"

Luka chuckled and kissed his way down her body. His lips closed around her swollen clit and Selene's eyes flew open. Her hips lifted, and despite her explosive climax only seconds before, desire and need flared bright once more.

"That's right, Selene. I have many plans for you this night. Starting. Right. Here."

***

Loki awakened first to the tickle of hair against his shoulder. The scent of wine, woman, and sex surrounded him. The hotel sheets were tangled around his legs and trapped thanks to the warm, slumbering human tucked against him. She slept with her back to his chest, her hair wild and full over the pillow.

For a while, as he contemplated the previous night's events and the deep sense of satiation in his limbs, he was content to rest one arm over her sleeping form and breathe in the subtle aroma in her hair.

How could one mortal be so beautiful?

He'd taken her again and again, and when they'd used up the last ridiculous condom, he'd showed her many other ways to earn her euphoric screams.

After studying his human for a while longer, he crawled away to obey his hungering belly and hunt for the room service menu.

One glance at Selene and a memory of their lunch the previous day cemented a plan in action. Food. A lot of it. He was famished, and the hungry dragon in him wouldn't settle for a pair of whipped cream filled crepes and a cup of coffee. And something told him the woman in the bed would want more too.

After ordering their feast, receiving it, and even paying before Selene showed the first signs of rousing, he settled on the edge of the bed and fiddled with his phone. The corporate world didn't care if it was a Sunday morning; they wanted his attention now. He sent texts, composed a few e-mails, then heard the sheets rustling behind him.

"Good morning at last. I thought you'd never awaken," he said, seconds lagging between realizing she was awake and that he should speak. He didn't know how to greet a human after sex. Did they want kisses and hugs, or would playful words suffice?

He had doubts about his decision to remain when she stared as if she were looking at his true form without the human disguise.

"Morning," she whispered back at last, voice husky. "How late is it?"

"Only a quarter after nine. I did not know what you preferred for your breakfast, so I ordered some of everything."

"Wow, you ordered enough for a small army."

A spread of pancakes, bacon, sausage, toast with jam, and eggs prepared two ways occupied the round table nearby. More food than one human, or even two humans, could possibly consume.

The corner of his mouth rose in a lopsided grin when her belly rumbled in approval. "It seems that was the correct course of action," he teased.

Selene sat up, holding the sheet over her breasts as if he hadn't kissed every inch of them already. "Thank you. I, uh… have you been up long?"

His smile wavered. Had she expected him to be gone? Would she prefer if he had been? Humans were so strange, each with their own different quirks, unlike dragon women who were easy to read. He'd have never stayed in a dragoness's hoard once their coupling was over.

"It's no trouble. I keep strange hours." He tapped the phone resting in his palm to illustrate his point, but then he slid it into the pocket of the trousers he'd thrown on to answer room service.

"It must be sort of annoying. Always being reachable. Always having work at your fingertips. Do you ever take an actual full break?"

"Irritating at times." He wondered how his underlings managed to do anything without him. "But rewarding to be in a position where others feel my input is valuable," he admitted. He'd come to blame Maximilian and Ēostre for such thoughts. Humans were no longer pests; he saw them as people, and since then, he'd no longer been able to play the role of the trickster who disrupted their lives for casual amusement.

She scooted down to the end of the bed. "Is some of that coffee for me? Or have you gobbled it all down?"

"I thought it would be rude to begin without you. I waited." And now had second thoughts. It would have been simpler to eave before she awakened, open a portal home, and eat there to his heart's content.

"Thank you. It was very thoughtful."

Closer and closer she slid, until they were beside each other, he cart pulled up in front of them. After a brief hesitation, she et go of the sheet and let it pool around her waist, breasts ncovered and free. Her leg brushed up against his, her arm ouching his side. The same electric current from before sizzled between them at the light contact. His slumbering cock stirred, nd he found his appetite for food waning.

What he really wanted was to feast on her again, to have his ace between her thick thighs while she trembled, squirmed, and begged him to bring her to completion. Then he wanted to show her how his cock would feel without a condom. He didn't see the point of such things, especially considering the sticky mess they made.

"I meant what I said yesterday. I had a great time with you," Selene said, oblivious to the rock-hard tension in his pants. "I, uh…" She blushed and took a sip of coffee. "I had a really great time."

"As did I."

His skin tingled and goose bumps arose over his chilled arms. He'd been warm and comfortable seconds ago, and one spark of contact left him unsettled and wary. The foreign sensations alarmed him and made the first few minutes of their shared breakfast awkward. He ate in silence, a famished dragon who had sustained himself on crumbs the previous day to avoid alerting her to his supernatural nature. After a night in bed with her, he couldn't keep up the act any longer.

If only he could have her again, but now was the time to escape. Nefertiti had never allowed him to linger long enough to dine with her and Mahuika had only used sex to manipulate him.

"I should be on my way," he murmured.

"Oh?" She twisted and glanced at the time. "Yeah, I guess you should. I need to pack anyway."

And if she needed to pack, he needed to clear out of her space. His soul yearned to kiss her again, but if he did, he'd hold her long after checkout, their bodies glistening over the disheveled sheets.

"It was a pleasure to meet you, Selene." He abandoned his perch on the bedside and shrugged into the shirt tossed over the back of a nearby chair. "Take care during your travels home."

"Same to you. With work, I mean, since you live here and all."

He lingered a moment and tried to make sense of his conflicting emotions. Who was she, this human female, to twist everything he'd ever known and send his world off balance?

Too disturbed to puzzle it out, he walked out of her life without another word and shut the door behind him.

***

Selene fell back against the sheets and squeezed her eyes shut once he was gone.

Holy crap. Not only had she enjoyed her first one-night stand, but she'd also shared breakfast with him. Making herself get up, she found three torn condom packets strewn around the room, tossed them away, and hurried into the bathroom.

After rushing through a shower, she dressed and haphazardly threw her belongings into her bags and suitcase. Selene verified her checkout over the phone then hurried with her luggage to meet Shelby.

"Oh man, how was it?" Shelby asked when she finally opened the door.

"It was great. Here, I brought you two bottles." She thrust her gift at her friend and pushed inside, promptly opening her suitcase on the desk so she could start her packing over again.

"Um, Selene?"

"Yeah?"

"I love the wine, but I'm not so sure about this condom in the other bag."

"What!" Selene rushed over, horrified.

"Why do you have a condom? Let alone a used one?"

"Um…"

Shelby's eyes brightened. "You little slut! You got trashed and got lucky, didn't you?"

"Uh, maybe." In her rush to tidy the room for the maids and dispose of the evidence to her crime of passion, one of the condoms must have landed among her things. Or maybe it had fallen there when Luka had tossed it aside. He'd been insatiable, a beast in bed.

After disposing of the runaway condom and washing her hands in the bathroom sink, she turned to find Shelby eyeing her with skepticism. "Is that why you booked your own room? Meeting with some mysterious lover?"

"No! I told you, it was part of the travel package I bought. Anyway, I met him at the wine tour. He was alone, too, and we kinda hit it off."

"Hit it off so well you continued to hit it all night?" Shelby thrust her hips forward and fell back on her bed, laughing and coughing all at once. "Guess it's a good thing I didn't go. So, what's his name? What's he look like?"

"Luka, and he… was hot as hell." She sighed and sank down to sit. "Like, cast of *Vikings* hot, long hair and all, but dark instead of blond. And his abs…" Her mouth watered. "He said he's in technology, but he looked like a friggin' model."

"Oh my God. Pictures? Where's your phone? Lemme see him." Shelby made a feeble grasping gesture with both of her hands, but Selene's face fell.

"I didn't take any."

"What! How can I gaze upon this majesty if you didn't even stealth shot him on the shuttle?" Shelby sighed. "I am very disappointed in you. Our friendship is over."

Selene laughed at her and returned to neatly rolling her rumpled laundry to create a snug cushion for the souvenirs she'd be taking home on the plane.

"At least tell me you got his number."

"Er…"

"Selene!" Shelby tossed a pillow at her. "Seriously?"

"What? It's not like he asked for mine either, and he had his phone out when I woke up." She went on to explain about breakfast, and how he'd then excused himself. "Probably for the best since, you know, I don't even live here. Long-distance stuff? Not gonna even try it."

Shelby relented. "Fine. At least you got goofy on wine and a long overdue lay. Please tell me it was good."

"It was fantastic, and that's all I'm gonna say about it."

"Fine, you wench. Now that we've got your gossip out of the way, I have some for you."

"I thought you were lying here sick all day. How do you have gossip?"

"Because being bored as hell with nothing on TV meant I surfed social media all day," Shelby shot back.

"Yeah? What's the latest drama?"

"Looks like Carlos knocked up some chick. She was all over his wall calling him the dad, and he's saying she's a liar and he doesn't want it. You really dodged a bullet when you ditched his dumb ass, girl."

"I did." It didn't even hurt anymore. Four years had dulled the ache and guilt of filing against her husband. She felt sorry for whatever woman was trying to claim him as a dad though, because he wanted nothing to do with kids. "You going to be okay when I leave?"

"Yeah, Joe is on the way as we speak, loaded with medicine and tissues for the drive back to Los Angeles. Sorry I got sick on you, honey."

"Like you said, it worked out." Still, she mourned the missed chance to take Luka's number with her—just in case he was ever in the area.

"Lucky."

"Sorta glad we ended up with different rooms. I don't need to take your crud back to my bakery either. Anyway, my Uber driver should be here soon to take me to the airport. Call you when I'm through TSA."

Selene's driver pulled in front of the hotel as soon as she hustled outside with her luggage. He chattered, a polite and sociable man who asked about her visit, how she'd enjoyed California, and if she planned to return. She didn't have a moment of free time until she reached the gate and claimed a seat.

With her cell out, she logged into Facebook and told herself it didn't matter, that she didn't need to see the drama that was her ex-husband and his train wreck of a life. But she did. Every so often, the insecurities crept in, and Selene had to remind herself that no amount of counseling and effort could have repaired what was lost between them unless Carlos wanted it too.

She skimmed the page, saw the argument, then logged out again before texting Shelby.

Selene: Saw the shit storm. Glad you told me.

Shelby: Ignore it. I hate that I told you.

Selene: It's fine. He can't hurt me anymore.

Shelby: You sure?

Selene: I see it as sweet karma. I hope she takes him for all the money he's worth in child support. Boarding. Talk soon.

Deep down, she hadn't logged on to look for Carlos. She'd been hoping to see a friend request from her mysterious, dark-haired stranger. There was none.

Chapter 3

The late evening breeze tossed Loki's hair and ruffled the feathers of the parrot perched on his shoulder. As the wind whipped a few black strands past Socrates, the African grey caught them in his beak and preened them dutifully. For some reason, Max's bird had taken a liking to him.

But there were worse ways to spend his time than in the company of Max and Socrates, although the former had prattled continuously and the latter wouldn't stop touching him. Sitting on Saul Drakenstone's veranda with a tall glass of dark beer in his hand, Loki glowered out at the field of zebras in the adjacent pasture as he thought of San Francisco.

Three months had passed and Loki still couldn't get Selene out of his head. She lingered in his thoughts, the specter of the best sexual encounter he'd had in all his life. She'd been genuine and open, her large and caring heart an intriguing change from selfish dragonesses.

If Selene were a dragon, she'd be Ēostre's equal. Perfect in every way.

Had he been buzzed? Or even drunk? It was possible, but he despised the thought of cheapening their night together by attributing it to only the alcohol.

Despite everything he ever believed about non-shifters, he'd surrendered to their animal attraction and found himself above the most gorgeous witch he'd ever crossed. Exactly where he'd wanted to be.

Now she haunted him.

Selene had smelled like flowers and wine, with the subtle cool burn of magic whenever he inhaled around her throat. And when they spoke, her gray-blue eyes filled with interest and she listened to him.

"You've been unusually distracted," Maximilian noted, jarring Loki out of his thoughts.

After concluding his second presidential term, the fire dragon enjoyed the return of his freedom. Max and Ēostre had dismissed their secret service detail and moved into a cozy beach house in Carlsbad, but certain duties kept him busy—especially the dragonslayers who had revolted against the leaders in their knightly order. Many had wanted to express atonement for their part in slaying innocent dragons over the years at Sirs Kay, Bedivere, and Pelleas's command.

"I'm not," Loki fibbed.

Max peered over at Loki. "I wanted to say you've been a great help in untangling the mess left by the dragonslayers, but you've also seemed agitated. Something on your mind about Merlin? Have you noticed another slayer surveillance from the rogue faction?"

Loki shook his head. "It has nothing to do with the occasional spy keeping tabs on me or the wizard. Merlin is a good man," he mumbled while questioning why he visited the Drakenstone estate. The beer, he told himself. Saul had better taste in beer than most dragons. Loki sipped from his glass and glowered out over the fields spreading to the distant horizon. "What is it? No longer President of the United States, so you've got to meddle in the affairs of others to compensate?"

Max frowned. "Snippy, too, I see. What? Don't like having the tables turned on you? Usually you're the inquisitive one. But fine, mope alone if you must. Far be it from me to show concern to my own flesh and blood."

"I'm not snippy," Loki gritted out, only to reconsider the claim. "Maybe a little." After his sheepish admission and another long drink, he relented. "When did you first realize you cared deeply about Ēostre?"

Max's mate Ēostre had once belonged to another dragon, an older, stronger fire wyrm with a taste for human flesh and violence. Of course, Ēostre had tempered his desire for ravaging the countryside, and years later, their bond came to an abrupt end when Sir Kay slew him in cold blood.

"I…" Max paused to stare at him, a suspicious raise to his brows. "I cared about her very much, long, long ago. But she belonged to Fafnir. You know that. You hounded me about it for near a century, rubbing it in that I coveted my dearest friend's mate."

"I did," he agreed. Reluctant to share his eye-opening experience with his cousin and expose himself to teasing, he drained his glass to the bottom then wished for another. Mahasti filled it, as she always did. If he didn't visit for Saul's kegged beer on tap, then it was certainly for the genie's services. "Ēostre is a good dragoness."

"She is, and I feel blessed to have my chance with her. It faded, you know, for a while. I was able to see her as only a friend. Someone to cherish from afar, and my love and desire for her waned. It came crashing back when she reawakened after her hibernation." Max smiled, lost in a happy memory; then he snapped his gaze back to Loki. "Why do you ask? Has some dragoness caught your eye? Approached you for a mating?"

Years later, and he still envied Maximilian. Envied him for being the more powerful volcanic dragon. For having the more prestigious company. For having the most beautiful and elegant dragoness to ever soar through the blue skies. And he envied him for taking what he'd wanted at last. If only he could do the same. Unfortunately, Selene was a mortal, and he convinced himself it had been only lust and a pleasurable night keeping her on his mind. He barely knew her. It wasn't real. No one fell in love in a single night.

Saul had. Saul and Chloe, over twenty-six years later, loved each other no less than the first time. Watching them coo over each other for a couple minutes could make anyone ill.

"No. Nothing of the sort, cousin."

Max sighed. "I'm sorry. It'd do you some good to find a woman and mate. You've been alone far too long, Loki."

Loki said nothing.

"If I may ask a question? Or perhaps give a suggestion… Don't aim so high. Look at Saul and Teo, both have found wonderful, strong mates. You can have the same, I'm sure. But, who am I to offer advice? Take it as you will."

"Don't aim so high?" He rose from his chair and fixed Max with a disbelieving stare. "Don't aim so high?" he repeated.

"Yes."

"Says the one who claimed the most powerful, wise, and beautiful of all dragonesses. I certainly shall remember to bear your advice in mind."

Why did he even dare to broach the subject with Max? He wanted to leave, but he was also starved for the assortment of livestock Saul had slaughtered. Glancing to the left, he saw the bronze dragon and his retainer Leiv chatting beside the coal firepit. A whole side of beef roasted beside several legs of lamb. Hamburgers and scotch eggs smoked on the grill. Humans certainly knew how to celebrate their strange holidays.

Max spoke quickly, perhaps sensing that he was losing the argument. "That isn't what I meant. Stop searching for perfection. You are so nitpicky when it comes to your women. Do you think I love my mate because she's brilliant? Because she's beautiful? It certainly helps, but if she were plain, I would still love Ēostre's bright soul and loving heart. You always seem to look at the richest of our kind. The brightest in color. The most magnificent to the eye. And do they ever give you anything more than a romp and disdain? No. Their haughtiness intrudes, always."

"I do not search for perfection. I merely seek the woman who is perfect for me."

With similar likes and interests, who enjoyed his company and saw beyond the wealth in his hoard. Selene had laughed at his jokes. Not at him, but with him. Somehow, she'd crept into his mind again when his thoughts should be consumed with dragon women.

"I met a human," Loki admitted at last.

Max's eyebrows nearly jumped beneath his hairline. He leaned back in his seat and patted the adjacent chair. "Well then... Why don't you tell me a little about this human. A name, to start, and maybe then how you met."

Skeptical, Loki eyed his cousin. His brows furrowed as he returned to his seat and convinced himself that the promise of food—not conversation with Max—lured him to remain. "Her name is Selene. We met at the wine tour in May when the twins were ill with the dragon pox and you weren't able to join me."

"Ah, yes, I was sorry to miss that trip, but perhaps it was for the best."

Loki waved it off with one hand. "Your cubs were more important." Another thing to envy Max for having.

"So... You've been seeing her since then? What's wrong with that?"

"I have not. To be honest, I doubt she remembers me. A stranger."

Max's eyes narrowed, then he leaned forward in his seat, lowering his voice to speak. "A human on your mind for so long? Did you bond with her, Loki? Did you do as Saul did and mark her before she even knew what it meant?"

He shook his head. "No. I may be many things, but I'm not that irresponsible." Then he gazed across the veranda into the green pasture where Saul's mate, Chloe, played ball with her youngest cub in his dragon form. Brandt had the golden gleam of his father and vibrant, red feathers. The couple's older daughter, Astrid, lay beside the pool while nursing her newborn infant.

How he envied them all. Maybe Saul had done the right thing after all, impulsive, yet right all along. Perhaps the ancestors had intervened and guided the reckless dragon's teeth.

"But you have not forgotten her."

Loki chuckled quietly. "I can't get her off my mind. The worst thing about it is, I know only her name and profession."

"Then you must explore what this means." Max rolled his eyes. "You more than anyone should know how easy it is now to find someone with only a name. Here," he passed over his tablet. "Pull up your Facebook account if you have one, or... er, hrm, you don't, do you? Here. Use mine." He leaned over and logged in. "There. Now search her name. Do you know anything else?"

Loki gave him a disgusted look. "I know her city and state."

"That is certainly more than her name and profession. I cannot believe you've yet to make a Facebook profile."

Loki growled. "Shut up. What use do I have for socializing with mortals over daily frivolities?" After a pause, he said, "Anura has almost convinced me to use Snapchat." He liked the filters.

With Max's tablet in hand, Loki entered Selene's full name and scanned the lists until he found her photograph. Her face smiled back at him from the lit screen. He tapped the profile and skimmed through an insightful post into her daily life. Her bakery had received its first order to cater a wedding, and she was thrilled. He wished he was there to wish her well. Instead, he shook his head and passed the device back to its owner.

"Finding her doesn't mean she'll wish to see me again."

Max accepted the tablet and skimmed through the wall of posts. "She has an interesting face," he observed.

"Interesting is a poor choice of words," he muttered. To him, she was beautiful, and her face haunted his dreams.

His cousin was no longer listening to him, prattling again. "And look, here's a link to her bakery, which so happens to have an address."

"Max," Loki said in warning.

"What more do you need? She's in Norfolk, Virginia. Easy enough to catch a flight, or take one yourself if you prefer. You can be there in less than a day. Minutes if you teleport."

"*Maximilian.*"

Max ignored him again. "Look here, she has a picture of wine from the trip. A surprise case, she said, with a huge thank you to her... to her mystery admirer. Loki, did you send wine? She seems happy enough with that, and grateful too. I'm sure she'd be pleased to see you."

With a sigh, Loki surrendered to his cousin's strange desire to nose into his business. "I may have, yes. She favored a particular bottle and was reluctant to pay. So I asked the salesman to charge me and send an additional shipment when she was in the bathroom." He shrugged. "She believed six hundred dollars for a half case to be excessive."

"No, as much money as an average human makes in a week's hard work is certainly not expensive," Max said drolly. "Why will you not visit her?"

"What if she believes I am stalking her? That is a thing, is it not, among the humans? Stalking? No one would believe I stumbled into her bakery by mere coincidence."

"Then tell her some of the truth. Tell her you were in the area, and you looked her up. You hope she doesn't mind. Or did you not part on good terms? How well did you get to know her?"

"We slept together," Loki said bluntly. "But no, I did not mark her. It would be a heathen thing to do, branding an unsuspecting woman." On the inside, he wished he had. Wished he'd told her to forget her flight and that he'd return her to Virginia on his private jet at her convenience if she'd stay another day with him. He closed his eyes and sank back deeper into the seat. "I don't understand what's wrong with me. I loathe feeling this way."

"Sounds like how I feel about Ēostre. How Saul missed Chloe. Teo and Marcy."

"Point made, old man." Loki grunted again.

"Then heed my advice and ask Teo how it felt. He resisted Marcy for years without marking her. Saul, well, we all know that boy had no self-control. And still lacks it."

"I will keep your advice in mind," Loki muttered, though they both knew it was his way of saying, "To hell with your ideas, I'll do what I want to do until I eventually cave and realize you've advised me well."

The pattern had served them over the centuries from their cub years into adulthood. To be honest, Loki had been startled when Max forgave him for his part in the entire sordid affair with Mahuika, though he'd kept bits and pieces of his interaction with her to himself, unwilling to discover how much the

Drakenstone family was willing to excuse. They'd accepted him as the strange and quirky, scholarly uncle who had no young of his own and sometimes read the children stories.

"Uncle Loki! You and Grandpa promised to come play ball with us!" Brandt called from the grass.

"Think it over. No one says you have to go today or tomorrow, but don't wait too long, or you might miss your chance with this one. Who knows how long a pretty lady like that will remain single." Max rose to his feet and stretched. "Now, ready to show the cub what it means to play ball?"

"Let's show the little one that his grandfather is much too slow to play."

Chapter 4

November dumped eighteen inches of snow on downtown Norfolk, Virginia. Selene leaned against the shop counter and watched the steady snowfall beyond the windows. The aroma of fresh pastry permeated every inch of her bakery, surrounding her with the smell of sugary confections and cinnamon-dusted delights.

Fat, white snowflakes plummeted to the ground outside. Because of the mess and hazard to her customers, she'd had Jacob, one of her employees, lay out a long rug from the door to the shop counter, then another there for messy feet. It kept her tile floors clean and prevented accidents.

Where had the summer and fall months gone? It seemed like only yesterday that she'd had her once-in-a-lifetime tryst with the man of her dreams. Then she discovered he was the fourth richest man in California. A couple dragons claimed two of the spots before him.

No wonder he didn't contact her and hadn't come away from the encounter wanting her number. Just the same, she'd felt empowered by her choice and had not regretted a moment of their night.

Now whenever she shopped at the market, her eyes darted to the magazine rack to look for Loki. Occasionally, she saw his face on a cover, and once she'd overheard someone murmuring about how unfair it was for a man to be so rich, intelligent, and sexy all at once. And smugly, Selene thought of the one day and night she'd had him to herself. It must have been as refreshing or him as it was for her, she thought. To talk to someone who didn't recognize him on sight and zero in on his money.

She'd even bought one of those magazines to learn a little more about him, discovering he'd avoided the public until recently and had only begun to accept interviews within the past three months.

What had changed? She lacked the arrogance to assume it was her doing.

Even if she'd dreamed about the handsome billionaire sitting down with her over cupcakes and coffee. She'd chalked those fantasies up to wishful thinking and dismissed them.

"That wasn't a bad sales day," Jacob commented. "I mean, you could probably hire another part-time employee for the lunch rush to help take some of these hours off your hands. With the way this place is jumping lately, I doubt it'd even touch your profits."

Selene's bakery in Norfolk's bustling downtown drew a big crowd each morning as people grabbed croissants, muffins, and coffee on their way into work. Shoppers popped in during the lunch hours for sweet treats and a midday caffeine pick-me-up.

With the increased business, she'd had to double her initial staff of two during the last month, and had just hired a fifth to pick up her slack. She'd been so tired lately, and couldn't manage a full day the way she used to.

She eyed the clock and considered taking off early. Jacob would close for the day. Not only was he a great friend and her first employee, but his boyfriend was a hoot. Lately, Will had begun playing his guitar in the corner during the busier hours, and the added ambience encouraged people to linger and buy seconds.

"You feeling okay, sweetie?" Jacob asked after he put on fresh coffee to brew.

"Yeah, a little tired is all, but I'm feeling really great otherwise."

"Glad to hear it... and, wow, would you get a look at the yum walking through the door?" He'd lowered his voice and stared over her shoulder. She whapped him playfully on the arm.

"Better not let Will hear you say—" She turned toward the hot subject worthy of Jacob's notice then froze.

It was him.

It was Loki Agnarhorn. Billionaire techie. Wine lover. Her one and only one-night stand.

***

Max phoned him to ask if he needed a pep talk. While Loki denied the necessity of it, his cousin's voice instilled a vague sense of relief and support he hadn't realized he needed.

Act natural. Just there for a visit. He'd already scripted the perfect excuse: while passing through town on business, he recognized her shop name and decided to take her to lunch.

That morning, he had trusted in his longtime servant to help him pick an appropriate casual outfit, the suits in his closet too formal for a personal reunion. After claiming all women loved leather, Anura had paired his cream-colored sweater with tailored jeans beneath a leather jacket. She'd taken such efforts with his appearance, he felt like a work of art.

Anura deserved a raise. He'd have to increase the staff's wages. Maybe double them.

He'd come to Virginia to speak at a conference, but Selene had been on his mind the entire time. Once his obligation ended, he'd taken a cab immediately to Norfolk's Sweet Shack, where he stood for ten minutes staring at the sign. Just beyond the door, Selene waited for him. So he pushed it open and stepped inside.

Loki had hoped she would be happy to see him, but what he received was the wide-eyed stare of a woman shocked to find her one-night stand in her place of business.

"Greetings," he called as he took his first steps. The smell of sugar cookies assaulted him, the air warm and fragrant with baked goods—with the smell of *her*. He caught a whiff of orange blossom, the smell he associated with her hair, and continued closer. "I'm told this is the only bakery with a decent double chocolate fudge muffin for twenty miles."

"I… you…"

A college-age man stood beside her, dark-skinned and muscular, with a football player's broad shoulders. The baby fresh scent of young sorcery floated around the boy in a haze. "I'd go as far as to say fifty miles, if not a hundred, sir. In fact, we have a batch about to come out of the oven in back, so I'll grab one for you." He vanished without waiting for Selene or Loki to respond.

"Sorry. Hi. I… I didn't expect to see you, Luka. You look… You look great."

"As do you," he replied. His eyes traveled over what he could see of her above the counter: her radiant smile and buoyant curls. Selene's twinkling eyes seemed more gray in the fluorescent lighting of her bakery than they'd been over the summer. Then, they'd been like the sky.

"How did you—? I mean, what brings you here? To Norfolk, I mean."

"The… ah, there was a conference," he babbled when he regained his wits. "I happened to be in town for a conference." He cleared his throat. "And I recalled you were a resident of Norfolk and thought I'd pay you a visit."

Of course, he hadn't planned to attend and had actually declined until he recognized how close it would place him to seeing Selene. Then he'd accepted in a rush and even agreed to be a guest speaker.

"Oh. But, I mean, how did you find me?"

"Facebook."

"Oh…" She chuckled nervously and ran her hand back through her hair. "So a conference, huh? That sounds…"

"Dull?" he suggested.

A hint of pink blossomed across the apples of her cheeks. "Well, dull to me I guess, but as you know, I'm not a techie."

"To call it dull would be an understatement," he replied. "Why anyone would pay to hear me speak is beyond my comprehension." And something Max would challenge as highly unlike him to say. While Loki had a reputation for his arrogance and love of himself, he wanted to make her laugh. Needed it, suddenly so desperate for her approval he felt sick with himself.

She smiled, forced. "Um, I have coffee. Would you like some? Two sugars and cream, right?"

If this was what it felt to find a soul mate, he didn't want it. And he did. With conflicting emotions guiding him, he gestured to one of her empty tables. "Only if you'll join me."

Her eyes darted around the bakery as if searching for an excuse to deny him. Seeing none, her eyes fell to the table in defeat. "Yeah, let me just get your coffee poured."

While he moved to a table, Selene disappeared into a back room. He waited quietly for her to emerge and minutes ticked by. Glancing at his phone revealed a text from Max.

Maximilian: Well?

Loki: She is pouring coffee for us.

Maximilian: Is she happy to see you?

Loki: No.

At least, she didn't appear to be happy, though he hoped it was on account of him startling her more than anything. His phone chirped again with another text when Selene emerged from the back with a tray and stepped from behind the counter.

"Perhaps, if you're not occupied this afternoon," he began, "you would honor me with din..."

His gaze danced over her legs, clothed in black tights and adorned by gray, fur-cuffed boots. Her simple, green knit shirt clung against her hips and belly. Her belly. Her rounded belly that drew his stare like a magnet. He couldn't look away.

"Here we go. Coffee for you and a muffin, still hot and gooey."

The worst indescribable sense of heartbreak shattered something in him, like an ice pick in his chest. No wonder she hadn't been overjoyed to see him. She'd moved on.

Max had been right, and he loathed his cousin anew for once again proving him wrong. Someone else had come along and done what he'd wanted. "I... thank you," he said awkwardly.

Selene bit her lower lip, but still managed a shy smile. Then she gingerly lowered into the seat across from him. "I know, I look like a whale."

He shook his head. "No, I would never call you a whale." He'd been in the mood for chocolate, but the sight of her swollen belly, the cost of his procrastination, had robbed him of all appetite. "Were you able to enjoy the wine for a while before...?" he asked while gesturing to her baby bump.

"You really didn't have to do that. It was sweet of you, but no, I haven't had the chance. My friend told me how to store them, so they've all been put away for now. I..." She blew out a breath and wrapped her hands around her water glass.

"You wanted them, and I felt you should have them." She could celebrate the birth of her little one with its father, he thought bitterly. He had no talent with forcing smiles so made no attempt. His neutral expressions made him appear brooding as Max was in the habit of pointing out.

"I wanted to thank you, but, uh... I didn't know how to reach you and then, well—" She huffed out a breath and peeked back up. "I saw you on a magazine."

"I know it was foolish to give you a false name, but I'm in the habit of it these days."

"No, I understand why you did it. I'm not mad, but I also don't want you to feel responsible. You don't *have* to do anything, and I don't need anything. So, it's okay."

The deserted bakery had felt inviting, but now it had become stifling. Too warm. Too cinnamony. The air was too sweet with the scent of the woman he wanted. "Responsible for what?" An awkward beat passed before he babbled, "You mean... oh no. No. You're not implying I did this, are you?"

Heat rushed up to her cheeks. "Look, I'm not in the habit of just rolling into bed with anyone. What happened... it was great. Crazy and impulsive, but great, and I haven't been with anyone else since. So, yeah, you did. But like I said, it's fine. I'm not going to come after you for *money* or anything."

Her words splashed him like cold water, stealing any elegant words from his mouth.

His cub? Could it be his? His mind raced back to their night together, and while he knew plenty about human contraception, he'd never worn a condom until that night. Weren't they supposed to be foolproof?

"You don't... you don't have to worry about it." Her voice became progressively quieter until she whispered and looked away. "I shouldn't have said anything. Stupid of me to assume you'd jump to that conclusion on your own."

"We used condoms. Several," he said bewildered.

"Yeah, we did."

"It couldn't be mine."

"Just forget it, okay?"

He stared at her, stunned. "I am not human, Selene. It cannot be mine, because it isn't possible." In the cases of all half-dragons he'd known, they were always conceived during a bonded relationship. Every single one of them.

Except for Arthur. They'd all assumed Astrid to be a special case since her own mother was human.

"It doesn't matter. It—" She stopped, blinked, and stared at him with wariness. "What do you mean, you aren't human? I mean, I know that there's, well, there's stuff out there. We all know it now, have for years since that dragon entered the White House."

"Exactly as I said. Which is why it is impossible for us to have conceived," he insisted.

"Believe what you want. You're the only man I've slept with in over three years, so I guess I'm having a miracle baby then. And you know what, I don't need you. I think you need to leave. Coffee and muffin are on the house. I won't take up any more of your precious ti—" Without finishing, she pushed up from her chair and bolted for the nearby bathroom door.

Months of watching the highlights of Astrid's pregnancy, as well as what he'd gleaned from movies and television, told him what was happening long before the sharp notes of sour vomit reached his nose.

Taking shallow breaths, he forced himself to stand and strode to the door. He knocked once he no longer heard her retching over the commode. "Selene? Please, give me a moment to explain."

Years ago, if anyone had suggested he would mate with a human, he would have called the notion preposterous and laughed them out of his company. Now, it was the sweetest promise he'd heard in months. While he knew some of the other dragons, such as Teo, were more devout toward the spirits of their fallen brethren, rarely did he spare them a moment of thought. Now, he found himself praying Selene was right.

Please let it be mine. I'd do anything.

Selene didn't answer his knock.

"Please."

Loki allowed a few minutes to pass before he opened the door. The unisex area had a single toilet and a sink, with neatly folded piles of washcloths laid out on a rack in place of paper towels. A flickering light mimicking a candle sat on a shelf above the sink.

Selene knelt on the spotless floor, hair held back with one hand while the other was braced on the seat. "I'm fine," she croaked, sounding as miserable as she looked.

"You're far from fine," he disagreed in a gentle voice.

At a loss, he thought back to the words he'd heard once from Astrid's husband, Nate. "When they're pregnant and hurting, you just do whatever you can to make them happy again."

So Loki knelt and joined her on the floor, gathering her dark hair in his hands as she vomited again. Max would laugh at him, the great god of mischief kneeling on a restroom floor. For Selene, he did it without complaint.

"It wasn't my intention to imply you've mated with multiple men. Though it isn't uncommon for my kind, I know for you humans, such things are held in low regard."

"Humans." Her hysterical laughter echoed over the bathroom tiles.

"Is that not what you are? A witch if not a human?" he asked, bewildered. What had he done wrong?

"Gods, you really are something else, aren't you? What then, werewolf? A mage?" With one hand, she tugged her hair free of his grip before rising to her feet. She washed her hands at the sink then fetched mouthwash from the cabinet beneath it.

He drew himself up afterward and watched her, wary, afraid her emotions would transition from resentment to fear.

Nothing had gone according to plan.

"The dragon who lived in the White House is my cousin," he said in an even voice. "Tell me what you need, and it will be yours. No price is too large, no request too great. What will our child need?"

Chapter 5

"I'm not looking for a handout." Tears streamed down her cheeks. She told herself it was from throwing up, but in truth it was mortification and the hurt caused by his implications, his outright haughty denial.

"Do all women view such things as handouts? Is it not what I am obligated to do? What any creature who called himself a man should do were he in my place, whether human or dragon?"

Dragon. He said it again, confirming what she'd hoped was a trick of her own hearing.

Cousin to the freaking former President. "I think I'm dreaming."

Selene turned away from the sink and stumbled, lightheaded.

When the world swam into focus again, two concerned male faces gazed down at her. She lay sprawled on the office couch. Loki pressed a cool washcloth against her forehead while Jacob glowered at him.

"What'd you do to her, man?" her friend demanded.

"I did nothing," Loki hissed. Jacob appeared unconvinced. Pressing his mouth into a thin line, he hovered by her and turned his worried eyes back to Selene. "Are you well? Is the little one well?"

"Hey, sweetums, are you okay?" Jacob helped her sit up and held a small glass of iced herbal tea out to her. "Small sips, okay?"

"Yeah, I'm fine. It happens sometimes. Little dizzy spells. It's normal."

Jacob rolled his eyes. "Nothing about this is normal, and at least now I know why. Sorta." He must have overheard, she thought, or Loki himself had revealed it.

Whatever, it didn't really matter.

"I'm fine," she said again to reassure them both. "But I think should head home. Jacob—"

"I'll close up. Are you okay to drive?"

"Yeah, I'm good."

"*I* will take her home," Loki cut in, stepping closer like a jealous dog guarding a bone. "And she will arrive much faster than by vehicle."

"I don't understand." She blinked again and sipped tea, brow furrowing. "My car is here."

"Would you like to be home now?"

"Well, yeah, but like I said, my car is outside."

Didn't he understand that? How did he expect her to get home? Riding dragonback?

"Just get her home safe," Jacob said. "But I swear, if you hurt her—"

Loki straightened. "You will what?" he asked darkly.

Selene reached out and put a hand on Jacob's arm. "I'll be fine. He's not going to hurt me, promise. We can talk tomorrow when I come in, okay?"

"Okay, yeah." Jacob passed her purse over. "Get some rest. And drink more fluids."

Loki held the bakery door open for her after she donned her winter gear. Virginia had grown so cold, she refused to step outdoors without bundling up in her jacket, mittens, hat, and scarf. She looked ridiculous, and adorable according to Jacob that morning, in a warm cocoon of heather gray and canary yellow.

"The lot is down around the corner. You don't really have to come with me. I'm fine."

Loki glanced at her. "It makes no matter to me," he said, guarded and quiet. The smiling, kind man from the wine tour was gone, a silent stranger in his place. "I will not trouble you for long, Selene, or force you to accept my help if you find my kind so displeasing."

"I don't find you displeasing," she muttered. "But I don't need your charity. You don't need to feel obligated to take care of me or worried I'm gonna come after you for money and stuff. I won't."

"Which vehicle do you drive?"

She held out her fob and unlocked a plain silver Kia. It had five years and sixty-five thousand miles on it, but it made decent gas mileage. She slid in and immediately fired the engine before cranking up the hot air. It always took a few minutes.

The dragon took the passenger seat, but everything about him looked at odds with her thrifty vehicle. He wore sophisticated winter wear and exuded class, probably accustomed to a driver and a limousine. She'd wore Target clothes in a secondhand car already fitted with a rear-facing infant seat gifted from a few friends.

"Tell me, Selene, why do you believe I sought you in this forsaken land of slush?" He gestured to the sloppy sidewalks with melting snow and salted ice. "For a chocolate muffin?"

"You told me why you came. You had a conference."

"I came for *you*. The conference was an excuse to see *you*. I cared nothing for being there and knew nothing of our cub."

Cub. The word was so odd. Her heart rate sped and breath quickened in the initial stirrings of a panic attack, requiring her to leave the car in park. "Baby," she corrected. "I'm having a baby."

"Baby then," he whispered, looking chastened, voice strained.

A cold fist closed icy fingers of guilt around her heart. Why had she said that to him? "I just need to be home, okay? Being sick made me feel disgusting, and I'm cold. I want my couch, fireplace, and a good book, along with a glass of almond milk and my pajamas."

"As you like."

A fireplace, book, and almond milk. Gods, those things sounded nice. Yearning for the idyllic scene she described to him, Selene closed her eyes. He touched her shoulder, and she didn't shy from it. Even enjoyed it, wishing to press her cheek against his chest.

She'd been a bitch to him. She knew it, but she couldn't bring herself to apologize just yet, afraid the moment she showed weakness, everything would collapse and she'd fall apart to irreparable pieces for him to pick up.

"Is this your home?" Loki asked, uncertainty in his silken voice.

Selene started to laugh. "The car? No, it's not my—" The laughter stopped when she opened her eyes.

The world beyond the Kia had changed from the city backdrop to a frost-blanketed suburban neighborhood. A kid across the street building a snowman gaped at the suddenly there vehicle, the forgotten handful of snow slipping from his fingers. The car idled in her driveway, a light snowfall drifting through the steel-gray sky.

"How did you...?"

Loki remained pensive and uncertain, and suddenly she felt a sharp ache for the confidence she'd admired during the tour. Her eyes darted from him to the house, which wasn't much, but it was hers, a red-brick residence with a covered porch and fenced backyard. Three bedrooms were too much for only her, but she'd loved the older style in the friendly neighborhood.

As a witch who had magic of her own, seeing it in use shouldn't have startled her so much. "Yeah," she whispered. "This is it."

The air in the car hadn't even warmed up yet. She turned the engine off and opened the car door, wondering if it was all an illusion.

"Come on inside, okay? I…" She sighed. "We should talk. I'm not doing a good job at that or being reasonable to you. I know it."

"Yes," he agreed.

Loki trailed behind her to the front door, and the moment she opened it, they were both besieged by two dogs. Baron and Dusty eagerly sniffed her fingers and shoved against her. Then they swarmed over Loki, a tidal wave of fur and eager, pink tongues.

"Baron, don't—no, get off him. No, don't do that. *Guys.*"

Too late, they'd fallen in love. Loki thumped back against the wall beside her door, and she could only imagine it was because he'd been taken by surprise, and not because he'd been overpowered. Dusty, her sweet but harmless Saint Bernard, was a shaggy sweetheart who weighed more than her. Possibly more than Loki in his human form. Baron on the other hand, topped the scales at twelve pounds, a mass of wispy, white fluff with glossy, black eyes.

"Your… beast is rather large."

"C'mon, Dusty, give him some room."

The two friendly dogs listened, backing off only enough for Selene to get the door shut. She locked it behind them.

"They won't hurt you, promise. They're softies. Er… I can put them in the other room for a few minutes to give you some space if you don't like dogs."

"I do not dislike them," he said. She imagined it was code for, "I do not know if I like smelly beasts."

"Okay, well, the Bernard there is Dusty. I picked him up from the local shelter. And this little guy is Baron. I found him last year on the side of the road, and he's been with me since. He's kind of a drama king and likes attention." As a single woman living all alone, they fulfilled the dual role of company and security.

"They are handsome." Loki touched the top of Baron's head like he was making contact with a snotty child. The dog yipped and pawed at Loki's jeans eagerly, but eventually backed off and hopped over to his bed. Dusty joined him and settled with an appreciative groan once Selene turned on the fireplace with the remote.

It had been her one upgrade to the house since its purchase, changing the original fireplace filled with ashes for a gas model. Sure, she missed the smell of a crackling fire, but she didn't miss the mess, soot, or hauling in logs.

"Would you like anything? I have tea, coffee, and juice. Or I could open wine if you'd prefer a glass."

"It would be rude to enjoy wine while you are unable." He paused and, after a few beats, asked quietly, "That is a thing, isn't it? Dragon women are different. Alcohol does not harm our young. It's little more than a treat for cubs. I give a little brandy to Maximilian's twins sometimes…"

She stared at him without knowing whether it was his impeccable manners and thoughtfulness or his references to female dragons that shocked her the most.

Maybe it was the fact that he'd admitted to giving alcohol to underage dragon cubs.

Patient as ever, he coached her in a gentle voice, "You invited me in to talk."

She gestured to the couch. "Please, have a seat." She sank down onto one end and tried to pry off a boot with her other foot. After struggling for a minute, she gave up and shrugged out of her jacket instead. "This is a lot to process all at once."

He glanced at the couch for a time with an indecisive, pondering look on his face before kneeling on the floor. Relief hissed from between her teeth in a grateful sigh when he removed her boot.

"I did not mean to do this to you," he said. The other boot came off, granting her toes freedom to move and wiggle. By afternoon, the boots that felt comfortable in the morning always became tear-inducing torture devices.

"I'm not blaming you. Accidents happen, and I'm the one who instigated the whole situation."

As she placed her feet over the ottoman, Loki rose from the floor and perched on the edge of the couch beside her. She envied his grace.

"Right. So. Talk. Can we start with, um, how you got us here? Nothing ever said dragons were magical. Well, I mean, obviously dragons are magical, but I never read anything in the paper about them doing actual magic."

"Many of my kind are born with specific gifts. Ēostre Emberthorn and I happen to share a talent for sorcery," he explained. "Though we excel at different aspects of magic. Her skill lies with the light and mine with the dark."

"I've always been of the belief that magic itself isn't light or dark, and that it's what's in the heart of the caster."

The observation earned a faint smile, gone from Loki's face s quickly as it had appeared. "Tell me truly, Selene. Do you want o do this alone?"

She released a long breath. It was the big question, and she aad no idea now that she was forced to face it head on with the only other soul in the world who had a say in the matter. Things aad been different when she thought him to be an anonymous ousinessman across the country who wouldn't care.

"When I was married—"

"You were married?" He blinked at her, bewildered. "Is he deceased?"

She shook her head. "No. I left him."

"Why?"

"We didn't want the same things. I wanted a family. We discussed it while we were dating, and he told me one day, but when one day came..." She shrugged. "His interest in the subject had waned. When I tried to compromise, he put it off. We couldn't agree about children at all."

"He was a fool."

Her mouth pressed into a tight line. "My family and friends agree with you. But he's part of my past now, and this baby means everything to me. Panicking wasn't an option, because I felt like I finally had the one thing I'd wanted all those years I was trapped in a marriage with my ex."

"Fair enough," he said. "But is there room for me as well? I ask because... among my kind, dragonesses hold all the power over our young. Once they've birthed our cubs and nursed them for so long, some lose interest in mothering."

"Are you suggesting I would—"

"No," he cut in swiftly. "Dragonesses are nothing like humans. I would not attempt to barter or purchase your...

baby," he said with apparent difficulty. "As it is not your culture, though it is mine."

Her brows shot up. "You sell your babies? Is that what's going to happen to the White House twins?"

Loki shook his head. "Ēostre and Maximilian are married and bonded. Why would she sell their twins to him?"

"But some female dragons do that? Sell their babies to the fathers?"

"Are there not surrogate mothers in human culture? Forever is a long time to live in loneliness, Selene."

"That's different. Some women can't have babies of their own."

"Neither can a man, and unlike mortals who may consider adoption or foster care, there are few options available to a dragon who craves an heir."

"And that's what you want? An heir?"

His gaze drifted to her mantle where a line of framed photographs detailed holidays and events with her mother, younger brother, and stepfather. "Your family is lovely."

"Thank you. You didn't answer my question, though."

"I was thinking," he murmured. "Sometimes it takes a moment to compose my thoughts, especially now when your regard for me has greater value."

"Oh…" She waited, giving him the time he needed without further pressure, all the while struggling to suppress the anxiety bubbling in her tummy.

"Many centuries ago, I entered a contract with a dragoness named Nefertiti. I paid her a quarter of the jewels in my horde—a value I cannot give you in modern American currency—for the privilege of mating with her one season. The pregnancy did not take." Loki spread his hands. "Had it worked, she would have weaned the child at thirty years of age and given it to me no questions asked. We have so few females, this is what we have been reduced to. Desperation."

She swallowed. "I... How few are they?"

"For every seven of us, there is one dragoness. We only discovered our ability to produce viable offspring with human women twenty-six years ago, Selene. A blink in our lifespans."

"Is that why you're being so nice, then? Because of the baby?"

"No. I do not want an heir. I want a companion, and I came to Virginia to ask if you might be mine."

He said it so matter-of-factly, she wondered if she'd hallucinated. "Your companion. You came to ask me to be your companion?" she repeated.

"Yes. Is that so difficult to believe?" Gone was the stoic face and neutral tone, replaced by unvarnished interest. His green eyes smoldered, startling her with the intensity of his stare. "After the day we spent together? Why should I not want you? You are vibrant and intelligent, your manners flawless. I can't describe everything I feel or why I desire you, because I don't understand it either."

Selene shook her head. "It's a strange title. Like concubine..." A tiny shiver crept down her spine, intensifying as memories of their time in her hotel room surged to her mind. Overwhelmed by a sharp, hot pang of hunger for him, she knit her fingers into the edge of her shirt and avoided eye contact. "This is a lot to take in, Luka—Loki. What do I even call you?"

"Loki will suffice."

"I need to think about this. Can we talk more about it tomorrow?"

Disappointment darkened his eyes. He shrugged. "We have only time."

"I'm going to shower and change. Will you be all right out here with the boys?"

And just like that, the wary apprehension on his face melted, abolished by a low, amused chuckle. "I am Loki. Your beasts will not cause any concern."

"Right. Loki, like the Norse god of mischief."

"No, I *am* Loki, and all tales told by the Norse were inspired by me."

***

The way Selene gaped at him, her mouth opening and closing in fishlike gasps, made Loki grin wider by the second. It never failed to amuse him when someone realized exactly who he was.

"Wait, if you're *the* Loki, does that means Thor and Odin are real too?"

"They are. I have fought with the true Thor, but I must confess, those movies have done nothing for his modesty since their production. He's insufferable."

"That means you're, like, hundreds of years old."

"Yes." Loki tilted his head and scrutinized her. "I expected less surprise from a witch."

"Barely a witch," she muttered. "So it's true then. Dragons are eternal."

"Not quite, but close enough. We don't die from old age, as the witches do, but once we perish, we are gone from this world for good. Our souls are not reborn as yours are."

Her eyes grew larger; then her fingers splayed over the round belly he'd been aching to touch since their arrival. "And our child? Will he or she be a dragon?"

"Well, it certainly won't be a wolf. If so, you are sadly out of luck, because someone has pulled that one over on me before." He said it gently, hoping sufficient humor had been infused in his tone.

Contrary to Norse belief, the great werewolf Fenrir had not been his son, though he'd wanted him and his siblings to be. Loki had loved Angrboda deeply, but giantesses were not known for their fidelity.

"What does this mean?"

"It will be a long pregnancy, Selene. Months longer than a mortal child. Chloe and Marceline both carried for almost a year."

"Who?"

"Apologies," he murmured. "They are the human mates of my acquaintances Saul Drakenstone and Teotihuacan Arcillanegro." Acquaintances? The word sounded strange to his ears after a year mingling among Saul's household. Friends. A decade ago, he would have never considered it possible. "Chloe is… family."

"Oh. Okay. So I'm not the first. That's good." She nodded and rubbed her belly, again luring him with the temptation to touch her too. He resisted, distracted by the pallor in her cheeks. "Yeah… Good…"

"Please, I can see I have overwhelmed you. Rest for a time, and we will speak more later." He rose from the couch and offered her both hands. She accepted his help to her feet and flashed a grateful, brief smile.

"I have a pile of takeout menus in the drawer there." She pointed to the side table next to the couch. "See if anything sounds good, and we can order when I get out of the shower."

"Take your time."

The moment she left, Loki slipped his phone from the holster and slid open the messaging screen to view the pile of texts left behind by Max. His sharp hearing picked out the distant drum of a shower stream rushing against tile. A door clicked shut somewhere between them.

Max: Well? Did you crash and burn?

Max: I hope you aren't in another bar drinking.

Max: You're drinking, aren't you?

Max: Well, let us know where you are once you're done so Ēostre and I can come retrieve you. We'd rather you not accidentally open a portal to Fort Knox again. That gold is not ours to nap on, no matter how shiny it may appear.

The messages each came five to ten minutes apart, revealing his beloved cousin had little to no faith in him. After rolling his eyes in exasperation, he swiped his finger over the screen a few times.

Loki: I'm not drinking. I'm waiting in her living room while she showers. Virginia is downright frigid.

Max: That sounds like good progress then.

If only he knew. Loki's fingers hovered over the touch screen. Did he dare tell his cousin about the cub? Or should he wait until he learned what Selene wanted to do? What would Max do in this situation?

He waited and held back the news related to their child.

Loki: I believe so. I've fared better than Saul at least, since she didn't shriek at me and send me away into the poor weather, so there's that.

Max: I'm telling Chloe.

Loki: Telling what?

Tattling? On him? Whatever had he done to deserve such treatment? He scowled down at the phone then checked out the menus she'd asked him to peruse. Nothing but pizza stood out as particularly appetizing.

A door opened and shut, squeaking noisily. He strained to listen for the sound of Selene's approach but heard nothing other than the muted sounds of her moving on the other side of her small home.

Max: Only the usual, cousin. Relax. You're usually in higher spirits than this when teased.

His shoulders sagged and he leaned back against the couch. Somehow, in the course of months, the entire dynamic between them had changed. He was no longer the aggressor and troublemaker, but a member of the family. A friend.

Someone to tease in playful banter. He breathed in a few steady breaths and let the panic subside.

Loki: You're right.

Max: Give a shout if you need us for personal references. I hear mortals do background checks these days when dating.

Grumbling to himself, he put the phone away and turned his thoughts to Selene. The dogs kept him company during her absence, the smaller fluffball edging closer by inch-long increments until eventually it had placed its front paws on Loki's thigh.

"I'm not your friend," he said to the white creature.

Baron moved closer, front half on his lap.

"That was the exact opposite of what you were supposed to do, pup."

The larger dog took it as an invitation to receive attention as well and moved closer, sitting at his feet and leaning against his leg.

By the time Selene emerged an hour later, clothed in her warm pajamas with her towel-dried hair loose and curly around her shoulders, Baron had sprawled across Loki's lap with his paws upraised, and Dusty had squeezed into the vacant couch space beside him. A small war had broken out between the two dogs, yipping and groaning at one another to determine who retained dominance over Loki's lap.

Selene chuckled. "Do you need help?"

"I do n—" The denial froze on his tongue. He cleared his throat. "Please."

"C'mon you two, leave our guest alone. Dinnertime."

The magic words summoned both animals away from his side. They leaped down and rushed to follow Selene into the kitchen. Loki ambled after them curiously with a stack of takeout menus in hand.

"There is a menu for a sushi bar here."

"Oh, no, skip that. I'm not supposed to eat raw fish." She frowned.

He crinkled his nose. The resulting expression must have been comical, because she laughed and took the sushi menu from his hands to set it aside. "Why not?"

"Because parasites. There's lots the doctors tell you to avoid when you're pregnant."

"There are not many options." He shuffled through the five menus.

"Drawback of a small town."

They settled for pizza, though agreeing to toppings wasn't as easy as making a choice about their dinner. The next dispute came over the bill once the deliveryman arrived with the three boxes required to satisfy his large appetite.

Loki only won the right to pay because the dogs distracted Selene long enough for him to pass over a few twenties to the delivery boy.

"Keep the change."

"Whoa! Thanks, dude!"

"No problem," he muttered before bumping the door shut.

While Selene hoarded her strange combination of salami and banana peppers with white garlic sauce, he enjoyed two meat lover's delights.

They didn't speak much over dinner, and deep down, Loki was relieved for that. She'd put on a Netflix movie from Saul's studio, a fantasy adventure he'd watched a dozen or more times already.

He'd have to take her to Saul and get her a tour of the studio. The appearance of the pixies made her eyes shine with delight, and he longed to introduce her to them.

Selene set her box aside on the coffee table and leaned back, eyes closed and expression sated. "I'm full."

"As am I."

"I'm not surprised. You ate two of those, but at least I understand why you ate like a starving man that morning."

"We have large appetites, it is true." He wiped his mouth and smiled. "Fear not, though. We do not indulge in so large a meal daily."

"That's good. I don't think my fridge could hold enough."

He agreed with her. Silently. The outdated fridge in her kitchen occupied a narrow space between the ancient stove and wall. He'd glanced at it in passing and wondered why the oven didn't close completely.

And then he wondered if her worries related to the fridge were a veiled invitation to stay.

"Tell me, Selene. Your scent reminds me of a witch, but you have spoken little of magic. Why is that?"

"Well, first off, I didn't realize I stank like magic."

"It isn't a displeasing smell."

"Thanks. As for not talking about it, what am I supposed to do? Introduce myself as 'Hey, I'm Selene and I'm a witch' when I meet new people?"

"Why not? Online dating sites have drop-menus for paranormal species now." The comment tumbled out before he could stop himself. He winced.

"I wouldn't know." She leaned back against the cushions and rubbed her hand over her belly. "It's not like you fessed up either," she pointed out.

"Dragon tends to intimidate many."

"So does magic, and I'm not really a practicing one."

Loki stroked his chin and considered her ambivalence toward the subject. "Are you so disinterested in your gift or have you merely lacked a teacher all this time?"

"No, it's not that. Not really. Jacob has tried to teach me a few things, but I can never make them work. My gift seems to be limited to empathy and mostly at night. Passive stuff. Sometimes a little ESP."

Jacob again. His brows drew together as he thought of the boy at her bakery. The way the male sorcerer had challenged him. Dared to threaten him. Loki had wanted to floss his teeth with Jacob, but respect for her place of business had deterred him.

Loki bristled. "You are close to this Jacob."

"He's my best friend."

"I see." His spine stiffened.

"He's gay."

"Oh."

Selene gathered up the leftovers and empty boxes, but he saw a cherubic smile on her face before she turned away.

"You're laughing at me."

"Maybe." She chuckled and continued toward the kitchen. When she returned moments later, her serene features remained at peace. "I should head to bed. I like to get an early start and arrive at the bakery by seven each morning to help the rest of the staff."

"May I remain here for the night? On this couch, perhaps? I will cause no trouble, you have my word."

"No," she said, tearing the rug out from under him, only to hold out both hands and in a rush say, "I'm not going to put you on the couch. I have a guest room. It's not much, and I need to put on fresh sheets, but it's way more comfortable."

Mute, he nodded and followed her into the hall over pea-green carpet.

"This is the bathroom here on the left. This first door here on the right is the guest room. I'm, um, making up the next room into a nursery, and that's my room at the end." Each room was on the small side, common in older houses. The guest room held a full-size bed and a small dresser, but little else. She crossed to the dresser and pulled out a set of sheets, cheery yellow with tiny daisies for a pattern. Feminine. "There's blankets in the closet there. Grab what you'd like."

As she fussed over the sheets on the bed, he crossed to her in a few long strides and set his hands over her wrists, stopping her cold. "Don't worry over my sleeping arrangements. I will manage. I am a dragon after all. I've literally slept on the floor of caves."

"Are you sure?" Selene asked with uncertainty.

"I am positive. Go and take your rest. There will be more to discuss tomorrow."

When she opened her mouth to speak, he silenced her by squeezing her hands.

"I'm going to kiss you now," Loki said, repeating the words she'd spoken to him over six months ago. And while he wanted to do far more than kiss her, he did only that, lowering his mouth over hers and coaxing her lips to part, gliding his tongue between them. Her tummy was round, but not so large he couldn't draw her closer to him.

He broke away first, despite his hunger for more.

"Goodnight, Selene. Rest."

"Okay…" A dazed expression came over her face, but he nudged her toward the door.

For a few minutes, Loki bided his time until the soft sound of her snores reached his ears. Afterward, he cast a simple muffling charm on her door to guarantee Selene would sleep undisturbed.

The work ahead of him seemed endless, the tasks too numerous and time short. He opened a gateway to his home in the kitchen where both dogs eyed the shimmering portal. Despite their proven fondness for following him around Selene's home, neither bounded through behind him.

He emerged on the other side in his own living room, a spacious den designed for optimal comfort and entertainment of guests, although he never invited anyone to join him aside from the Drakenstones. The long bar curved beside a 500-gallon aquarium installed in the wall. The television spanned another wall. The thin pane home theater screen was capable of airing 3-D movies.

The window shades had already been drawn by his faithful servant who stood beside them with the cord in her hand. "Good evening, Master!" Anura chirped.

"Good evening, Anura. I have need of you." He paused and considered the task ahead, then added, "As well as the others. At least three more."

"Even William?"

"Yes, please."

His assistant assembled a small team and, after some direction, they pushed through the portal with buckets filled to the brims with supplies.

"The mother of my cub deserves a spotless home. She shall worry over nothing," he decided before removing himself from their working area.

His servants cleaned through the night, bleaching counters, refinishing the hardwood floors of her formal living room, and even wiping the blades of every ceiling fan. They beat rugs outside and moved like dustbusting locusts from one room to the next, including her garage. The scent of lavender essential oil filled the air with its calming aroma after a round of carpet shampooing lifted years of age from the carpet.

Loki supervised from the front room with a cup of coffee near at hand.

"I am ready to prepare breakfast," Anura said. She presented a silver tray covered with neat bowls and plates holding the ingredients necessary for stuffed crepes and eggs.

"Cream cheese and blueberries. Selene dislikes strawberries. The eggs must be scrambled, but use a liberal amount of cheddar cheese. Grated." He remembered it from their breakfast so long ago. He remembered everything about that meal with startling clarity, and her preferences remained in his mind.

"Of course. I will make the change and get this started."

"Thank you, Anura."

"The driveway has been shoveled and garage organized, my lord. Will there be anything else?" his butler asked.

"The dogs, William. Take the dogs to be groomed, please."

"As you wish."

It was with satisfaction that he looked over the transformed house. He'd done everything he could to prove he would be a suitable and providing mate. Now he only needed Selene to awaken and see.

Chapter 6

Selene awoke to sunshine against her curtains, the warm glow diffused through the opaque, cream linen. With absolute silence throughout the house, she hadn't stirred once, making it the best night of sleep she'd enjoyed in weeks.

A glance at the clock showed the hour to be a quarter past nine, long past the time her alarm should have buzzed. If she'd set it at all. Had she?

"Crap. Look at that, making your mommy late already. I don't know if I'm coming or going anymore," she said. A tiny flutter in her tummy seemed to be the baby's response.

Parting from her cocoon of blankets and body pillows, she rolled out of bed and stepped into the fluffy slippers beside it before opening her door. The dogs weren't there to greet her.

Maybe Loki had let them out into the yard to pee. She tried to imagine him walking the pair down the salted sidewalks and giggled at the image in her mind of the aristocratic dragon leading her Saint Bernard and fluffy Maltese by their leashes.

After taking a step into the hall, a strange sense of wrongness surged over her. She paused, turned around in a full circle, and frowned. A shiny, high-tech carpet shampooer replaced the vacuum she'd kept by the nursery room door, and the hallway light had been fitted with a bright, new bulb.

The fragrance of lavender encompassed her, entwined with refreshing mint, and then she heard unfamiliar voices in her kitchen.

As a woman living alone, she kept a baseball bat by her bedroom door for protection and a gun in her nightstand. She reached for the bat only to stop short and consider the situation.

What sort of burglar brought in cleaning supplies?

A murderer maybe. Dexter had broken into her home to slaughter her, and he'd brought a shampooer to remove evidence of the crime.

Bat in hand, she crept down the hallway on tiptoe and peeked around the corner into the kitchen.

The room sparkled.

The sink was empty, dishes cleaned and put away, counters wiped, faucet literally shining in the sunlight coming through the window over the sink.

"What the hell?" That's when she spotted a young man and woman in matching uniforms wiping down the walls in her breakfast nook. Both were slim and short, lean with impressive muscular definition straining their uniform pants in the thighs and legs. The girl wore her chestnut hair in a tight bun, and neither looked aggressive or intimidating. "Who the hell are you and who let you in here?"

The man shrieked, dropped his rag, and became a fluffy bunny that hurtled from the kitchen and into the dining room.

The girl also froze, a rag trapped between her hand and the wall. Her large eyes stared at Selene and her chest moved with rapid breaths.

But she didn't shift and bound away. She recovered quickly and dipped into a polite bow.

"Good morning, Madam Selene. Master asked that we tidy your home. Is this to your liking?"

"Is it to my liking?" Her home hadn't been as tidy since the day she'd moved in.

The woman curtsied again. "Yes. Master thought you would be pleased. I am Anura, Master Loki's chief maid."

Loki's voice drifted in from the front room. Selene strode past the maid without a word, too stunned to even speak, and pulled open the closed door leading to her living room. Like her kitchen, the informal space had been transformed, but this time with a new addition.

The dragon sprawled lazily in the embrace of an immense, leather recliner, a laptop resting on his thighs. A glass of dark, plum-colored liquid sat in the holder on the left armrest, and Baron lay on the right. Loki cradled a cell phone between his shoulder and ear while his fingers flew across the keyboard.

Baron wiggled his head beneath Loki's hands, urging his new friend to abandon the keys to pet him instead. His efforts were rewarded with a few scratches behind one of his shaggy ears.

"Yes, yes, I know, but tell them I couldn't give a rat's arse whether they're in need of my opinion this morning. They'll have to make do on their own for now, as I have pressing personal matters requiring my attention and shall not return until I'm good and ready. Yes. Yes, good day to you as well, Scott." His eyes raised to Selene, and he froze. "Good morning."

While her traitor dog loved up on the mighty dragon, Selene wondered if she was having a nervous breakdown.

I can't deal with this right now.

It was too early for drama, and she needed orange juice to get her sluggish head moving. Turning about on one foot, she crossed back through the kitchen and yanked open the fridge. Even that had been wiped spotless and decluttered. It had also been stocked with fresh groceries. She found the orange juice neatly set between her milk and cranberry juice.

Looking through the cupboard for a glass revealed more displays of cleaning and organization. In fact, she couldn't find a cup at all. She found plates and bowls where her coffee mugs and water glasses usually were.

"Where the heck are my gl—"

"Here, madam. It made more sense to put them here, closer to the fridge."

"They're *my* cupboards," she snapped, immediately regretting her harsh tone. It wasn't the girl's fault. The blame belonging to her lord and master.

Selene cleared her throat, uttered a quiet "thank you" to the flinching, timid girl and accepted the glass without making a bigger fuss.

"Master asked that we wait until you've awakened before we proceed with the remaining rooms. Shall I make your bed now, Madam Selene?" she asked helpfully.

"No. I can make my own bed, thanks. Please don't touch my room."

Loki approached from behind her. "Good morning," he repeated. Anura glanced at him and shrugged.

The male bunny peeked through the threshold from the dining room.

"Please take no offense. Her mate frightens easily," Loki explained.

Selene froze, glass of juice raised toward her mouth, and stared at her stove. It wasn't right. She had an older, glass-top model with stained white plastic knobs. Or that's what she had. The one sitting there now was stainless steel and glossy black. With two oven compartments. It must have cost hundreds of dollars more, beyond her budget.

"Where. Is. My. Stove?"

"The other stove didn't shut easily so I replaced it."

Anura scooped the male bunny into her arms, gathered his clothes, and hurried out of the kitchen. A door opened and shut, and then the two were gone.

"You seem to be upset, Selene. What's wrong?"

"My stove was fine." Sure, it had been old and the oven door never fully closed, but it had been hers. "What gives you the right to come into my home and change things?" Fury overwhelmed any appreciation for the hard work the two cleaners had done.

"It didn't close," he said, bewildered. "Would you prefer the original stove?"

Dusty darted inside through the front door as another servant arrived with his cheeks red from the cold. "The groomer is ready for the second pup, sir. I ought to have taken both at once after all. He was more than willing to push us to the top of the schedule."

"I had a feeling he would accommodate us," Loki said.

Her dog hurried up to her, wagging his tail and sporting a dog-bone patterned bandanna around his neck. He was brushed to a burnished copper gold color and smelled like sandalwood and citrus. He'd been trimmed and shaved, the mats behind his ears gone.

"You took my dog to the groomer?" her voice squeaked up an octave. The man bowed to her then traded one dog for the other. Baron went off happily, not a complaint out of him.

"They were unkempt."

"I'm going to take a shower." Distrusting herself to say anything more, she spun around and stalked down the hall.

Like everything else, her bathroom had been cleaned top to bottom. The shifter cleaning crew had straightened general clutter, repaired the broken toilet paper holder, and replaced her worn towels with fluffy new bath sheets.

Selene closed her eyes and counted to ten. The knobs didn't squeak when she started the shower. Her large walk-in shower shone bright, the grout white again through some miracle she'd never been able to achieve. She sat down on the built-in bench after angling the spray, ducked her head into her hands, and fought back the urge to cry.

How dare he? How dare he come into her house and change her things without asking, as if they were his to do with as he wanted?

Just who did he think he was?

***

Loki moved to the bathroom door and rapped. "Selene?" When she didn't answer, he knocked louder, before he cracked the door and raised his voice to be heard over the thunderous rain of the showerhead. "Selene, may I enter?"

What would Maximilian do in his place?

If Selene was his fated mate, he couldn't afford to chase her away. Couldn't scare her off. He had to do everything within his power to show her she would be cherished, loved, and adored. No task was too large or too small, her comfort his greatest priority.

Asking what she wanted never came to mind.

"Selene?"

"Yeah, I'm fine," she called out. "I just need to get cleaned up is all. I... Dammit. Can you pass me my soaps and stuff? I didn't even pay attention, and they're not in here."

Loki stepped inside and shut the door behind him. The bathroom had already fogged with humidity hanging in the air, but he heard her over the drumbeat of the showerhead. With her shower caddy in hand, he stepped over her discarded clothes, pulled open the frosted door a crack, and passed her things inside.

"Thank you." She sniffled. "I'm good now."

"You're crying, and unless everything I've ever learned about women is wrong, that's hardly good," he replied.

He hesitated. Any idiot, dragon or human, knew women could become more emotional during pregnancy, but he didn't think hormones were guiding Selene's emotions this time.

"What can I do to make you happy?"

"You can stop taking over my life," she wailed, voice wavering. "Look, I appreciate the cleaning crew. I do. It was a thoughtful gesture, but this is my home. My mess. My crazy disorganized organization. I c-c-can't even find my cups anymore."

"My servants will happily fetch whatever cup you desire, Selene." After a pause, he added in a gentler voice, "Even I would."

She said nothing, but the sobbing continued.

At first, he'd wanted to feel only anger and resentment that she had tossed aside what he felt was a fine gift.

What would Max do? The answer crept into his thoughts. Max would counsel him to be patient before he said anything rash.

"It will not happen again, Selene. My apologies. I…" He stopped, embarrassed. "My staff will return things as they were."

The sniffling subsided. "No. They already did all the work. Just please talk to me first before you decide to go changing stuff in my house. How would you feel if I went into your office and moved everything around?"

He chuckled quietly and leaned his back against the wall adjacent to the shower and looked forward, gazing out the small window there instead of at the shadow of her on the bench. "We'll return the original stove. Upsetting you was never my intention. I only wanted to alleviate your burdens and to make your life easier."

"It's a great stove. It's just... You don't have to buy me things. You don't have to spend money on me, I mean. It's too much, and I could never pay you back."

Loki flinched. "Why should you owe me anything in return? The cost of the stove is inconsequential. Our child is priceless."

He counted his heartbeats while waiting for Selene to answer. Several passed at a slow and sedate, draconic rhythm before she whispered, "Thank you."

As he exhaled a relieved breath, he tilted his head against the wall and closed his eyes. He'd never struggled in all his life to speak as kindly to a human as he did with her. "What do you know of dragons?"

"Not much beyond the general stuff most of us know in the paranormal community. President Emberthorn was a great guy. He did a lot of good things for the country. Obviously, you all can take a human form and knock a plain old human up. I'm still not exactly sure how that works."

If this was love, fearing for another person's safety, he wanted nothing of it. He'd been too ignorant to realize. "Many dragons go their entire lives without having a single cub. Then there are some like my cousin Maximilian who father several. And others who conceive with human women the first and only time." He gazed at the shadow moving on the other side of the frosted glass door. "Will you allow me to stay by your side?"

"Do you want to?" she asked.

"Did you believe me to be joking when I said I came to find you? Maximilian and I discovered your Facebook page months ago, and I've been planning to seek you ever since. The cub is an unexpected gift." He waited with anticipation churning in his gut.

"Yes," she whispered, eyes closed and head bowed. He watched her silhouette, tempted to throw open the door to join her. "Yes. I want you to stay. I... I'm terrified. Not because I've found out this baby is part dragon, but because I'm pregnant and I'm alone."

For a while, they were only two people sharing the same space without further conversation as he searched for what he thought his logical, older cousin or his sentimental mate would say. Nothing wise or beautiful came to him.

"I can't promise there won't be times I drive you crazy, because there will be. I am the god of mischief after all, but I'll try my best. That I will promise."

"I gotta admit, you're a lot better looking than that actor who plays Loki... er, you. And that's saying something." The water switched off.

"Thank you. I think."

"Could you pass me a towel?" she asked. After a hesitant pause, added shyly, "One of the new ones please."

"Of course." And he did it without peeking, respecting the boundary between them. "I will dismiss the staff as well, though I insist William continues to take your creatures to the groomer as needed. They smelled of things I will not name."

With a towel wrapped around her, Selene emerged from the shower, water droplets glistening over her bare shoulders. He gazed down at her, then set his hand on her waist above the towel, desperate to touch. She didn't withdraw.

"Okay, yeah, I guess that's fair. Thank you. Dusty looks amazing." Selene tilted her head up to watch him in return, nibbling her lower lip. "I'll be out in a few minutes, okay?"

"I've overwhelmed you with too much at once."

"A little, yes."

His fingers didn't rise from the towel, and he wondered how much her body had been changed by motherhood. Like a mental tattoo, the vision of her naked beneath him had been etched into his memory, a sight he could never forget. He swallowed and fought against his common sense to release her.

Insanity had brought him to Virginia, and the same insanity—the raw need and an urgent hunger for her—drove him to slant his mouth over Selene's lips. He kissed her hard, nothing coaxing or gentle about it, feverish and passionate.

The towel was a hindrance, so he shoved it down until one breast was bared and spilling over into his palm. Still, it wasn't enough. He wanted more, craving her with a desperate intensity. A single sweep from his thumb was all it took to harden her nipple. The dusky peak tightened beneath his touch, and Selene's satisfied moan sent a jolt straight to his stiffening cock.

A polite rap against the door broke them apart, both startled by the interruption. His deep and vocal growl made Selene's eyes widen. She stumbled back and bumped her hip against the bathroom counter.

"Master?" Anura called through the door. "Should we return things as we found them?"

Loki's eyes darted to Selene. She shook her head.

Calming, he dragged a few deep breaths through his nose. Anura knew no better, and he controlled the irritation in his voice before responding. "No. Leave it as it is. Please pass word to the others that you're dismissed."

"As you wish. We will take our leave, until you have need of us again. Breakfast awaits on the table."

Selene hitched her towel up, tightening it around her chest. "Breakfast sounds nice, so I guess I should get dressed.

He raised a brow. "What happens now?"

"I get some clothes on, make sure Jacob knows I'm okay, and then I suppose… you tell me everything I need to know about having a dragon baby."

Chapter 7

Sir Pelleas shoved open the bakery door with his shoulder and strode inside with his hands in his pockets. After lurking a frigid hour across the street, snowflakes dusted his shoulders and stood out against his black hair.

Circulated heat and the aroma of homemade goods welcomed him into Norfolk's tiny slice of baked heaven. Behind the counter, Selene Richards loaded a fresh assortment of cupcakes beneath the glass display. She glanced up at him and smiled.

"Good morning. Welcome to the Sweet Shack. What can I get for you?"

He smiled back at her and stepped up to the counter while feigning interest in her sweets. An enormous chalkboard on the wall behind her displayed menu items and prices not featured under the glass. "An espresso and one of those chocolate croissants will be fine, thank you."

"Sure thing. If you aren't in a rush and don't mind waiting a few minutes, I can serve you a fresh croissant from the batch coming out of the oven."

Perfect. "Of course." It gave him a valid excuse to linger, although he didn't dare to press his luck and remain long enough for the dragon to return. After all, it wasn't time to move forward with their plans.

Pelleas paid in cash and explored the products on the shelves to his immediate left. The store sold everything from chocolate-covered nuts to variety packages of cookies.

So why the hell had a dragon visited her? Over the years, the dragonslayers had observed Loki keeping all manner of strange habits and even odder activities, but he'd never gone out of his way to play escort to a simple human.

Providing service with a smile, Selene delivered his coffee instead of calling him to the counter. "Here you are. It's hot, so take care."

"Thanks." He sipped it, filling his mouth with bittersweet caffeinated brew. "So how far along?"

"Excuse me?"

He gestured to her rounded belly and grinned. Her eyes dropped to his scarred hand. A juvenile dragon had slashed it open to the bone a few years ago, and he was lucky to have kept it. "The baby. How far along are you?"

"Oh, um, six months." A soft smile curved her lips and she ran a hand over her bump.

"Ah, close then. Such a wonderful thing."

"It is, thank you." Selene chuckled and returned to the counter. "That's an interesting accent you have. Are you from Italy?"

"You have good ears, signorina. Yes, I am a visitor to this country, though I've found Americans to be quite welcoming during my travels. And beautiful. What a lucky man he must be, this husband of yours."

He hadn't seen a ring, but that was hardly uncommon these days. Selene flushed and bit her lower lip, making a noncommittal sound rather than giving him a reply, which he took to mean she wasn't married or engaged. He sipped his coffee and turned his attention away, feigning interest in the newspaper left behind on the table by a previous customer.

A young man emerged from the rear of the bakery, built like an athlete with the fashion sense of a metrosexual hair stylist. He restocked the paper cups while eyeballing the woman behind the counter with him.

A small enchantment on Pelleas's Bluetooth earpiece boosted all the sounds in the room, including the low-voiced conversation happening behind the counter.

"Hey, Selene, you want me to take over for a bit? You're looking a little pale."

"No, it's fine."

"Yeah, well, if you pass out behind the counter, I'm the one who's gonna get roasted by your boyfriend," the other worker grumbled. "Literally."

Selene swatted him. "Loki wouldn't do that."

"He threatened to do it. He's protective of you and the baby. Like, crazy protective. Pretty sure I'd be a pile of ashes if anything happened to you on my watch."

"It is not 'your watch' thank you very much. I'm a grown woman, and I can look out for myself."

"Tell that to the dragon who's been escorting you to and from work for the past four days."

That was all he needed. Pelleas swallowed down the hot remnants of his espresso, wrapped his croissant in a napkin, and stood up.

"Have a lovely day," Selene called over. "Watch your step outside."

"Thank you, signorina. A wonderful day to you as well."

Pelleas hurried down the road and to his rental car. Once inside, he cranked the engine. Chilly air rushed through the vents and gradually warmed. He hit speed dial on his phone and waited.

Sir Bedivere answered. "It's about time you checked in."

Pelleas dropped his exaggerated Italian accent and set the device in the cup holder. "Stuff it. I have the intel."

"What'd you find out?"

"It looks like our dragon is about to become a father. Look into Richards again and check her for any travel activity to California."

"How far back are we going?"

Grinning, he threw the car into drive and pulled away. "About six or seven months…"

***

Over the course of the week, Loki teleported Selene to work, kissed her cheek, and went to handle his own business affairs. The moment she called to say she was ready to go home, he appeared at her side and whisked her away.

He refused to allow her to drive on the icy roads, claiming it to be an unnecessary risk and that he was saving her gas money she could otherwise save for their child.

At the start of their strange relationship, he retired to her guest room, sometimes excusing himself to his home in California, although she'd awaken by morning to find him in her kitchen with an enormous tumbler of espresso.

Then there were the times she crawled into bed while he lounged in his recliner with his laptop, only to wake up and find him in the same place. She wondered if he slept at all.

"Have you been awake all night?" she asked the third time she came out and found him in the same clothes.

"Dragons are crepuscular."

"What?" Her eyes crossed.

"We prefer to be awake during the dawn and twilight, though some of us merely remain awake throughout the night. Remaining active during the morning is… displeasing, but not impossible." He sipped his coffee again and resumed reading the screen. "However, it would be difficult to manage an entire company while remaining asleep during the day, so Max and I do what we must."

"Did you sleep at *all?*"

"No." He continued typing. "I'll be fine."

"If you stay up during the day for work, why don't you sleep at night then?"

He shrugged. "Were I able to break hundreds of years of habit so easily, I would, but I've only operated in a human guise for three decades, unlike Saul Drakenstone. I believe he's feigned at mortalhood since the 1950s."

"The movie tycoon?"

"Yes."

"Wow." She flopped down on the couch and drew a blanket over herself. "It's the weekend, why are you working?"

"Business doesn't stop for the weekend," he muttered, though he closed the laptop and set it aside without so much as a glance. "Well then. You asked me to be present this Saturday, so what are your plans for us today?"

"Nothing, really. Can't we just spend time together without something planned? Watch movies on the couch maybe?"

Loki didn't respond at first, making her wonder if the request for a quiet day in offended his delicate, dragon sensibilities. "That is what you want?"

"To spend time with you, yes, but only if you want to."

Within seconds of settling beside her, and before Selene could shift to make room for him, Loki slid his arm beneath her knees and scooted her into his lap. His strength startled her and she squealed, throwing both arms around his neck.

"There."

"What was that for?"

"Aren't you more comfortable? I have seen you rub your back after sitting on this couch." His nose wrinkled.

That he hadn't replaced it went a long way in showing how much he had taken her words to heart about changing her home. It endeared him to her a little more each time he resisted his natural impulse to take control.

"I am," she told him, voice soft. "I guess I'm used to you keeping a certain distance from me."

Since their heated moment in the bathroom, Loki had made no move to touch her again.

"I believed you to be ambivalent to my presence," he admitted. "So I have tried to give you space."

She looked down. "No, it's not that. Though sometimes I really do dislike being touched. It's weird. Hormones have been doing all sorts of crazy things to me lately."

"What things?"

"Midnight snacking, for one. And then there are days I get annoyed if someone so much as brushes up against me, while the next day I just wanna lean against Jacob or my mom for the contact."

He grunted. "You may lean on me as much as you wish."

She chuckled. "Trust me when I say you have nothing to feel threatened about, okay?"

"I understand homosexuality. It's certainly nothing new. However, my place is by your side, and I was under the impression such responsibilities are *mine*." He placed his palm against her stomach, articulate fingers outstretched over the curve. The baby, their baby, wiggled and did one of its strange flips, almost as if sensing the man on the other side.

Enchanted, Loki tilted his head and studied her stomach, features glowing with pleasure. "The little one recognizes me."

"It looks like he does. Or she."

His brows raised. "Do you have a preference?"

"No, not really. A little girl or a little boy would be perfect either way. What about you?"

"I… do not know. I have seen how daughters wrap their fathers around their finger, and I have seen how sons get into all manner of mischief."

"But you've wanted a child for so long, surely you've thought about it," she pressed.

"Exactly so. A child, Selene. It did not matter to me whether I fathered a son or daughter, either one would be cherished."

His warm hand curved over her stomach and their child gave another little nudge. The intermittent kicks and fluttering sensations, like butterflies, made her giggle. Equally enchanted, she laid her hand over his and enjoyed the comfortable silence as they shared the moment together.

"We should tell our families," she finally said.

Loki grimaced. "Must we?"

"Look, I don't know about you, but my mom has been helping me through these past few months. She deserves to know."

"You're welcome to tell your family whatever you'd like. I meant *mine*."

"Ashamed you knocked up a human?"

Baron crawled onto the couch beside them and exposed his belly, forcing the dragon to give him attention. He sighed and stroked him lazily. "Considering half of them have knocked up humans, no. They're hardly in any place to judge."

"What's the problem, then?"

"You'll see."

"That sounds so ominous."

"They'll want to meet you," he clarified.

"Okay…"

Loki raised a skeptical eyebrow. "You won't be intimidated by a room filled with dragons?"

"Of course I will be, but I'll have you with me."

"Then I suppose there is no time like the present. Pack for two days."

"Wait, what?"

"We can leave as soon as you're ready. Besides, it will be warmer in California. Not much, but there won't be snow at least. I've lived enough of my life in snowy conditions to appreciate the Californian climate."

"We're gonna show up at your family's place, just like that? Don't you want to call first? Make sure they're home or something?"

"It's Saturday. Chloe doesn't allow Saul to work during the weekends. They'll be home with Brandt."

"Smart woman. I like her already."

He grimaced. "I will try to curb my habits. Anyway, she's a perpetual gossip, and once we arrive, the others will be there shortly thereafter."

"Might as well get it all over and done at once, huh?" She patted his leg and crawled off his lap. "I'll go get cleaned up."

"You look fine as you are," he told her.

"I need the bathroom mirror so I can fix my hair. It's a mess."

Loki rose, looked her over with a critical eye, and then he changed. He shrank in size and Selene gaped at herself. He'd become her doppelganger. Her mirror image.

"Now you can see yourself. How's this?"

Loki must have gazed at her through permanent beer goggles, because his perception of her beauty struck her as airbrushed and flawless. No one could possibly see her that way.

After the initial shock wore off, Selene frowned at him. "Disturbing."

But she guessed that was part of the charm and what drew her to him. His sense of humor and the little things that always made her laugh, even when she wanted to stare at him stoic and serious.

"What? I am simply providing you a look at yourself." His grin on her face had to be one of the freakiest things she'd ever seen.

Finally, the laughter bubbled out of her. "Would you stop that?"

Being with Loki sometimes reminded Selene of babysitting her younger cousins years ago. She bit back the urge to laugh at his sulky expression. "Fine." He became himself again, or rather, the dark-haired, green-eyed Loki she'd met during the summer.

Selene moved closer and rose on tiptoe to kiss him. "I want an actual mirror. Besides, I'm in my pajamas. I can't meet your family in my nightclothes."

Loki caught up to her in the hallway before she could enter her bedroom to shower and swap into respectable clothes for meeting a family of dragons. His arm circled around her waist, and instead of stiffening, she leaned back against his chest.

"Selene? One thing before you go?"

"What's that?"

With Loki's next step, they pressed flush together and his other hand anchored her against him by the hip. Breath ghosted against her ear as his lips skimmed the edge. "Part of me wants to show you off, but I also enjoy hoarding you to myself. I could never be ashamed of you."

"Loki…"

"And I hope soon you trust me to share your bedroom again. Nothing about my want for you has changed."

Trust him in her bedroom? Didn't he know she'd been fighting against the urge to drag him inside ever since she first brought him home?

***

Within a breath of leaving her home in Virginia, they stood on a stone porch with an extravagant overhang. In the weeks since Loki had begun his strange ritual of delivering her to and from work, she'd yet to fully adapt to instantaneous travel.

The scent of late-autumn flowers perfumed the air as pink, trumpet-shaped daphne grew in magnificent numbers beneath the glass windows spanning the front.

She breathed in the glorious fragrance of jasmine and orange-blossom—her favorite scents—then sighed with longing. She hadn't expected the deep contrast between the weather in Virginia and southern California.

"This home is beautiful."

"It is a very lovely home, though I must say I favor my own." His lips parted to speak again; then he quieted, saying nothing further.

By endeavoring not to smother her, he'd almost moved too far in the other direction.

"Will you show me your house too?" Selene asked impulsively.

His eyes warmed with pleasure. "Yes. I would be honored."

"Are you going to knock or are we going to stand out here? They can't be that scary. Or is that why we arrived outside instead of inside?"

He chuckled. "Maybe I was giving you a chance to back out. Although we tend to visit one another without prior arrangements or calls, it's impolite to teleport into another's home without forewarning." With his left hand in hers, he raised the right and pushed the doorbell.

A blonde woman answered the door. "Hello, Loki, and…" The chipper greeting died on her lips. Her blue eyes dropped to Selene's round tummy then drifted to their linked hands before going back to Selene's stomach again. "I can see you've been busy."

He glowered at her. "Hello, Chloe."

"Well, don't stand out there in the cold. Come in, come in." She moved aside and ushered them into a spacious receiving hall with a high, cathedral ceiling and a split staircase leading to the upper level. "Here, I'll take your coats, and then we can have proper introductions."

The place looked like a mansion, nicer than any place Selene had ever visited. Chloe took her coat and hung it in a long closet near the front entrance. Loki hung his own.

"While it's always a pleasure to have you around, Loki, aren't you going to introduce us?"

He hesitated. "Yes, yes of course. This is Selene, my… Selene, Chloe Drakenstone. She is Saul's human mate and has borne him two fine and healthy children."

"One of which you'll see soo—"

"Oh man, Uncle Loki's here!" A strawberry-blond child came tearing around the corner and crashed into Loki's legs. "Uncle Loki! Hug, hug!"

"Greetings, little one."

Loki crouched down and swept the tyke into his arms. A warm sensation of longing fluttered inside Selene's chest when she imagined him doing the same with their little boy. It would be a boy. Something in her heart told her it would be, though she'd be equally pleased to have a daughter.

"Ease up, kiddo. Why don't you take your uncle and his friend into the living room while I get some refreshments. Is there anything in particular you'd like, Selene? I have ginger tea, lemonade—anything you want really."

"Oh, um, mint tea if you have it, and it isn't any trouble."

Before Selene could say anything else, the little boy took her and Loki by their hands and tugged them from the foyer.

Every step into the manor introduced her to new wonders of wealth and luxury. Yet everything felt homey and cozy, unlike the severe atmosphere of a museum she'd once experienced when visiting Carlos's rich grandmother. A pile of colorful Lego pieces in different themes occupied one corner of the room while several finished models were spread out across a Persian rug.

Loki gestured her to a loveseat. The plush fabric cradled her in comfort as she sat down and sank back against the cushions. Her couch couldn't compare.

"I see you finished several sets in my absence. Well done, Brandt." Loki took his place beside her and smiled at the boy.

"But I saved the best for you," Brandt said proudly. Although he was no larger than a three or four-year-old in physical shape, he spoke with the eerie intelligence of an older child. "You're supposed to help me with the castle."

"And I will, but not today."

"Awww."

"I won't mind if you help him," Selene said. Brandt beamed at her, and she smiled in return.

"Then perhaps a little later."

"Okay! I'll go get the box right now so it's ready!"

Brandt bolted from the room.

"He's very verbose for—how old is he? Four? Five?"

"Brandt celebrated his seventh birthday this past October, Selene."

"But he looks so much younger."

"Half-dragons, like Astrid and Brandt, mentally develop as expected, but remain behind their mortal peers physically."

Selene ran her fingers over her round belly. "I guess I should have figured that when you told me my pregnancy would last longer than normal."

"In hindsight, concealing you from them appears to have been a foolish notion. As Chloe has weathered two pregnancies of this nature, she will be able to answer any of your questions far better than I can."

"Chloe tells me congratulations are in order," a jovial voice boomed toward her.

Within seconds of glancing at the blond Viking lookalike, Selene recognized Saul Drakenstone from photographs of him online. He'd been one of the first dragons to come into the open.

Panicked, she started rising from the seat to greet him, but he shook his head and approached.

"No, no need to rise. I can see you deserve your rest," Saul said.

Loki grinned. "Quite considerate of you."

Saul's smile widened, and he gave Selene a wink. "So it would seem Loki's hidden you from the rest of us for quite some time. What a pleasure to meet you, Selene."

He shook her hand, his fingers warm and grip strong. The friendly smile on his face instantly put her at ease, and she sighed in relief.

"Thank you, Mr. Drakenstone."

"None of that. You may call me Saul. Welcome to our home. Anyone dear to Loki is dear to us as well. It shouldn't be long before my mother and Max arrive. Any second now, in fact."

Time with Loki made it easy to recognize the sensation of an opening portal. Magical white noise filled her ears and the buzz of it raised the fine hairs on the backs of her arms. Selene glanced toward the open space in the living room in time to see the gateway snap open, trimmed with glittering silver sparkles resembling a million diamonds. A man and woman stepped through, each one holding a child.

Maximilian Emberthorn, former President of the United States, beamed at her from beside his wife. Was she supposed to bow? Stand and salute? What did a person do when meeting the former leader of the country?

"Oh no, don't stand on our account. What an exquisite pleasure to meet you at last, Selene. I've heard only the most pleasant things about you," Maximilian said. "In the event that he's told you nothing of me, as I highly suspect he hasn't, I am Max and this ravishing beauty beside me is my mate Ēostre."

"P-pleasure to meet you both," she stammered.

Loki curled his arm around her waist, leaned close, and whispered, "I warned you."

"We'll have to throw a celebration dinner, of course," Ēostre said, smiling warmly. "Chloe and I shall get to that now."

"I've already asked Leiv to butcher a pair of goats," Chloe said from the doorway.

"Oh, no, you don't have to do anything special for me," Selene protested.

"Please, we insist," Saul said. "My daughter should be here shortly."

The same buzz filled the air and another portal opened, though the ring shone like liquid gold instead of stardust and silver.

"I swear it's perfectly safe," the voice from the other side said. "Don't be a baby. You're a knight for crying out loud."

"Did they say knight?" Selene whispered against Loki's ear.

"Yes. Astrid's mate is a reincarnated Knight of the Round Table."

"Oh… Oh, of course he is." Because how could anything else not get any stranger?

A handsome man stepped through first, eyes closed and an expectant wince on his face. Saul chortled and grabbed him by the arm.

"No pool landing this time, son. Come, meet Selene." Saul gestured to where she sat. "Selene, this is Nate, my son-in-law, and this beautiful lady is my daughter, Astrid, and their son, Arthur."

Selene's gaze moved from Nate's smiling features to the blonde stepping through the portal with an infant in her arms. She looked like Chloe. Too much like her. They could have been sisters, although Loki had warned her they were mother and daughter.

Was that what she had to look forward to now because of their baby? The rest of her life eternally frozen at the age of thirty-six?

The thought of it spun the world around her, leading Selene to clutch the armrest with one hand and Loki's thigh with the other.

"Selene?" His voice rose in alarm.

"I need some air," she whispered. A staccato drumbeat pounded in her head to the tempo of her heart.

The room swam as she tried to stand, wavering enough to make her stomach flip and tighten. Then Loki had her in his arms and consciousness blurred away.

Chapter 8

Petrified by Selene's swoon and unfamiliar with the frailty of humans, Loki rushed her away from the others and into the guest room he favored while visiting. He lowered Selene to the bed then hovered over her until she stirred and showed the first signs of rousing from the faint.

Loki frowned down at her. "Are you well? Is the little one?"

"I'm fine," she assured him. "Just tired is all."

"I am sorry."

Selene gave him a hazy, fragile smile. "It's not anyone's fault. It happens sometimes."

"What can I do for you?"

"Nothing. I need to sleep for a little while, is all. Is that okay?"

"Of course. You take as much rest as you require, and I will sit here—"

"No. Go see your family. I feel awful for fainting on them like that."

He smoothed her hair back from her brow. "They overwhelmed you. As far as I am concerned, there is no reason for *you* to feel awful."

Loki remained beside her until her breaths evened, smoothing his hand up and down her back. Assured she was asleep, he tucked the blanket around her shoulders and exited the room.

The most motherly of them, Chloe and Ēostre, jumped to their feet the moment he returned to the living room.

"Is she all right?" Ēostre asked.

"She is asleep, no thanks to you lot. Could we not crowd her? I can hardly blame her for needing to lie down after she's been assaulted by each of you in turn. Perhaps time your arrivals at respectable intervals next time someone has a—" He stopped. What did he call her? His mate? She had yet to accept, though she enjoyed his company, and seemed reluctant to take any more steps.

Maximilian frowned. "I suppose that would have been wise. Apologies, Loki. We were all so eager to meet her."

"You act as if you've never met a human before," he grumbled at them.

"We are truly sorry," Saul apologized.

Chloe sighed. "I am too. Sorry. I just couldn't wait to let everyone know you'd found someone."

"As fortune would have it, I did warn her this would happen. One can hardly expect anything different from you."

Saul nodded. "She woke me to share the news."

"No fancy dinner. No party. No one else is to be invited to gawk, am I understood?"

Nate raised his hand. "Permission to speak, sir?"

Loki grunted and took a seat on the empty chaise. "I am neither your superior officer nor your teacher. You need not raise your hand or call me sir."

"Oh, right. So, uh, Merlin might have been over when we got the call…"

Loki dropped his face into his hand and sighed. "Well, at least the wizard has the decency not to pop up in a rush."

"I'm sorry," Chloe apologized again.

The irritation dwindled and left exhaustion in its wake, too many chagrined and apologetic expressions surrounding Loki to remain angry with them for long.

After all, they'd assembled because they cared. Because they loved him. Because at some point, he'd become a part of their family, and now he was as beloved as Nate, Maximilian, and everyone else connected by marriage.

Loki sighed. "No, no, it's fine. Very well then, a dinner, but no large celebration, please."

Chloe relaxed. "Of course. Is there anything you think she'd like?"

He spouted off a list of Selene's favorite things with ease, and afterward, everyone but Saul and Max drifted from the room.

"So…," Max began. "You're to be a father."

"I am."

Saul leaned forward. "But you have not claimed her?"

Loki shook his head. "I only discovered her this past month, Saul. I had no idea she carried my cub, and this isn't to be rushed."

"No, that wasn't my concern," Saul said. He stroked his chin. "This invalidates our theory. If she's become pregnant without a bond, I cannot understand why some dragons, such as Thor, who sleep quite frequently with humans, do not have a score of children."

Loki scowled at him. "That is because Thor sleeps around with any human who catches his fancy. Selene may not be my bonded mate, but she is still *mine*."

"Then perhaps it is the potential for a bond, not the bond itself," Max muttered.

Saul agreed. "She also doesn't smell human."

Loki straightened. "You noticed it as well? She genuinely believes herself to be a witch of some sort."

"She smells like magic, but not any sort I'm familiar with."

"It strikes me as familiar, but eludes my memory," Max said. The older fire wyrm gazed at Loki with a thoughtful expression. "Has she discussed much with you regarding her origins?"

"A mortal mother, father unknown."

"It could be the father perhaps."

"Or a grandparent. I haven't interrogated her and don't plan to."

Max held up both hands. "I meant no offense, Loki."

He sighed. "No, the apology is mine. I realize I've grown quite protective of her."

Both dragons grinned at him.

By dinner time, Selene had roused with an appetite. She joined them in the dining room, seeming more at ease and less likely to panic again. Loki appreciated his family's restraint. No one bombarded her with questions or asked more than what was expected in polite conversation.

"Can we build my castle now?" Brandt asked.

"Don't you want to wait and have dessert?"

The boy considered the offer, then shook his head. "We can build it before dessert. Mom always makes us wait for our food to settle."

Beside him, Selene laughed into her water glass. "My mother does the same thing."

"I do hope there's dessert for me," an unfamiliar voice spoke up.

Selene jumped in her seat, but no one else reacted to the appearance of an additional diner, an old man with a grandfatherly smile and silver hair. Neither his crow's feet nor laugh lines detracted from his handsome features.

Freaked out by the arrival of another teleporting stranger, Selene reached for Loki's hand.

Nate chuckled and leaned back in his seat. "Leave it to a wizard to appear in time for sweets."

The stranger stroked his white beard. He wore a royal purple three-piece suit, and no one but him could have pulled it off without carrying a pimp cane to complete the ensemble.

"Am I fashionably late?" he asked.

"Very. Everyone else swarmed her at once," Loki said.

"Ah. I expected they would."

"Selene, allow me to introduce you to a good friend of mine. Merlin, meet Selene."

"Wait, you mean like *the* Merlin?"

"The one and only Merlin. A great pleasure it is to meet you, Selene." Merlin rose from his seat, swept back the edge of his shoulder cape, and bowed. "I must say, it is nice to see you with some companionship, Loki, especially a companion so lovely to the eyes."

Selene blushed. "Oh, well, thank you."

They all adjourned to the family room with strudel and ice cream, though Loki held off so he could help Brandt with his Lego set first. Selene eventually joined them on the floor and helped sift through the tiny blocks whenever they needed a certain piece. She had a knack for finding what they overlooked.

"How *do* you do that?" Merlin asked. He occupied a nearby leather recliner and had been watching them the whole time.

Selene looked up and shrugged. "What? You mean find the right piece? I dunno, they just sorta jump out at me, almost like they come to my hand."

"Fascinating."

Loki stared at the wizard and frowned. He figured if anyone knew about Selene's magic, it would be Merlin, but the great sage appeared as puzzled as the rest of them. Or he was playing dumb.

They finished the set with half an hour to spare before Brandt's bedtime. The grateful child took his newest creation to the table where he kept all his models and happily entertained himself.

Loki assisted Selene to her feet and took a seat beside her on the sofa.

"Go ahead, dear, I'm certain you have questions." Merlin smiled cheerfully from his seat.

"I sorta wondered if you were going to take over the covens, I guess. I mean, you're Merlin. They say our magic came from you."

"Yes and no. I was one of the first, and I taught many and passed on my gift to my bloodline, but even my magic came from somewhere." The wizard chuckled. "As for the rest, no, I have no intention of taking over anything. That is not how I work. I may teach an apprentice now and again, but that is all. Why do you ask?"

Selene shrugged and laughed, tucking her hair behind her ear in a self-conscious gesture. "No real reason. It's expected for witches in the States to register with one of the three main councils. Jacob hates it. Says it's restrictive and very cliquish once you get into the higher levels."

"Jacob?"

"My best friend. He's a witch."

"A bold one, too," Loki added with reluctant respect. "Bold enough to stand up to me."

"I'd love to meet him one day soon. For now, however, the hour grows late, so I shall take my leave. It was lovely to meet you, Selene." Merlin rose from his seat and bowed. Unlike the dragons, the fabled wizard had no need for portals. He simply vanished, there one second and gone the next.

"The old man is right, it is time to retire. You can have my room," Loki offered.

After saying their goodnights to the rest of the family, he led the way upstairs. Drakenstone Manor had become a home away from home, and he was always made to feel welcome. "If I have your usual room, where will you sleep?" Selene asked.

"Another room I suppose."

"You don't have to. The bed is big enough for us both."

"I would not wish to presume…"

"Which is why I'm inviting you." She patted the sheets beside her.

Loki shrugged out of his clothes and eased beneath the blanket.

Selene stared. "Are they magic?"

"Excuse me?" He focused his puzzled gaze on her.

"Your clothes. Do you conjure them up out of thin air? That's the first time I've actually seen you remove anything since we met in California." Her gaze lingered on his chest, trailing over the defined muscle and lingering where the sheets pooled around his waist.

He laughed. "No. Though I've been known to conjure armor and other objects in the past, those are merely temporary constructs of sorcery. I summoned these clothes while you were preparing for the day." He snapped his fingers. The clothes folded over the nearby chair vanished. More appeared in their place in different shades of charcoal and burgundy.

"Okay, that is seriously cool. Witches can't do stuff like that."

"Our magic is completely different." He shrugged and settled back against the pillow. He didn't know whether to invite her closer or not. Pregnancy had made her shy.

"I like your family," Selene said.

He turned his head to look at her. "You do?"

"Yes. Astrid and Chloe offered to take me shopping tomorrow."

He let out a breath. "That is good. I'll give you my card."

"You don't have to do that."

"But I wish to. I don't want you to settle for anything less than what you want simply because it is beyond your usual means."

Selene remained quiet and still beside him and for a moment until he thought she had fallen asleep.

"Thank you," she whispered. Making the first move, she crawled closer and placed her palm against his chest.

Relief surged over him, loosening the tense muscles he'd held since joining her in the bed. He drew her closer and kissed her brow. The sound she made, pure satisfaction, sent a stiffening pulse below his waist.

He ignored it. Her comfort meant everything.

"You and this child are the greatest gift I could ever receive. It is I who should be thanking you. Now get some rest. Tomorrow will be a busy day if the girls are taking you out."

***

Despite Loki giving her unlimited access to his Centurion credit card, Selene made reasonable and responsible choices as she was dragged from store to store. A few new tops to accommodate her growing belly, comfortable leggings, and slip-on boots.

It wasn't until Astrid took her into a specialty children's shop that she experienced the sudden urge to go hog-wild with Loki's money. She flitted between the various crib displays and gazed with longing at the varied bedding patterns.

"The jungle animals are adorable," Selene said. "But I also love this patchwork design."

"You can always order both." Astrid grinned. "I mean, we have more than one set of sheets for our bed, why shouldn't the baby?"

Selene sighed. "You're a horrible influence."

Divided between cringing and wanting to cheer when she saw the total, Selene fished out Loki's credit card and made peace with herself.

Loki would get his wish after all. Babies were expensive business, and if she didn't want to deplete her nest egg, she'd have to allow him to bankroll her pregnancy. With his help, she walked out holding a receipt for a crib with a matching dresser and changing table, new animal print curtains, and two bedding sets to be delivered.

"Lunchtime," Chloe sang. "I'm starved, so I know you are."

"I'm craving Chinese like you wouldn't believe," Selene said.

"Well, there are at least two choices in the food court or we could drive over to a nearby restaurant I know," Astrid offered.

"Here is fine since it took forever to find parking. Which brings to mind a question."

"Shoot."

"If you can portal to wherever you want, why do you even bother driving?"

Astrid shook her head and sighed. "The Anti-Mag Fields. Most of us had that kind of protection around our homes and personal property before, and we'd create the wards in a way to allow ourselves and loved ones through. But when Grandpa made the Supernatural Right to Privacy Act guarding our identities, we had to give the mortals something in return."

The answer was so obvious, Selene felt herself blush. "Okay, makes sense. I remember now how everyone was freaking out about bank robberies and home invasions when the paranormals first came out. As if you all would just start pillaging now that we knew you existed."

"Right. I mean, if it makes them feel safer, that's great. There *are* some bad dudes out there, and we should all be protected anyway."

Chloe chuckled at her daughter. "And sometimes it's easier to drive like normal people than to appear into the middle of a parking garage and freak everyone out. Saul never developed a knack for creating portals, but Mahasti would teleport us everywhere. Now she's been reigned in, too."

After riding to the upper level in the elevator, they crossed to the food court and found Chinese-style carryout in abundance. They chose the place with the best lunch-hour deal, ordered meals, then settled at a table.

"Have you two discussed bonding?" Astrid asked after a few quiet minutes of the girls sating their ravenous appetites.

"Bonding? Well, we've been trying since he showed up, I guess. It's…" Selene sighed. She had few female friends; Jacob was the closest person to her. "It's strange, you know? When I met him, I thought he was the hottest guy I'd ever meet. I was mad at myself for letting him get away without asking for his phone number."

Wrinkles creased Chloe's brow. Her daughter leaned forward across the table, cupping her chin against both palms. "But now?" Astrid asked.

"He's sweet, and he makes me laugh. Every day we're together, it feels more like a dream. Now I don't know what to do… and I get the distinct feeling I'm misunderstanding what you asked me."

"Just a little," Astrid replied. "I meant a soulbond, not bonding as friends. Obviously you've already bonded as a little more than friends, right?" She gestured toward Selene's stomach.

A surge of heat flashed over Selene's body.

"Has he mentioned a soulbond to you at all?" Chloe asked.

"Nooo," she said, drawing the word out. "Should he have?"

Astrid and Chloe exchanged looks.

"What? Does that mean something bad?"

"No, no, no," Astrid rushed to say. "Not bad. Odd, is all."

Chloe picked up where her daughter left off. "Most dragon males, well, they don't waste any time forming a bond. It's a natural instinct."

"And I'm guessing I would know if he had?"

Both blondes nodded. Chloe looked around then tugged aside the neckline of her sweater. Selene leaned over and made out a red mark against her shoulder. "It looks like an animal bit you."

"If you consider a dragon an animal, you aren't far off the mark. They bite you and infuse you with part of their soul, hence the name. It doesn't hurt, honest. Aches a little afterward, kind of like a tattoo does."

It should have terrified her. Instead of striking fear into her heart, Selene's stomach quivered with rising nausea. "If it's natural instinct for him, does it mean something bad if he hasn't offered it to me? Does it mean he doesn't want me?"

"No, no, no," Chloe said quickly. "Maybe he's waiting for the right moment."

"Nate and I waited months before we did it."

"But he's never even mentioned it."

"Soulbonds aren't made lightly. As I said, they're gifting you with part of their soul. You become linked. I'm sure, given everything that's happened, that he's trying not to overwhelm you. Hell, Saul bonded to me before I even knew he was a dragon."

"And everyone still gives Dad shit over it."

Chloe reached over and gave Selene's arm a comforting squeeze. "Talk to him about it if it will make you feel better. I imagine, Loki being who he is, that he's resisting the urge for your comfort. He doesn't want to scare you off."

"What if he only cares about the baby?"

"Trust me. If he only cared about the baby, he wouldn't be giving you his credit card or staying by your side. He'd be sending checks and waiting for it to turn eighteen. He was furious with us for upsetting you."

Selene shook her head. "I wasn't upset."

"Well, for making you faint. And he was right, we all sort of forgot to consider your feelings in our excitement."

"You guys didn't do that. I faint a bit." She tucked her chin and toyed with the edge of her camisole, frowning. "My doctor was worried about the baby at first because the pregnancy wasn't progressing as expected. But I wanted to wait it out and see what happened."

Astrid grinned. "I'll give you the name of my doctor. She has experience in dragon pregnancies."

A few words of protest sprang to the tip of her tongue, a natural inclination to refuse. Then relief swept over her. At last, someone who could answer her questions. Someone who knew what they were doing. "Thank you."

"And you don't even have to worry about her being on the opposite coast since Uncle Loki can send you by portal to appointments."

"Still getting used to that."

"Hey, it beats Air Djinn. I'll never grow accustomed to that," Chloe said.

"Huh?"

Chloe laughed at her bewildered expression. "You met Mahasti last night."

"Yeah, is she not a dragon?"

"Nope, she's a djinn. Her husband Leiv is a bear shifter. Sorry, we didn't want to overwhelm you again with an info dump of who we are and what we do."

"No, it's fine. Shifters I'm familiar with. I had no idea there were djinn around, though."

"Very few," Chloe said. "And they don't like to advertise it since greedy people hunt for their lamps to enslave them."

Learning about their unique family intrigued her, and with every new discovery, Selene feared less. They'd accepted her and included them without argument or questioning. Her eyes burned, and a few tears slipped beneath her lashes.

Chloe offered her a tissue from her purse.

"Sorry. I get so emotional."

"Hey, the great thing about pregnancy is you have an excuse and never have to apologize for crying, wanting weird foods at strange hours, foot rubs, baths, or anything else," Chloe said.

Astrid snickered. "Yeah, Mom got busted horking down raw meat from the fridge."

Selene stared.

"All that stuff about raw fish and meat? Ignore it," Chloe said.

Selene stirred the noodles and shrimp in front of her. "I can eat sushi again?"

"Go to an all-you-can-eat buffet if you want. In fact, even better, I'll ask Mahasti if she'll pick us up some food from this Japanese place we discovered about a year ago. To die for."

"I'd love that."

"Perfect, dinner's decided. Now then, it's time for the next big question." Chloe leaned forward and lowered her voice, expression serious. "Are you ready to tackle the baby clothes shops?"

Chapter 9

Shortly after dinner with the generous Drakenstone family, Selene joked that Loki would have to roll her through his portal. Once she'd hugged her new friends and Loki had sent her shopping bags ahead to his estate, he escorted her through the shimmering gateway.

Then she stepped into paradise, her feet touching down on a manicured lawn bordered by ornamental trees and hedges of varying sizes and colors. Spotlights scattered around the property lit everything brighter than an amusement park.

Selene sucked in her breath and stared. A sprawling compound stretched before her with oversized windows and a pair of beautiful French doors. To her left, the jacuzzi bubbled near a spacious pool edged by stone tiles and swaying palms.

"Is that a waterslide?"

Loki's lips turned up at the corners. "It is."

Her eyes flicked left and right, taking in each sight as it registered in her mind.

As she panned left, she saw a tennis court beside a stretch of white sand.

"Do you even play beach volleyball?"

"Astrid brought her friends to play over the summer."

"But do *you?*"

He shook his head. "My real estate agent prompted me to purchase the property due to the location. It's quite private, and she knows my true identity. You won't find many other people for the next ten or fifteen miles, and the ones who do dwell nearby are all shapeshifters or paranormal creatures of some kind."

Selene walked forward as if she were exploring a dream, half convinced she'd fallen asleep and fantasized the past three weeks of her life.

"This isn't real."

"It's my home," Loki said. "Your home as well if you'll have it and me."

His words made her turn and pause. Live with him? Her heart and soul screamed yes, but her mind had other nefarious plans. "What's a soulbond, Loki?" tumbled from Selene's lips.

He froze. "Excuse me?"

"A soulbond," she repeated.

After rubbing his face with one hand, he gave a low groan. "Chloe has a big mouth."

"She and Astrid mentioned it."

"This is a talk meant for inside. Please."

With a hand held lightly against the small of her back, Loki guided her up a short flight of steps to the French doors she'd been admiring. The inside of his home was as beautiful as the outside, with open-beam, vaulted ceilings and burnished wood trim.

"You live here alone?"

"I live here with my staff, so I'm never truly alone."

As if summoned, Anura stepped around the corner with a silver tray in her hands. The slim woman smiled and bowed her head to them. "I have your evening drink, Master, and herbal tea for Madam Selene."

"Thank you, Anura. That will be all for the evening."

"Shall I leave these in your den?"

"Yes."

Every step of the way amazed Selene, from the polished floors in the great room beyond the entrance doors to the thick carpet beneath her feet when they reached his man cave. She couldn't think of another way to describe it. The wood-paneled walls gleamed and a faint lemon scent hung in the air.

She breathed in the smell of real wood. Cords of it had been stacked beside the crackling fireplace.

"This is a lot for one man."

"Technically, I'm not a man. I'm a dragon."

"Point taken, I guess, but unless you stretch out in your dragon form…" There seemed to be enough room to house a dragon in the vast den.

"Sometimes I do on the lawn during the summer, but never indoors. There wouldn't be enough room to hold me, even here."

Selene tried to picture a basking dragon beneath the sun, but without any idea of what Loki looked like, she clawed mentally at visuals. "Will I get to see you before summer?"

"If you like."

"I do," she blurted out, continuing to speak in a rush. "I would love to see what you look like. What color are your scales? Is it true you have feathered wings?"

"Black, and yes." He took his rum from the tray on his desk in one hand and Selene's mug in the other.

"I imagine they're beautiful."

"Beautiful is a word no one has ever called me," Loki said, chuckling.

Selene accepted her tea, and then they settled on a leather couch with a television screen stretching across half of the wall in front of them.

"Hello, Sif."

"What may I do for you, Loki?"

"Play music at volume three, please." With the mood set and absolute privacy granted to them, Selene fidgeted and circled her finger around the rim of her tea mug. A delightful fragrance wafted up to her—sage, jasmine, and mint.

One glance from him made her reconsider drinking. Her mouth went dry, and her tummy did a small flipflop of anticipation when he studied her.

"How much did Chloe tell you?" he asked.

"Bonding is a natural instinct for you."

"It is."

"But you haven't bonded with me. Haven't asked or brought it up."

"I did not wish to frighten you away, considering you never contacted me and seemed to have no intention to ever do so."

Heat traveled up her neck, and she dropped her gaze. "You never gave me your full name to find you, and when I saw your picture on that magazine, I figured you probably had a legal team prepared for this kind of thing."

"I have an excellent legal team, it is true, but I've never employed their services to handle expectant mothers."

"Yeah, well, I didn't wanna sound like some crazy lady looking to get ahold of your money, especially since we used protection."

"That we did, but…" He stroked his hand over her round belly. "If we bond, it should be a choice made between us both, not an accident because I have lost control."

"Like Saul."

His lips quirked. "Chloe has a *very* big mouth."

"So you keep saying." She sipped her tea and studied him. "Were you ever going to bring it up?"

"In time, yes. Resisting you is… It is quite trying, Selene, but respecting your boundaries means more than my own pleasure. Which brings me to a question of my own."

"Yeah?"

"Would you *desire* to be bonded to me? Knowing now what it means?"

Did she? Selene gazed into his green eyes and knew exactly what she wanted.

"Before I answer, I want to see you."

His dark brows drew close together. "Am I not here before you now."

"No. The real you, scales, wings, big teeth and all. The real Loki when you're not a businessman or entertaining me."

"What makes you believe this isn't the real Loki?"

"You're a dragon."

His mouth turned up at the corner. "Yes, but was I a dragon first or a man first? No one really knows."

Exasperated, she gave his shoulder a gentle nudge. "Now you're only messing with me."

"I am," he admitted with a cunning smile. "As is my nature."

Considering his impressive title, she relented and allowed him his playful victory over her. If she could accept his billions and his multi-million-dollar compound, she'd have to take the entire package. "Please? I want to see your dragon shape."

"As you wish," Loki murmured, a mysterious air to his voice as he led her by the hand outside onto the yard. He put distance between them before he turned to face her again, making her wonder how large a dragon he would be.

"Loki?" she whispered. "Why are you so far away?"

"I'd prefer not to harm you. Last chance to change your mind. Some humans aren't able to confront even a non-aggressive dragon."

"What happens?" she asked.

"They faint. Sometimes the fight-or-flight response forces them to flee."

Selene swallowed. She'd fainted enough times over her pregnancy, would one more time really change anything. "Will you catch me?"

A hint of a smile touched his lips. "Of course. You may always count on me, Selene."

He hesitated a moment longer, at least, it seemed that way to Selene. He watched her for a while across the yards between them, breathing slow, measured breaths. Then he transformed, and the sophisticated businessman was no longer six feet of eye candy, but several thousand pounds of scaled behemoth towering above her.

The air left Selene's lungs all at once, a low whoosh she barely noticed. She stared up at him with wide eyes and staggered back a step. The blood rushed in her veins as the cold fingers of a fainting spell grasped to pull her under.

His hand—or his claw, rather—against her back supported her as he'd promised. The tips never touched her, though each talon was as long as her forearm and gleamed black.

"Have I frightened you?"

"N-no."

He'd been modest when he described his scales as black. They were, but a ruby edge trimmed each individual scale, and they glowed beneath the lights dotting the property. She reached for him at first, but fell short of caressing his snout.

"Is it okay to…?"

"Please." He met her the rest of the way and touched his warm scales to her hand.

"Having a dragon of my own is far better than having a billionaire boyfriend," she murmured.

"Perhaps, but as luck would have it, you do not need to choose, Selene. I am both."

She searched his face for similarities between the man and the dragon, humanizing his emerald eyes and drawing familiarity between his angular human features and the slim taper of his snout.

"Your horns are beautiful." She touched one of them, finding it smooth and polished beneath her fingers, like obsidian glass. "*You're* beautiful."

"I am?"

"Yes."

He dipped his head to her and settled on the lawn. With his wings tucked against his body, long flight feathers drifted against the grass, speckled with scarlet down. The initial spike of terror dimmed and faded until only tranquility remained. Joy mingled with the warmth spreading in her chest until she stepped forward against him.

When she placed their cheeks together and stroked her fingers across the softer, supple skin of his face, a rumbling motor sound came from the dragon's chest.

"You purr!"

"I am Loki, god of mischief. I do not purr."

She kissed his snout. "You purr, and I love it."

"I suppose I do," he admitted.

Selene blinked the tears away again, reluctant to ruin their moment with another emotional fit.

"You are happy with me?"

For a confident god of mischief, troublemaker, and all-powerful dragon, she heard the yearning in his voice tinged with disbelief.

"Yes," she whispered, "and I do want to be bonded to you. I want us to be a real family. Every day with you has been special,

Loki. Your devotion to me. The way you make me laugh. Every time your kindness defies my expectations, I realize… that I already love you."

Warm scales were replaced by even warmer skin and cool cotton. His arms wrapped around her. Somehow, he'd even brought his clothes back again during the transformation to a man.

He nuzzled his face against her throat and breathed her scent, inhaling a deep breath into his lungs. "I never tire of holding you, and I want to hold you for the rest of my life, Selene."

Loki carried her from the majestic lawn and into the house. All the while, she tried to take in the view along the way to distract her anxious mind from their impending bond. Tried to focus on his smell, the masculine musk of him that was a hint of earthy soil and a woodsy scent like the cozy fire in his den. Above all else, Selene tried to ignore the way he devoured her with his green eyes each step of the way.

The bedroom was a marvel of hardwood and glass. A pair of doors led to a deck beyond the windows spanning the rest of the wall. At the push of a button, a gentle whirring noise carried heavy draperies into place and concealed the outside world, though the room remained lit by the fireplace crackling nearby.

Gray silk sheets contrasted against the navy-blue comforter spread over a king-size bed dominated by a dozen pillows. She fell in love with it the moment he set her on the edge. It was soft as a cloud, but firm, and much better than the mattress she'd longed to replace at home.

Glossy black bookcases flanked both sides of the bed, each shelf filled with a variety of titles. Leather-bound classics sat beside dollar store paperbacks and plastic sheathed comics.

"Do you like it?" he asked.

From the corner of her eye, she caught him unfastening his shirt. Her gaze honed in on him, instantly reminded of having his bare muscles beneath her hands in the hotel room months ago.

"Yes."

"You can change whatever you wish."

Selene shook her head. "It's perfect." *He* was perfect—which was reaffirmed the moment his trousers fell and he stepped free of them. The orange glow cast from the hearth created shadows against the dips and planes of hard muscle.

How could any one man be so beautiful? So sexy? His sculpted shape put Michelangelo's David to shame. In *every* way. Her gaze followed the muscled indents defining his hips, like an arrow leading to his cock.

Once she kicked off her shoes, she stood and unfastened her jeans, thankful she hadn't grown large enough yet to require the stretch top pants. Her fingers hesitated at the hem of her shirt. "I—no one's seen me since…" She gestured to her stomach. "You."

"I will be happy to be the only one who ever sees you again." His fingers caressed the round curve. "You have nothing to fear with me, Selene. No need for insecurity. You will always be remarkable in my eyes."

He peeled her blouse away, revealing the lace-trimmed bra beneath and the naked curve of her tummy. Except for fleeting moments of confidence, she hadn't felt attractive in weeks. But with Loki standing before her naked and gazing through lidded, bedroom eyes, there was no other way for Selene to feel.

"You are radiant." After removing her bra, he supported her heavy breast with his palm and dipped his head to kiss the tender tip. When her core tightened in response, his nostrils flared.

He trailed lower with each kiss, drawing her jeans down her legs. His whiskered chin tickled against her hips as he freed each ankle in turn.

"I have dreamed of this moment," he whispered.

"Y-you have?"

"Mm-hmm." He nuzzled the front of her matching lace panties and kissed her through the semi-sheer fabric. Selene gripped his shoulders with both hands to keep her weakening knees from dropping her to the floor.

Loki nipped her hipbone and caught the edge of her panties with his teeth. Inch by teasing inch, he drew them down. Her body tingled from head to toe with goose bumps as he guided her to the mattress.

He caressed her belly, letting his fingers slide beneath the curve until he touched between her legs. Agile, eager fingers pressed inward and stroked, teasing. "When I bite you, it may be without warning."

"It's all right," she whispered, wriggling beneath his touch. "I'm ready."

The deep timbre of his chuckle curled through her. "No, you're not."

A hot flush spread up from her toes to her ears. Loki grinned at her and dipped down, claiming her lips while his fingers continued their wicked work. He brought her to the brink of orgasm, slowed until her body settled and the tension coiled in her limbs relaxed, then repeated the process until she thought she couldn't take any more.

"Loki, please."

"Please what?"

"I need you inside me."

"Is that all?" His thumb circled around her sensitive clit. "Tell me what you want, Selene."

"I want you to make love to me. I want to have your mark. I want..." She moaned and writhed again, overwhelmed by desire.

A final flick brought her over the edge. She bucked beneath his touch and grabbed a handful of the silken sheets, riding out the rippling waves of pleasure.

Her dragon gave her no time to recover, rolling to his back and pulling her onto him. Selene blinked and braced her hands against his chest. His black hair spilled around him like an ebony halo, framing the image of masculine perfection. She recalled trying to take this position that first night they met, but Loki had been the one in control and unwilling to surrender it.

"What...?" she asked breathlessly.

"I want to see you when you come. Every time." Strong hands at her waist lifted and guided her back down over his stiff cock. Without a condom between them, she discovered the ecstasy of his hot, silken skin within her.

And every inch of him felt divine. His head tilted back against the pillows, and with her next movement, she sheathed him completely, joining their bodies tight. Her dreams and memories hadn't done him justice.

She also couldn't move, dedicating the first moments of penetration to savoring every exquisite inch. Her walls fluttered around him, and he flexed in response, groaning a low, primal sound in his throat that aroused her as much as his lustful eyes.

Loki scooped both of her breasts into his hands. "These are magnificent." They'd only felt heavy and cumbersome to her, but his touch ignited a spark of ecstasy, and she couldn't imagine telling him to stop.

He touched her everywhere but where she needed it most, kissing the dark areola and skimming his lips between her full breasts. When he finally took one tip between his teeth, the delicious heat of his tongue against the tender nipple dragged her to the brink of orgasm.

"Loki," she gasped, startled by the amount of sensation in so tiny an area. His tongue flicked over stiffened flesh, and then he alternated between them, sending zips of pleasure lancing straight to her core.

Consumed by her own needs, she slid up and down the thick shaft with increasing speed, rising with a flex of her thighs and clenching her inner muscles tight as she returned.

The hunger for Loki never faded, even when exhaustion seeped into her limbs. She moved atop him at a frenetic pace while her breasts bounced beneath his palms to the wild tempo. Her aching thighs screamed for relief.

One hand dropped away, and he patted her thigh. "Off."

"Off?" His bewildering request put a falter in her sinuous rhythm. Her hips briefly stilled. "Are… are you having second thoughts?"

Loki's hands slid around to cup her bottom and he sat up, green eyes bright and fierce in his face. "I'm not."

Dominant as he'd been the night they met, he raised Selene from his body and placed her on her back. His cock swayed as he stood, slick from her body and standing proud for her to see. She only had a moment to admire him before Loki grasped her by her ankles and dragged her over the sheets to the edge of the bed.

The blissful reunion of their bodies brought her back from the bedding. Selene tilted her head back against the mattress, grasped the covers, and held on tight while her tireless mate made love to her. Each thrust brought her closer to completion, setting fire to her blood and burning through her soul. Loki lifted her right leg over his hip and used his free hand to stimulate her clit. His rough padded fingers circled over the tight nerve bundle and nearly undid her.

"Loki! Loki, I'm so close!"

"Tell me I'm yours."

Hers? How could she possibly want anything else? "Yes! Mine! You're mine, mine, mine, mine!" she wailed.

He bit her without any preamble. No warning. Sharp teeth sank into the plump flesh of her upper left breast. Whether or not it left a stinging, angry mark or bled was the furthest concern from Selene's mind.

Not when her body sizzled from within. All her mental preparation for the act amounted to naught. The initial pain lanced through her chest in a fleeting burst, but the force of her climax banished it with cresting waves of pleasure. It crashed over Selene, radiating through every nerve fiber until she was awash with ecstasy.

Pain ceased to exist, bled away by the most fulfilling rapture she'd ever experienced, molten bliss coursing through her body from head to toe until she screamed. She'd never orgasmed so strong in all her life, and for one moment, she thought it would never end. It shuddered through her, and her body convulsed beneath him. Loki wrapped both arms around her body and held her as closely as their baby would allow.

"Loki!" She lost track of how many times she called his name. She screamed it until she was hoarse and her cries left as a soundless moan. An undeniable heat scorched through her body. Lost to the sensation, she grasped at him with one hand and ripped the sheets with the other.

When coherent thought returned, her cheek was smooshed into the pillow and Loki regarded her with concern, his face inches away.

"What happened?"

"You passed out for a moment." He stroked a stray curl off her cheek and smoothed it back behind her ear. Then he grinned, a smug and arrogant look she knew all too well. "Did I please you so much?"

She swatted at him, a weak and half-hearted smack of her hand against his shoulder. "You know you did, so I'm not going to buff your ego any further."

Loki lifted up on one elbow and leaned over her. He traced his fingers down the curve of her neck and across her shoulder, then down the slope of one breast. The mark he'd left against her skin tingled beneath his gentle touch, inciting a hard clench of her core as pleasure rippled through her body.

Another sweep of his thumb across the bite brought a muted explosion and left her seeing stars as the next orgasm swept through her. All without a single penetrating touch.

"Holy crap!" she gasped.

Her mate chuckled, leaned down, and kissed her while she came down off the incredible high.

"Is it like that every time?" she asked when she could think again.

"Not quite. The first time is always the most intense, or so I've gathered from my conversations with other dragons."

"Wow."

"Wow indeed. It seems orgasms make your magic come out." He grinned and gestured to a hole seared into the comforter.

"I did that?"

"You did." The dragon then turned to reveal his back to her. A silver handprint shone below his shoulder, and the skin had the texture of a burn scar. "Here as well, though I suspect this means our bond was reciprocated."

Aghast, she jerked up into a sitting position as sharply as her belly would allow. "I'm sorry. I didn't mean to hurt you!"

"Hurt me? Hardly. I…" He hesitated for a moment. "It makes me happy to know I wear some mark of yours as well."

He left the bed then returned with a washcloth from the adjacent bathroom. With tender hands, her lover bathed her lower body. "If it makes you feel any better, we get to do that again in thirteen years. Dragons celebrate a reclaiming of sorts, although our bonds never break during our lifetimes, they can fray and weaken over time."

"Dragons are amazing," Selene murmured. "I *feel* amazing." A drowsy haze clouded her thoughts, and despite her desire to remain awake to chat with her new mate, exhaustion swept her under and into the realm of sweet dreams—dreams of dark hair and green eyes set in a tiny face.

***

Loki awakened first, which he considered a gift once he realized the time provided an uninterrupted moment to admire his human mate. Selene had always been radiant to him, but now she positively glowed with life once the bond connected them.

She stirred as he lazily circled his fingers over her back, gazing up at him from beneath the disheveled curls of her hair. Then she squinted at the bedside clock. "You're up early."

"Mm, I don't sleep here as often as I once did," he admitted. "When I am not in your home, I often slumber in my hoard."

"With all of your jewels and stuff?"

He chuckled. "Yes. And books. I like to collect them."

"So I've seen, not that I had much chance to read any titles."

"I have many, but I keep the most precious with the rest of my treasures." Except now, the only treasure he cared about was the one beside him. The rest meant little in comparison.

"Do you think…?"

"Think what?" he asked when she trailed off.

"Nothing. Never mind."

He rolled Selene to her back and leaned over her. "You can ask or tell me anything."

"I wondered if I could see it, is all. Your hoard."

"At any time," he agreed. "Perhaps I should give you some perspective regarding my wealth and what it means to me, Selene."

"Okay."

"Given that I have shared half of my *soul* with you already, what value do you think I hold for my hoard—mere physical possessions acquired through no extraordinary means?"

"Point taken."

"I am glad you understand." He dipped his head and nibbled the delicate skin across her collarbone. "Nothing in the world holds a higher value to me than you and our little one. I would give up everything in my hoard if it meant keeping you safe."

"Wow. You really mean that, don't you?"

"Every word, *skatten min*." He kissed her shoulder. "My treasure." His lips ghosted down to the slope of her left breast. "My Selene."

He guided her up to her knees, with her back against his chest and her breasts perfect handfuls in his palms, and made love to her again. Selene clutched the headboard and cried his name with every thrust, until they both reached their release together and sank back to the rumpled sheets.

As she slept, he admired the dark fringe of her lashes against her umber skin, the angle of her cheekbones, and her cupid's bow mouth—lips he couldn't resist kissing time and time again.

When she roused the second time, Selene drowsily glanced up at him. "Did I doze off?"

"You did." His grin widened. "I enjoy wearing you out."

"Ha, ha. Makes you feel all-powerful and mighty, doesn't it?" She rolled onto her back.

"I am all-powerful and mighty, and if you find that hard to believe, I will gladly show you again."

"Tempting, but…" Her fingers found her phone and she activated the screen. "Oh no! I wanted to return to the bakery today!"

Feigning nonchalance, Loki chuckled and slid from beneath the covers. God of mischief? She made him feel like the god of seduction, because her eyes darted to him and followed his path to the closet. "Then I will take you. Perhaps you will allow me to linger for a day to assist with your bakery."

"You'd hate it," Selene said, laughing. She slipped from under the sheets to join him and peer into the majestic collection of suits and fine attire hanging in the walk-in closet. "You own enough clothing to fill a men's warehouse."

Loki raised both brows. "I could never loathe anything you love with such passion."

"Pokémon."

"Most things," he corrected.

"What's not to like about cute, strange-looking creatures?"

He sniffed in disdain. "For all of the time humans spend seeking strange and magical creatures that don't exist, they could befriend any one of us."

Selene placed both hands against her hips and gazed at him shrewdly. "Are you saying you'd be social to a human who met you in your dragon form?"

"Yes. I have a great amount of respect for anyone able to confront me."

She made a small sound in her throat.

"Working in the bakery means getting messy. You might get flour all over your nice clothes."

"I own jeans." He peered into the distant depths of the closet. "I think. Anura will know where they are."

"I'd almost forgotten about her and the others. The house is so quiet."

"They have their own homes on the property. Families. I do not keep them confined to the house, though there was a time in dragon history when things were different. A regrettable time, I'm afraid, when we were all very different people."

"So they aren't 'slaves' then?"

He shook his head. "I consider them employees who are bound to me by their own preferences and mine. Anura and William's parents once served on my staff, as did their parents before them. Among the shifters, it's common for those who would be considered prey to band together. Often they swear themselves to a more powerful creature for protection."

"Like a dragon."

"Yes."

"So you are their lord, and they are the vassals."

"In a way, yes."

Anura lived up to his expectations, and within seconds of her arrival, she unearthed clothing Loki had never seen. Jeans, simple T-shirts, sweats, and other styles of casual clothes left neglected over the years.

He and Selene shared a shower together in the immense walk-in, and once they were dressed for the day, he opened a portal directly to her office at the bakery.

"Selene!" Jacob rushed over once he overcame his shock at their arrival. He wrapped her in a familiar hug and Loki ignored the internal prompt urging him to obliterate the interloper.

"You're okay? You're feeling good?"

"I'm fine, Jacob, see? A few days rest and I'm good as new."

"And him?" Jacob nodded toward Loki.

"Long story that we'll go into later. For now, Loki wants to learn what we do each day."

The boy's brows rose before he turned a skeptical eye toward Loki. "You want to work?"

"Yes."

"Really work? I mean, you know you'll get dough under your perfect manicure."

A low growl bubbled from Loki's chest, but Jacob didn't back off. If anything, he stood taller and stared him down without backing away, until Selene moved between them and placed a palm on both of their chests.

"Down, boys. Put all that testosterone-laden aggression into kneading some bread."

He would knead a hundred loaves if it meant putting the insolent pup in his place.

Selene led him into the kitchen and introduced him to each of the appliances. And somehow, for her, he managed to tie his hair beneath a cap with the shop's logo, though it pained him—and her too apparently—for him to put it all away.

They discovered Loki had a knack for multitasking, so she put him on the donut fryer and asked him to keep an eye on the cookies in the oven after providing enough training for him to remove the sheets of chocolate chip delight to the wire cooling racks when the timer finished.

On the opposite side of the kitchen, he kept tabs on Jacob's progress with the bread dough. Selene also sold artisan breads to a local deli.

He used the morning to soak up as much knowledge as he could about her place of business, tolerating Jacob's persistent presence over his shoulder whenever the boy lurked behind his shoulder to observe.

Trusting them alone in the kitchen, Selene retreated to the front to handle customers.

"Need any help over there?" Jacob asked.

"I am fine," Loki replied. "Tend to your own tasks."

Jacob tossed the next ball of dough onto the counter and kneaded it with his hands. "Just offering, man, no need to be snippy about—"

Poof. The gentle, audible sound accompanied a flour explosion, like nuclear winter contained within a three-yard radius. It covered Jacob in white from top to bottom, clinging to his hair and face, and even covering the kid's apron.

Loki maintained a neutral expression while operating the fryer, refusing to look away.

"The fuck? How was that even possible?" Jacob demanded, staring down in horror.

Loki grinned and tucked his chin. So what if it was childish? It was also damned satisfying.

Selene entered from the storefront, stopped in her tracks, and stared. Her gaze drifted between the two men and settled on Loki. Jacob stalked from the room toward the direction of the exit doors leading to the dumpsters behind the bakery.

"Clean it up." Selene put her hands on her hips and stared him down.

"I did nothing."

Her brows rose and she crossed her arms over her chest, an unimpressed general inspecting her troops. "Is that why you're grinning like a five-year-old?"

"I'm not." Dammit. He wiped the smile off his face again, appearing stoic and serious, though the damage had already been done, and he sighed before confessing. "Maybe I did a little."

"I expect my kitchen to be spotless again. *Without* magic."

"But—"

"No buts. You clean, Jacob gets that bread going. I have afternoon orders to fill." The bells chimed, signaling the arrival of the lunch-hour rush. Selene spun and stalked away.

Jacob returned on the tail end of her orders with the scent of magic clinging to him and the excess flour gone. "Damn. She has that mommy thing down already."

Loki grunted at the enemy and focused on sweeping the fine mist of flour covering the floor with a push broom. Aside from carving out his own hoard and working over a pile of electronics, he'd never done a minute of labor in all his life.

"Use that broom instead. It'll be easier to get beneath the table," Jacob suggested.

Loki made another inarticulate sound but grabbed the angled broom. He'd seen his servants clean a million times before, quite literally, and mimicked them with little effort, though it felt strange to be tidying a place after himself.

And a little empowering to do it without magic, though he'd never admit it to anyone.

Loki eyed Jacob with suspicion when the human stepped over and crouched to sweep a pile of crumbs and flour into the dustpan for him. "Why are you helping?"

"Because this in my kitchen, too, and, well, you got me good. Least I can do is help." He glanced over the counter.

"Besides, you look ridiculous cleaning up after yourself. I expected you to snap your fingers and summon a squad of shapeshifters."

Loki sniffed. "Selene has not allowed it."

Jacob's grin widened and his blue eyes crinkled at the corners. "Wow. She *has* tamed a dragon. I'm kinda jealous of her."

Loki narrowed his eyes. "I am hardly tamed."

"Uh-huh."

"Maybe a little," Loki admitted, sighing.

"Look, Selene is my friend, and all that matters to me is she's happy. You seem to be doing a bang-up job of that so far. So can we have a truce? Call it even now?"

Studying him, Loki considered everything Selene had told him about her friend, especially the boy's sexual preferences for men. "You truly have no interest in her?"

"Sweetheart, if I had my choice between the two of you, I would rock your world. Selene is a friend, and only that."

"Uh, well, in that case, friends we shall be."

"Good. Glad to have that out of the way."

They worked side by side while loading dough into greased pans. Jacob broke the silence first, speaking up in a nonchalant tone. "So... I kinda found my boyfriend balls deep in another man this past weekend, and I'm on the road to moving on. You wouldn't happen to know any dragons with... different tastes, do you?"

"Balls. Deep..." Loki blinked and gaped while his mind processed the very vivid picture Jacob had painted for him in so few words. "Did you skin him?"

"Tempting as that may have been, I didn't want to go to jail." Jacob paused as he slid a tray of bread pans into the oven.

"I burned his stuff and his clothes. You know, since I paid for them and what the good Jacob giveth, he also taketh away."

"That's it?"

"He was still in them." Jacob's grin widened as Loki blinked at him in surprise. "Didn't burn him, of course, since that'd be very, very wrong, according to the law… But he and his buddy left in bedsheets, and I'm satisfied."

"Good." He looked at the man with new respect. "As a matter of fact, I might know someone who would appreciate your spunk."

He'd have to place a call to Apollo that evening. If his memory was right, Zeus's son had a fondness for the pretty ones.

Chapter 10

The remainder of the week passed in a strange haze. At night, they alternated between her house and Loki's estate, taking the dogs along with them to California. Her beasts enjoyed his company for some strange reason, and they grew on him, despite the larger canine's tendency to shed on everything he touched.

Loki sighed and studied the ivory world beyond the passenger side window. Virginia's weather reminded him of Scandinavia's cold north before he'd followed his cousin Maximilian to America.

Also reminded him of why the hell he left Europe behind. "Must we drive?" he asked.

"Yes," Selene told him in a placid voice, as if she'd answered a child.

He puffed his chest out. "William would be happy to drive you wherever you desire. There's truly no need to do it yourself."

"I like driving," she told him for the hundredth time. "And I don't mind the weather. Besides, it's not like we're going long distance. An hour. Two tops with traffic."

"We've been in the car for an hour," he muttered darkly.

Selene patted his knee and continued driving.

"How do I greet your mother?"

What if they didn't like him? He'd been absent from Selene's life for six months of her pregnancy.

"How do you greet anyone you want to impress? Say Merry Christmas and just be yourself."

"I do not impress, Selene. I intimidate most normal humans." He sighed.

Selene bit her lip and huffed out a breath. "Look, I had the same worries meeting your family. Just be the same charming man I fell for over wine. And if you're going to cause any trouble or play pranks, save them for my little brother. Anthony loves that kind of thing."

"Give me a little credit to know when to show restraint."

The car paused at a stop light, granting Selene time to stare at him incredulously from the driver's seat. Sensing it was time to shut his mouth, Loki fiddled with his phone for the remaining fifteen minutes of the drive until they reached a quaint neighborhood with shoveled drives and snowmen decorated lawns.

Strings of multicolored lights wrapped around the low iron fence surrounding the front lawn of a humble, two-story home. Selene pulled up to the curb, turned the car off, and released a quiet breath.

"Okay. Let's go do this. We can come back for the presents later."

Loki helped her from the car and tucked her hand into the crook of his elbow as they made their way up the sand-strewn walkway to a door with a pine wreath. Selene let them inside with her key and paused to stomp the sand from her boots.

He followed her example before assisting her with her coat. Selene pointed to the entry closet.

"I'm home!" she called out as she unwound her scarf, passing it over to him to hang with her coat. "Huh. She must be in the kitchen, then. Sound carries weird in the house."

"Mom, is that Sele—" A young man stepped around the corner and froze midsentence with his mouth gaping open.

"Hey, Anthony," Selene chirped. "Merry Christmas! I'd like you to meet—"

"Dude, I can't believe I'm meeting you. Holy shit. I was at your conference in the city last month. Like, I watched your talks on software advancement!" Anthony blew her off completely.

Loki's eyes brightened and he straightened his shoulders. "Oh?"

"Yeah. Your discussion on augmented reality software apps was fascinating. I'm basing my final report in coding on it. Oh man, I can't believe you're here... with my sister?" The realization dawned on the teen that Loki hadn't appeared on a whim inside his house.

The corner of Selene's mouth quirked. "As I was saying before you interrupted me, Anthony, I'd like you to meet Loki, my, um, fiancé."

"No way." His eyes dropped to his sister's stomach then flew back to her face. "Really? *This* is the mystery wine dude?"

"Yup."

"Who the hell sleeps with a billionaire and doesn't know it? Have you not seen the magazines all over my room?"

"Who can see anything in that pigsty?" she shot back.

Loki watched their exchange and grinned.

So many years in the technology sector had made it easy for him to forget there were people who looked up to his works and his advancements in programming, that the invitations to their conferences weren't mere lip service.

An older woman, roughly in her fifties from his reckoning, stalked into the room with the airs of a person accustomed to breaking up sibling arguments. "What's all this commotion out here? Are you two fighting already? Honestly, it's Christmas."

Her brother whirled and gestured wildly with his hands. "Selene brought home Loki Agnarhorn, Mom. She brought home a *genius*. A billionaire genius!"

Selene rolled her eyes. "His money isn't what interests me."

She had proven that fact multiple times, both frustrating Loki and endearing her to him. Selene could be trusted with his hoard, unlike a female dragon who would have swallowed as many jewels as she could down her gullet the moment he turned his back.

A dragon's hoard was the most valuable gift he could share with his mate, and Selene's visit was long overdue. He'd have to take her soon.

Her mother drifted closer, warm brown eyes trailing over Loki's face then his business-casual clothing. He'd donned a burgundy shirt tailored to his broad shoulders and trim physique, tucked into designer slacks.

"Is this him?" she asked Selene.

"Yes, Mom."

And for the second time in all of Loki's life, it mattered to him what a human thought of him. The older woman's kind eyes lingered on his face.

"Well then, it's a pleasure to finally meet you, young man. I tried to convince her to contact you, but as you've probably discovered, the girl is stubborn."

Loki chortled. "Incredibly."

Selene glared at him.

"Mom, this is Loki. Loki, my mom."

"Call me Anita. Anthony, don't you think it's rude to hold our guest in the hallway? Run out back and tell your father Selene is home with her man."

"But he's chopping wood and it's cold out there."

"All the more reason to go out and help him."

Anthony sighed. "Fine."

Loki stepped forward and clapped the teen's slumped shoulder. "I'll help."

"That's mighty kind of you, Loki." Anita smiled. "As for you, young lady, you can help me in the kitchen. You may be pregnant, but there's nothing wrong with your fingers."

***

Her mother's cheerful blue and yellow kitchen hadn't changed since Selene was a kid. The same lacy curtains hung in the window over the sink, and the doorframe leading into the hall had little hash marks in red and black, each one marking her and Anthony's height over the years.

One day, her baby's height would be recorded in the same manner.

"So, are you going to tell me about him?"

Selene pushed her hair back behind her ears. "I really, really like him, Mom."

The understatement of the year came out of her lips of course, but she didn't have the nerve to admit she'd bonded to an immortal dragon and would be having a magical baby. A magical dragon baby who would one day breathe fire and cast spells.

"He's asked you to marry him?"

Technically... "He did," she fibbed. "That horse has kinda left the barn already though, you know?" She touched her stomach and tried to imagine donning a pretty white dress and marching down the aisle in front of their friends and family. The thought twisted her nerves into knots.

"You'd be a beautiful bride, belly and all, but don't feel like you need to rush."

"I was hoping you'd feel that way about it. Maybe once the baby is here, we can have him in the ceremony with us." Selene returned to her duty at the counter, slicing cucumber for the salad. "I really don't know what else to say, Mom. He's wonderful. I know you always told me, if something seems too good to be true, it usually is, but with him, I keep waiting for something bad to happen and it never does."

"He's not... normal, is he?"

Selene shook her head. "He's not human, if that's what you mean. How'd you know?"

Anita's gaze drifted to the window and became distant. "He reminds me of your father in ways. The way he carries himself. Power, charisma, and charm just ooze off him. I can see how that"—her mother pointed to her stomach—"happened."

Grumbling, Selene tucked her chin and focused on her task, even if her belly lacked the appetite for diced tomatoes. "There was also wine. And we *did* use protection. I wasn't that drunk."

"Oh, you don't have to answer to me. You're grown," the smiling woman said before tucking the pan of brownies into the oven. "So what is he? A sorcerer like your friend Jacob? I do like that young man."

"A dragon."

Her mother startled and slammed the oven door shut. "Really?"

"Yup. Fangs, wings, and all."

"We're going to need more steaks."

Selene laughed. She leaned over and pressed a kiss against her mom's cheek. "I'll go grab a few more from the freezer. I've seen him eat, and trust me, one steak isn't going to cut it. We need like five of these."

"Five?" her mother echoed.

"Five, Mom. He can put away a four-pound pork loin on his own. I wish you could have seen the way my freezer looked after a single trip to the market with him."

Her mother's eyes twinkled with amusement. "Nothing wrong with a young man who can eat his fill. I'll have your father run out for another couple sides of ribeye then."

"Don't put yourself out, Mom. You don't need to cook half a cow for him."

"But I want him to feel welcome and part of this family. Oh, Selene, you don't know how happy I am that you found him. I thought... well, I worried you might end up like me, is all. Don't get me wrong, I wouldn't trade you for anything, but it was lonely at times. My folks weren't so understanding."

Blinking the tears away from her eyes, Selene wrapped her arms around her mother and hugged her tight. "I know, but you were the best mom any girl could ever ask for."

"Moooooom! Selene's new boyfriend can do magic!" Anthony called from the hallway.

Anita leaned back and stared at her.

Unable to control her enthusiasm, Selene grinned at her mother. "Did I mention he's a sorcerer dragon?"

Accustomed to Selene's occasional bouts of magical activity over the years, her family treated Loki no different than they'd interacted with her previous boyfriends. Although her mother's husband shared no DNA with her, he'd raised her for most of her life. As a true father fulfilling the role left by her sperm donor, he took Loki aside after dinner and personally welcomed him to the family.

In the privacy of her old bedroom, she tugged on an old nightshirt while Loki undressed. He had laid their single small suitcase on the dresser and unpacked it himself. The simple task made her grin.

"And then he told me, dragon or not, that he'd have my skin if I hurt you."

Selene chuckled. "That's Dad." It touched her to have not only a close friend, but also a father willing to threaten a dragon on her behalf.

He joined her in bed once she slipped beneath the sheets, although the narrow mattress barely fit the two of them. "I respect his devotion to you. He appears to be a good man, as does your brother."

With the worst behind them—meeting each other's families—Selene exhaled a sigh of relief. Little else remained aside from waiting to welcome their child into the world, and with four months left of an almost year-long pregnancy on the horizon, they had all the time needed to prepare for his arrival.

The next day, the Richards household threw in every effort to make Loki part of the family. They enjoyed the traditional family Christmas breakfast of fried potatoes, berry French toast casserole, cheesy scrambled eggs, and bacon. Then they sat around the tree and exchanged gifts. Anthony shadowed her mate, her mother pampered them with another sensational dinner, and Loki entertained her brother by critiquing his current projects.

Her mother and father embraced them both at the end of the visit with pleas for them to return soon and visit at any time. She drove them home shortly after dinner, completing the hour-long trip in silence while Loki napped beside her.

She'd never caught him asleep. Not once in all the days since he'd located her had she ever seen him close his eyes for more than a few moments. First to rise and last to sleep each time they lay down beside each other.

He stirred when she pulled the car into the driveway. Blinking the drowsiness from his green eyes, he glanced out the window and stared. "Are we home?"

"Yup. You slept the entire time."

"I'm sorry."

"For what? Even a dragon needs to rest sometimes, Loki. It's okay." He received so little of it, and she frowned, wishing she hadn't taken him away from his hoard.

The dragon frowned, indicating it certainly wasn't okay by his perception. As much as she appreciated his doting, she didn't want it done to his detriment.

Eager to change the subject, Selene cleared her throat. "Did you enjoy yourself at Mom's place? They loved you, and not just because you offered Anthony a paid internship with Ragnarok."

"He's a bright boy. If his true desire is to attend school in California, I will do all in my power to help him succeed."

"Honestly," Selene added.

Loki rolled his eyes then helped her from the car. "Yes, honestly. I can do your sibling the courtesy of removing the obstacles to his success, but he must earn a place at my company with ingenuity and good grades. I'm not easily impressed."

After listening to his brutal honesty, she smiled and imagined her brother among the geniuses at Ragnarok Enterprises. Her mate had made her brother's longtime dream come true.

Without any preface, she kissed him then murmured, "You're amazing."

His brows rose, a split second of bewilderment on his handsome face. In those moments when she gained an honest reaction from him, she always realized how much of his bravado and confidence was an act, a show for his own protection.

The surprise faded, giving way to an uneven smile. "Of course I am. Come on. Let's get in from the cold."

Once they traversed the iced path and entered her frigid home, Selene made up her mind.

Her new beloved needed self-care as much as she did, and in the coming days, she'd find out a way to guarantee he received it.

Chapter 11

Loki had known for a while about the humans watching him. At first, he tolerated their spying and allowed them to observe his life from a distance, knowing they would never have the balls to confront him in an attack. In the wake of Watatsumi's death, all the dragons had exercised absolute vigilance while in public.

With Selene in the picture, things had changed, and he took pleasure in giving them the slip. Maintaining a presence back in California meant they'd never have a reason to set eyes on his mate and child.

But how long could he keep his new family secret from them?

As Loki made his rounds through the building he owned in downtown San Francisco, he sipped a cup of coffee and paused to chat with the staff in the lower level. Eventually, he stepped outside for a breath of fresh air and to make his usual public appearance. Not far away across the traffic-laden street, a man stood in the shadows of a store overhang while feigning interest in his cell phone.

Loki knew most of the spies by sight. One glimpse was enough to recognize the dark magic staining their souls, and he had to wonder when Merlin intended to do something about it instead of sitting on his laurels.

A year ago, when the Knights of the Round Table discovered their interim leader had gone rogue, the order had been left in shambles—until Astrid's husband Nathaniel stepped up to the plate. Since the kid was the reincarnated spirit of Sir

Galahad, he was the purest of heart among the humans. The best one for the job.

Aware of the eyes on him, Loki meandered down the road to purchase a newspaper from a street vendor. He lingered outside long enough to watch the underling report in, and then he returned to his office to dial Nate.

"Sup, Loki? What can I do for you?"

"You can convince your blasted wizard it's time to act against the dragonslayers. There's another lurking beyond my building."

"Bedivere or a human spy?"

"A human spy with the usual aura, but what does it matter if it's one of them or their masters? The fact of the matter is, they're out there. They're watching and reporting. They know our movements, but what do we know of theirs?"

"Not much."

"Mark my words, Nathaniel, sooner or later they will strike, and what happened to Watatsumi will occur again. You must help me to convince Merlin it is time to act in our own best interests."

"Merlin's been locked away in the archives doing research."

"On what? Bedivere? The titans?"

"I don't know. I'm not his babysitter," Nate snapped, then sighed. "Sorry. Sorry. I've been dealing with phone calls all day about this same thing. A few of the older knights were contacted by Pelleas. He tried to convince them to join up, and I'm sad to say one or two considered the offer."

"What?"

"Like it or not, the knights have been hunting dragons for their last couple of lives. Now that we have a truce, some of them are feeling restless and don't know what to do with themselves."

"Don't know what to do? So murder is their alternative to boredom?"

"I never said I agreed with them or understood it. Anyway, that's what's happening here with us. Percivale and I have been assigning the ones we trust to tracking down Pelleas and Bedivere, while we send the others to assist with shifter affairs."

Loki snorted in disgust. "There are worse creatures in the world than dragons. Perhaps I should awaken a few to give your friends ample activities to pursue in the meantime."

"You're a real grouch, you know that? We're doing our best, but it's not like you're having any better luck with Bedivere, so back off a little."

"Sooner or later, they will act. What will you do if Astrid becomes the one in their crosshairs? Or Arthur? He is the true leader of the knights, after all. And unlike Watatsumi, I will not throw myself on the altar as a sacrificial lamb regardless of how many humans are present when it happens."

"Fine," Nate barked into the phone. "No one is asking you to be a martyr, just a decent person. If you don't like how slow things are moving, put some work into this operation yourself." The knight hung up on him.

Resisting the urge to crumple the phone in his fist, Loki growled in disgust and tossed it onto the desk instead. Taking his anger out on the device wouldn't improve the situation, nor would it change the fact that he'd abused the one man who deserved it the least. He owed Nate an apology. Not now, while their tempers still simmered, but later, he'd have to phone his friend.

An hour later, his mood remained volatile, his phone calls snippy, and his orders curt enough for his assistant to enter with a note addressed to him from most of the department working directly beneath him.

Please go home, sir. Signed, your adoring staff. P.S. Your mate called and would like to speak with you.

Damn. He would have ignored their plea and remained an hour longer to be a prat if Selene wasn't included in the note. He rose from the seat, punched the intercom button, and said, "You win this time."

"Excellent," Georgia replied.

"Using my mate is a cheap trick."

"Actually, Ms. Richards phoned me directly about an hour ago and inquired about your daily work schedule. I was asked if I'd shoo you home about now if you weren't too busy to leave early. She wanted to surprise you, and you know what, it couldn't have come at a better time."

He ended the call, stowed his laptop into his briefcase, and left the office via portal. He stepped into the home in Virginia seconds later to a wet-nosed welcome from Dusty. Baron scrambled down from the couch and yipped.

Loki set his briefcase aside and petted both animals. "Selene?"

"I'll be out in just a minute!"

A delicious aroma wafted to him from the kitchen. He ventured inside and discovered an array of cooling, chocolate treats awaiting him on the counter. Everything from chocolate chip cookies to decadent cake decorated a silver platter, and a folded card beside the variety tray displayed Selene's handwritten message.

I love you.

All of this for him? "Selene?"

"Give me one moment!" She sounded out of breath. Rushed.

His brows pushed together again, but he waited until her approaching footsteps reached the kitchen's entryway.

She wore pink lace and chocolate silk, a tight bodice molded against her generous bosom. The rest of the babydoll nightie skimmed the top of her thighs and revealed mile-long legs he ached to caress. Rose-gold dust glittered against her upper chest, but he smelled scented sugar from a distance.

Loki's belly growled, and somehow he was simultaneously hungry and starved for her at the same time. He crossed to her in a few strides, compelled by raw, animal attraction. With all other things forgotten—slayers, Nate, insubordinate but loving assistants, and even dessert—he kissed her, discovering cocoa-flavored lip balm.

After the devouring kiss ended, his mouth trailed down to her throat. Even her skin tasted like chocolate. It wasn't fair that she'd combined two of his favorite things.

"I know you're fond of my chocolates at the bakery, so I made something when I returned from work."

"You did this for me?"

"Mm-hmm."

"But why?"

"Because I love you."

His growing appetite rumbled again in protest, but his left hand rose to cup her breast. They'd become sensitive enough for her to guide his hands away recently, and he was afraid to touch them, afraid he'd hurt her. Instead of flinching as she had days ago when he'd tried to initiate sex between them, she encouraged him by lifting the other hand to join it and arching her back. Her eyes closed.

"Gentle."

How gentle did she expect him to be when he was bursting with excitement?

And why did every moment of intimacy with Selene thrill him as much as the last? It never grew old.

"This garment is very pretty, but I would appreciate it the most on the floor."

Teasing, her index finger trailed down the middle of his chest, following an invisible line until she reached his belt. His cock jumped, stiffening hard as a branding iron.

Selene glanced down at the noticeable bulge. "Not yet, naughty dragon. You have to eat your treats before you get your dessert."

"Will you not share these with me?"

He tried to kiss her again, but she held up one hand and pressed two fingers to his lips. "I will on one condition."

"What's that?"

"We enjoy it at your hoard."

Although he had promised to take her to his hoard soon, part of him had dreaded what she would think when she saw his centuries-old collection. Would she think him selfish to amass such vast quantities of unshared wealth? Would she see him less as a man and more like the beast he truly was?

His heart thumped, mood split between eager and apprehensive. He hadn't tidied it in decades. Sharing his mortal home with her had been easy, and while he'd already vowed to share every cent of his treasures with her, showing her was another matter altogether.

Selene gazed up at him and smiled. "Well?"

He kissed her fingertips. "All right."

Bypassing the trapped entrance to the hoard and opening a portal directly to its central chamber, the rift in the middle of her kitchen revealed the polished stone floor of a darkened room. Selene lifted the tray and grabbed a bottle of red from the counter—one they had shared months ago, but she hadn't yet dared to taste.

"The floor is cold," he warned her.

Stalactites pointed from the high ceiling, each one glittering, their surfaces polished to a mirror sheen. With magic, he'd created a subterranean palace made of black marble, an underground lair filled with otherworldly beauty.

Her eyes widened as she turned around to take in their surroundings. "This is... I've never seen anything so beautiful. But where are the jewels and gems?"

Loki took the tray from her and set it on a low table carved into the ground. It arose like a stalagmite from the gleaming floor and had only two chairs. "This is only the main chamber. I mostly hold art here and dedicate each room to another collection."

"Is it a good place for our picnic?"

"As good as any," he replied.

"In that case, I'll need the blanket on the couch. And, um, there's one more tray in the fridge. Will you get those for me?"

"Of course."

In two trips, he retrieved everything Selene wanted. His mate spread out a blanket over the floor and then arranged the pillows for them to recline.

"Do you remember our lunch during the wine tour?"

"How could I forget it?"

Selene uncovered one of the dishes to reveal an array of sliced meats and delectable cheeses. He scanned the wooden charcuterie board replicating their first meal together, a combination of salami, chorizo, smoked salmon, French soft-ripened cheeses, hard cheeses from Spain, onion jam, pita chips, and toasted bread slices.

"How did you...?"

Her eyes twinkled. "A little help from Mahasti. I asked if she'd pick up an order and bring it to us in Virginia."

"You're amazing.

He leaned in to kiss her, but Selene dipped away. "Dinner first."

"Dammit."

Selene grinned and handed him the wine bottle to uncork. "Tell me about your day," she urged him.

"My day..." He considered the slayers, his argument with Nate, and his snippy attitude. "No, no. Tell me about yours instead."

"Oh come on, that's not how this works."

"My day was..." He tilted his head down and searched. "I'm not proud of my behavior this day and owe a good friend an apology."

She touched his knee. "Do you want to talk about it?"

"I was curt with Nathaniel when I shouldn't have been. He has issues of his own to work out with the knights, getting them reorganized and such, and I shouldn't have lost my temper."

"The fact that you recognize you need to apologize is good. Just don't wait too long to set things right between you both."

"I will tomorrow."

"Nate's a great guy, and he'll understand that you had a bad day."

Her confidence and optimism became infectious, lightening the burden on his heart within moments. "You're right."

Selene poured generous glasses of the rich and fragrant cabernet sauvignon. They sipped, fed each other morsels of food, and dug into the assortment of baked goods without shame. Loki polished off every cookie and most of the fudge brownies.

"This has been perfect," he said, leaning back on his hands. Until Selene entered his life, he hadn't realized how empty and lacking it had been. Each day prior to meeting her seeming bleak and flavorless.

She crawled onto his lap. Straddling his hips, she unfastened his shirt and pulled it from his trousers. "I think you'll be more comfortable without these clothes."

Her busy hands unbuckled his belt then tugged it from the loops, undressing him with an aggressive edge he didn't recognize. His mate wasn't docile in the least, but she'd also never manhandled him.

"Selene?"

She shoved him back against the blanket and crawled off him onto her knees beside his body. A sharp yank tugged his pants down to his knees. Two more removed them and his socks.

What in the name of the ancestors is she doing?

Selene moistened her lips with her tongue, an unspoken promise of what was to come. "My turn for dessert." After shifting between his spread thighs, she dragged her nails down the inside of his legs. Bowing down brought her to the perfect level to kiss the tip of his cock, and he sucked a breath between his teeth when her lips parted to envelop the smooth head.

The last time she'd done that, they were in a hotel room, drunk off wine and each other.

"What are you doing?"

Her tongue swirled around the tip, tasting the single, clear drop of precum. "Appreciating you."

"You don't have—"

"Oh, but I want to," she assured him. The kittenish smile on her face left no doubt in his mind that she meant every word.

Her fingers took the place of her lips, the long and thick length of him jutting up from her fisted grip. She laid a path of tender nibbles down and up his straining shaft, interspersed with tiny licks and delicate kisses.

He ached hard and ready, desperate for any part of her to slide over his cock. The moment her mouth touched him, he gave a preemptive, appreciative groan of relief. *Thank the ancestors. Finally.* Her teasing had been the most exquisite torture, but torture nonetheless.

Loki's fingers closed around a handful of her hair. He groaned and writhed beneath her tender ministrations, brought to the brink of ecstasy each time her lips dragged over his shaft to meet the crown.

Her gray eyes rose to hold his gaze, and he trembled while watching her lick him in a series of expert strokes. Then she engulfed him anew, sheathing the complete length.

"Selene," he groaned. He tilted his head back, the muscles in his neck drawn taut and jaw clenched. Slowly, his hips rose from the blanket. Restraining himself pushed him to his limits when what he truly wanted to do was thrust deeper.

She made a quiet sound, almost like a purr, and the reverberations rippled across his slick flesh, shattering his control.

"Stop." He tried to warn her, barely able to gasp her name. "Love, no more. I can't—"

Clutching a handful of the blanket, he thrust up and climaxed, each hard pulse greedily taken into Selene's mouth. He pumped shallow strokes, a victorious growl rumbling through his chest at the moment of release.

While he'd wanted to spend his seed inside her, she'd given him the next best thing.

Sagging back against the blankets, he released a shuddered breath and tried to focus his eyes, a near impossible task when Selene still had her mouth upon him. She suckled the last few drops and came off him with a quiet pop.

"I… You…" He couldn't form words, brought down by his mate and her wickedly talented mouth. Selene crawled up over his body and grinned.

"Good. Now you can sleep."

"But—"

"I want you to sleep, because you can't take care of me and our baby if you're also tired. Please?" Pleading eyes gazed down at him. Resigned to giving Selene her way, he nodded.

He had no bed in the hoard, but after she rose from his lap, he gathered the blanket and pillows from the floor then led the way to his treasure room. The door to her home remained open behind him, a way for her to travel back and forth as needed.

Selene gasped.

"What?"

"There's so much… *everything.*"

The jewels of his precious hoard no longer impressed him. Piles of gold coins—a mix of Aztec gold, British sovereigns, and other currencies from around the world—glittered beneath the magical lantern lights glowing throughout the chamber. Selene dragged her fingers over a glossy ruby, only to jerk her hand away and shoot him an apologetic smile.

Loki took the same jewel from the waist-high pile then placed it in her palm. "No. It's yours. Every single thing here is yours."

"Loki, I can't take this. It must be worth a fortune."

"And so are you. You are my one true treasure, more important than anything I could collect in all of the nine worlds. Never doubt that."

Selene's eyes shimmered with unshed tears. "I'm so lucky to have you."

"No. We are lucky to have one another. For I count myself blessed from the moment you entered my life, and doubly blessed for the child we will soon welcome into the world."

He wiped away the tears spilling down her cheeks with his thumbs and leaned down to kiss her. Selene melted against him. Then a tiny bump kicked against his middle, breaking them apart. Selene laughed and ran her hands over her belly.

"It looks like our baby shares the sentiment."

Captivated by the baby's movement, Loki spread his palm across her stomach. Their child rewarded him with another strong kick. They never failed to awe him. "He recognizes me."

"He does," Selene said. "Now sleep for both of us."

Unable to deny her, Loki surrendered and adopted his draconic form. In his larger body, he stretched across the gold and wriggled until the coins shifted beneath him to create the perfect cushion. His aching back decompressed, and all the stress of maintaining human appearances melted away. And then there was Selene. She smiled up at him, his fearless and beautiful mate. The mother of his child.

"Promise you won't roll over on me if I sleep close to you?"

He grinned. "I don't move once asleep, but I have something better to offer than sleeping beside me."

Her brow raised. "Oh?"

After wiggling onto his back, he fanned out one wing and exposed the downy surface to her.

Once she settled upon the softest, warmest feathers with her blanket and pillows, Loki allowed the sweet melody of gemstones to lull him to sleep.

***

Awakening once in the middle of the night, Selene took the portal home to use the restroom and let the dogs out to potty too. Grateful she'd returned, they rushed inside and promptly passed out again in their beds once finished.

When she returned to Loki's chief treasure room, she found her dragon undisturbed, still sprawled upon his back like a gargantuan, feathered kitten.

He didn't stir when she kissed his nose, and she didn't know whether it was typical for him to slumber so deeply or if it was testament to his sleep deprivation.

After a moment of studying his sleeping face and trying to imagine their child, she crawled back into her makeshift bed, pulled up the blanket, and returned to sweet dreams.

With Loki's wings cradling her, Selene slept until a few rays of sunlight streamed over her face through a cluster of fist-sized holes in the rocky wall. He still hadn't awakened, prompting her to complete the usual morning activities at home. She sipped herbal tea while the dogs ran outside, took a quick shower, and then she returned.

He still hadn't moved.

She caressed his face then parted from his side to explore the rest of the cave.

Lanterns lit the way. He'd promised her the hoard was safe and that she'd come to no harm while she explored. Picking her way through, she occasionally stopped to admire a marble bust, a portrait, or some strange piece of history worthy of a museum pedestal.

In the next room, she discovered everything from Japanese artifacts to Scandinavian relics. He had shelves filled with scrolls and leather-bound books. A few stone tablets occupied places of honor on slanted display tables. Each alcove she peered into revealed another wondrous treasure.

A golden trunk caught her attention. She approached slowly, lured by the way the light glinted off the engraved lid.

"I really hope that isn't the Ark of the Covenant," she muttered. Wary of melting off her face, she stayed away from the exquisite yet suspicious golden chest.

A grumble from her belly prompted her to return to the house through the stable portal. She enjoyed a day of blissful silence, caught up on her reading, and slept whenever the mood struck.

By the second day, she grew bored with her solitude but occupied herself with rearranging the nursery decorations and reading poetry to her growing dragon. On the third day, she returned to the hoard and found Loki still hadn't budged an inch.

Was he okay? Selene blinked at the motionless dragon, and a sense of panic overrode all reason, terror clawing through her chest.

What if he'd needed sleep so badly he'd gone into hibernation? What if he slept for months and missed their son's birth?

No. He needs a day or two of rest, that's all. He'll be himself again soon. Light glinted off his glossy scales, accentuating the ruby-edged luster.

"Don't sleep too much longer," she whispered as she stroked his snout.

One large, green eye blinked open.

"Loki!"

With a groan, he rolled onto his belly. The wealth of coins beneath him clinked together, and a few glittered from beneath his scales where they'd been lodged during his slumber. "Was I asleep for long?"

"Only two days. Enough for me to realize I should have asked how long you normally sleep in this form."

He gave her a sheepish look and transformed to his human body. "Two days is unusual for the nap I intended to take, but you were right. I did need to rest and hadn't realized how much I had deprived myself during these weeks at your side."

Missing the warmth of him, she leaned close until Loki took her in his arms. Her fingers traced over his muscled chest and the lean lines of each defined plane, dip, and chiseled angle. "Please don't do that again. Don't suffer in silence for me."

"I won't. Will you return with me each week as I rest?"

His reassuring kiss eased the tension in her chest. Relieved, she nodded and swallowed the thick lump in her throat. "Yes."

He squeezed her closer, as close as her growing belly would allow, and kissed the crown of her head. "As I slept, I thought about Nathaniel and what I would say to him. I also realized there are things I should tell you."

"Like what?"

"There are many dangers in my world, and it is regarding one of them that I quarreled with Astrid's mate. You already know he is a knight."

"Yeah. One of King Arthur's knights, who just so happens to be his son in this lifetime. Still getting used to that."

Loki chuckled and looped her arm through his. They walked together to the next chamber. "Yes, it is a tad confusing. Similar, in a way, to the witches and their reincarnation, but different in the fact that it is confined to bloodlines. Witches are not always born to witches."

"So what does this have to do with danger?"

"Not all the knights are as honorable as Nathaniel, or Galahad as you would know him from the tales. Two have broken away from the order and seek to destroy all dragons. They've had their goons following me for months. But always in California," he added hastily. "Guaranteeing your safety and that of our child is important to me, so I continue appearances each day for them to see me."

"Who are they?"

"Pelleas and Bedivere. They are the authority figures behind the Anti-Dragon Movement, which you have likely heard of. Everyone has, it seems."

"I remember reading about them in the news. Didn't they try to assassinate the presi—Max?"

"They did and nearly succeeded. It was an awful time for dragons everywhere when we realized the driving force behind the Anti-Dragon Movement. During King Arthur's reign, the knights were benevolent figures and quite fair to us, I must admit. They could have slain me for any number of infractions against humankind, but tolerated my hijinks."

"You weren't a murderer."

"No, I've never murdered in cold blood. Caused trouble, drove others to commit crimes with my mischief, but I never did it myself."

"So, wait a second. Do you mean all the knights were against you guys? Nate, too?"

"Yes and no. The knighthood had been misled by Sir Kay and his two co-conspirators, Bedivere and Pelleas. Nate and Astrid discovered they had confined Merlin to an unnatural sleep and bound Arthur's spirit. I became involved when Maximilian asked if I could break the curse. I did." He shrugged, as if he hadn't admitted to rescuing the most powerful wizard of all time.

"Wow." At times, it felt like she lived in a fairy tale. "So, you fought with Nate because…?"

"Because I felt as if he were not doing enough to track down Pelleas and Bedivere."

"What happened to Kay?"

"Dead. We won that battle and brought the knights back to the side of justice, but the two escaped with Gaia's aid. They've practically disappeared off the face of the planet, but we know they're watching, biding their time for their next strike."

"Gaia…? Gaia, as in the titan?"

Loki nodded.

"So… Merlin is real. The titans are real. Does that mean your golden box over there is the real deal holding the ten commandments?" She pointed to the artifact in question as they passed.

Loki tossed his head back and laughed. The deep rumble flushed heat to her cheeks. "No, it isn't the Ark of the Covenant."

Selene relaxed.

"It's Pandora's Box."

"That's no better, Loki!" Keeping her distance, she stared at the chest again. She'd always thought Pandora's Box would be smaller. Even a plain and disinteresting box of no particularly interesting design. "Why do you even have this?"

He grimaced. "The last person to open it is forced to hold it until the next dumb twit makes the same mistake. You wouldn't believe how long it took to put everything back." He paused. "I don't recommend opening it."

Astonished by his admission—and also overwhelmed—she stared at her mate and tried to imagine the mysterious "things" he'd hunted to the ends of the Earth. Did she want to know what the box held? Unable to form a coherent sentence, she nodded instead.

The warmth of Loki's chuckle tousled her hair before he kissed her temple. "I was a foolish, brash young dragon, and Pandora charmed me. She beguiled me long enough to free herself from the burden of being the box's caretaker."

"What's inside it?"

A moment of silence passed. "I don't want to tell you."

"All right." His reluctance to share the box's contents told Selene everything she needed to know. "Then, may I suggest a better use of the rest of our afternoon?"

"What did you have in mind? Another picnic?"

Selene beamed up at him, hoping to pull off an impish smile. "Tell me about the paintings in your gallery. I saw the Birth of Venus, and if it's real, I'm dying to know how it came into your hands."

"Oh, I assure you it's the real thing, *skatten min*. As for how I acquired it, it's a long story."

Chapter 12

Selene's belly grew larger with the passing weeks, proportionate with her developing love for the new dragon in her life. As January faded and February came upon them, so did the projected due date of a normal nine-month human gestation. A couple regular customers remarked on her long pregnancy, but she only smiled and said the baby would come when he was ready.

Although her life had changed in multiple ways, she refused to allow Loki's riches to change her. The normalcy of working in the bakery became her anchor, a safe place to remind Selene she'd remained in control of her life. By day, she ran a successful business, and at the close of the afternoon shift, she returned to her mate—eager to return to his arms.

The icy fingers of winter melted away to spring, bringing verdant leaves to her garden and tender buds to the floral bushes outside. Children who had made snowmen rode their skateboards and bicycles down the peaceful streets, and she enjoyed evening strolls hand in hand with Loki as they walked the dogs.

As the weather warmed, Selene gained the opportunity to introduce him to neighbors and envious housewives who drooled over her charming new live-in boyfriend. Whenever she thought someone would recognize him, their eyes skimmed over him without recognition.

"Why is it that no one has put together two and two and realized you're a friggin' billionaire? Susan's son was playing on one of your handheld video game systems while she talked to us, and she didn't even blink."

Loki shrugged. "A spell. It's a minor cantrip designed to alter their perception. It wouldn't work on another magical person, such as you. Besides, do you recognize every billionaire in the world? Would you recognize, for example, Bill Gates?"

"I recognize a man when I've fantasized about boning him."

"Point made."

Her steps slowed once they reached her house, and she frowned at the hydrangea planted beside her side stoop. No matter how much she watered the bush, the leaves always drooped and the flower clusters browned on the edges. At times she considered pulling it up, but she loved the bluish-purple blossoms.

"What's wrong?" Loki asked, following her gaze.

"Wishing I had a greener thumb, is all. This bush was here when I moved in, but it always looks like crap after a couple weeks."

Loki crouched beside the wilting plant and ran his hands across the dirt beneath it. "It needs more acid, is all. You can mix some of these pine needles in the soil to help feed it."

Reminding her of a time-lapse video, the wilting hydrangea lifted and brightened, then the spindly leaves unrolled into lush foliage. Pink and periwinkle blue flooded over the browning flower clusters.

Selene's mouth fell open.

"Why didn't you tell me you could do garden magic!"

"You never asked. My mother is a black dragon, and earth magic is our forte."

Selene placed both fists against her hips and stared at him. Why did anything about him surprise her anymore? When he'd mentioned his magic aligning with the dark, she'd imagined necromancy and shadowplay. "You're impossible."

Loki grinned. "I thought you would appreciate the view as you crochet. Of course, I can undo—"

"No, no! Don't you dare!" She touched a silken petal and leaned closer to breathe in the floral fragrance. "They're beautiful, Loki. Thank you."

"You are welcome. If you're ready to return inside, I'll draw you a bath."

"Actually, I feel great now that I've had some fresh air, and I think I'll visit Astrid after all." She'd felt sluggish and overtaxed that morning, but sunlight and warm air had rejuvenated her. "If she hasn't made new plans anyway. We were going to see a movie and visit the teahouse."

"Of course. I'll open a portal to her home as soon as you're ready."

"You're the best." She lifted to her toes and kissed his cheek. "I'll call her right now. Do you think… could you go spruce up the other hydrangea by the front porch? Please?"

"Your wish is my command." His exaggerated, gallant bow made her giggle. While he rounded the house to the front porch, she went inside and fetched her phone. A quick text exchange with Astrid confirmed their previous arrangements.

By the time she freshened up in the bathroom and grabbed a snack, Loki had come inside and waited for her on the couch. Baron had claimed his favorite spot across Loki's lap and Dusty lay across his feet. Selene never tired of seeing him trapped beneath the two furry lugs.

"Astrid said you can open a portal inside her place. What are you going to do all day?"

"I haven't paid a proper visit to Merlin in months. I may do so when these two allow me to stand. Enjoy your afternoon with Astrid."

One casual gesture of his hand opened a sparkling rift to Astrid's living room. He didn't complain when Baron pawed his shirt or crawled onto his chest to nose his cheek. The months had changed him, too, replacing the uptight businessman with a laidback dragon.

"Love you," she called over her shoulder. Selene didn't think she would ever get used to traveling from Virginia to California in a single step. All those years of commercial flights, and all she'd needed was her own personal dragon mage.

Sometimes, she wished she'd met him before Carlos, but she'd been a different person then, a different young woman with no ambition and drive, still tumbling through life and unable to decide what she wanted.

Would he have loved her the same way?

The delectable aroma of sugar cookies welcomed Selene to San Diego. She stepped into the apartment to see Chloe on the couch with Arthur on her lap and her half-dragon son, Brandt, beside her. Both children appeared to be absorbed with the dinosaurs on the television.

"Oh, hey, Chloe. I didn't know you were here."

Selene took the seat beside the other woman and greeted her with a kiss to the cheek.

"Nate is the duty officer on the ship tonight, so I came over to watch Arthur and have a break from Saul," Chloe explained.

"A break?"

"Yeah. I love him with all my heart, but sometimes dragon affection can get, well, a little overbearing. Plus, he can be an insufferable know-it-all."

"Oh, yeah, I learned early on not to ask Loki about anything remotely technical or related to software. He starts going into details about maintaining this or that and my eyes glaze over."

They shared a laugh that sent her baby into a flurry of activity. Her belly rolled and the skin stretched as one little foot kicked out.

"Ow! That one hurt a little." The other foot must have bounced off her lower rib. She winced, shifted, and massaged the spot, but didn't dare to complain.

A strong baby was also a healthy baby, and she'd never take her child's health for granted.

"Are you okay? I can't believe you're still on your feet," Chloe marveled. "By the ninth month, I couldn't leave the house without Saul putting me in a wheelchair."

Selene's eyes popped open wide. "Really?"

"Really. I spent the last month on strict bed rest, but… you look great. I mean, really great." Arthur reached up to grab a fistful of his grandmother's hair. Chloe gently unwound it and loosened his chubby fist.

"I have moments where I'm ridiculously tired, like this morning, but a short walk outside fixed that right up."

Chloe tilted her head. "Well, Merlin and Loki did mention you have something magical and different in your blood. Maybe you're from Krypton."

"Well, I don't think I'm from a fictional alien planet, but I'd totally rock the red boots and miniskirt if I could fit in them right now." She felt pudgy and swollen, but Loki gazed at her with bedroom eyes regardless of how large her belly grew. He'd only become more innovative when it came to their sexual positions, taking her in a variety of ways that applied no pressure to their baby.

Astrid stepped into the room and fetched her purse from the couch arm. She'd donned a breezy pink and white, floral-print sundress. "You'll be in heels again in no time. Ready to go?"

Once they were in the car and en route to the theater for their action flick, Selene turned Chloe's words over in her head again.

"Hey, was your pregnancy difficult at the end?"

Astrid shook her head. "Not really. No more difficult than I suspect most pregnancies would be. Why?"

"Your mother said hers was rough and she had to go on bed rest right about now."

"She did. So did my Aunt Marcy. Mom almost died, but Dad's got some of Grandma's white magic, and he was able to heal her before the blood loss was irreversible. It was... God, I shouldn't be saying this to you. I mean, you seem fine, so I don't think what happened to them is going to happen to you." Astrid blurted it in a rush as color surged to her cheeks.

"Loki warned me the pregnancy may become dangerous, but he never said..." Selene closed her eyes and bowed her head forward, her good mood and humor bruised by the weight of her heavy thoughts. "Why am I different?"

"I don't know, hon." She pursed her lips then reached over to touch Selene's shoulder with one hand. "Maybe it's a witch thing? That still makes you a paranormal, in a sense. Mom was a plain old human. Aunt Marcy, too."

"Barely a witch," she muttered. "Times like this, I really wish I knew who my dad was. *What* he was."

If he wasn't a dragon or a shifter, then what was he? What else could possibly be out there?

They drove with the top down in Astrid's new car, a sporty convertible painted cherry red with golden stardust accents across the hood. The wind whipped through Selene's hair, and she enjoyed the California sunshine against her skin.

They made it with ten minutes to spare before their blockbuster.

"Crap," Astrid muttered.

"Don't tell me you forgot to pee before leaving home."

Astrid's sheepish smile provided the answer. "Guilty as charged. Be right back."

Wanting to remain in the open and easy to find in the unfamiliar theater, Selene perused the posters decorating the carpeted corridor while the dragoness hurried away toward public restrooms.

They had time. At risk of missing only a few of the previews for upcoming flicks, or even a few advertisements, she glanced at a pop-out advertisement for an upcoming kid flick. Would Loki enjoy bringing their little one to the theater? She hoped so. He had a fondness for movies, and he'd even brought her home an animated underwater flick from the Redbox one evening.

A familiar dark-haired and handsome man crossed Selene's path. "Excuse me."

"It's no problem. Sorry about that. I take up so much…" She tilted her head and gazed into his brown eyes, recognizing him from memories of winter in Virginia. "Don't I know you?"

"Ah, I do not believe so…?"

"No, I do know you. From my bakery in Norfolk." Her eyes dropped to his hand and the deep, gnarly scar over the back of his knuckles, like something had almost taken off all his fingers. "It *is* you."

The man's eyes lit up with recognition. "*Signorina*, what an unexpected surprise, seeing you again so very far away." He took her hand and brushed a kiss across her knuckles.

"I have family here," she said. "You?"

"Work, *signorina*. Work. It takes me all over the world. Are you here to see a movie or leaving?"

"About to go in, actually."

"Please, you must allow me to buy you a popcorn, or whatever else you like." He steered her by the elbow away from the hall toward the front counter.

"That's sweet, but you don't have to. Besides, I'm waiting for my friend."

"She will see us here, no?" His charming smile brightened his eyes. "Tell me what you both would like. My treat. It is the least I can do for such a beautiful expectant mother. The baby is due soon, yes?"

"Soon," Selene agreed. Her pulse pounded in her ears and her palms grew damp.

It took her a moment to realize he was veering her toward the longest concession line, the end close to the exit doors. A niggling voice of doubt whispered a warning in her head.

She didn't want to go anywhere with him, to get popcorn or anything else.

"No, I'm fine," she insisted as she withdrew her arm.

"Selene, get away from him!" Astrid's voice cut through the general din of the theater lobby like a sharp knife, amplified with power.

A cold burst of terror coursed through her veins. The world around her exploded into brilliant white light. Unable to see, she stumbled back against another customer. Startled cries came from every corner of the spacious lobby. People bumped into each other and cried out in panic. Alarms went off.

When Selene's vision cleared seconds later, the man was gone and Astrid was standing beside her with a blazing sword in her hand, one arm shielding her eyes. "Call Uncle Loki *now*. Tell him the knights are here."

"What?"

"Just do it, Selene, and don't move from this spot unless Loki or I come and get you."

Astrid sprinted away.

The slayers. For months, they'd all warned her about the danger of the bloodthirsty fallen knights, but she'd hoped to never cross paths with one. Cold fear pulsed through her chest as her trembling hands dialed Loki on the phone.

"Calling so early, my treasure?" His voice sounded amused. "Shall I come get you?"

"The slayers are here!" she blurted. "Astrid ran off after one of them, Loki. Please, you have to do something. I—" The phone clicked dead. "Loki?"

Selene paced the floor, among the first of the theater-goers to regain her vision. A couple people huddled, and a security guard who had been outside the lobby during the attack called for everyone affected to sit on the floor.

A scuffle at the doors alerted her to another problem. She glanced toward the commotion.

"Selene!"

Loki burst through the entry doors and plowed past the security officers trying to calm the frantic crowd. He pulled Selene into his arms and cradled her head against his chest.

"Are you all right? Did he hurt you or the baby?"

"No, I'm fine, but I knew him. He was in my bakery months ago, and Astrid ran after him."

"You never mentioned this."

"I didn't realize he was a... a dragonslayer." The tears came hot and fast down her cheeks. "He was just a customer. I don't... I don't think to tell you about every customer."

"Shh, shh." He stroked her hair and gave her another gentle squeeze. "Of course you wouldn't, and you shouldn't. You had no idea." He kissed her brow and held her, but even the warmth of his body failed to assuage the terror building in her chest.

"Astrid is out there looking for him. What if he hurts her?" What if she died like their waterdragon friend in Japan? "You have to go help her!"

"I will. First, I am taking you to Drakenstone Manor."

Her large belly trembled from the quick pace of their steps. Outside, a crowded sidewalk teemed with terrified people. One of the same guards who had tried to prevent Loki from barging inside held out a hand.

"Excuse me, sir, but we need everyone to remain until the police arrive."

Although he never changed forms, Loki drew himself to his full height. Every intimidating inch of him seemed larger than before, and his eyes glowed bright. "Dragonslayers targeted my pregnant mate within this establishment, and I will remove her from the premises at my own discretion. Challenge me further and learn how it feels to be crushed beneath a dragon's claw."

The guard gulped and stepped back.

Unimpeded, Loki opened the door and allowed Selene through. He ushered her toward the sidewalk and away from the throb of the Anti-Mag Field.

"Gods, it's Astrid." Her voice trembled in relief as her friend approached them from the direction of the street. Perspiration shone against her brow and she moved with a slight limp.

"Where is he?" Loki snarled.

"Gone. He got away. He did some kind of magical thing with the vines growing on a nearby billboard, and it came crashing down. I barely shifted in time to catch it, otherwise it would have creamed a dozen mortals." She rubbed her shoulder and grimaced, her features tight with pain. "I kind of caught it with my back."

"I am taking you to your grandmother," he said, giving her no option to argue. Loki opened up a portal in front of the gawking spectators. "Both of you."

Ēostre met them on the other side. Her pale eyes widened when she saw Astrid's disheveled appearance and Selene's tear-streaked face.

"What happened?"

"Pelleas tried to grab Selene from the theater," Astrid answered.

"I'd never have believed they'd be so bold as to grab a pregnant woman in public." Ēostre gestured them all over to the couch. She and Max shared a quaint home on the beach in Carlsbad, preferring it over a larger mansion, though Loki was certain that would change when the twins grew older.

"They do not seem to care any more about staying quiet," Loki said. "He caused quite a scene and tried to injure many, including Astrid."

Ēostre nodded in understanding. "Let me take a look at you."

"See to Selene first, Grandma."

"No!" Selene protested. "I'm fine. Shaken, but fine. Astrid's the one who caught a billboard on her back."

Astrid relented and remained still while her grandmother tended to her bruises and scrapes. Loki kept Selene in his arms but guided her to sit on the couch. His hand remained on her belly, circling in soothing strokes.

"Where is Nate? He should be alerted to this new development."

"He was doing recon with Percivale," Astrid replied. "He's been pushing himself hard this past week because they thought they had a lead on Pelleas."

Loki grumbled. "No doubt a clever ploy to keep him busy while they made their real move."

Selene's hold on him tightened and she turned her face into his shoulder. Now that the immediate danger was over, exhaustion swept through her. While the others discussed options and who to talk to, she found her eyes drifting shut.

"Why don't you take her home?" Ēostre said.

"Yes, please," Selene agreed in a sleepy slur.

"Yeah, she's had enough today, Uncle Loki. I'll call Nate and tell him what happened." Astrid sighed. "I'm sorry our day out was ruined."

Selene forced herself to open her eyes and smiled at her friend. "I'm just glad you're okay. It wasn't your fault."

Loki rose and picked her up, cradling her like a princess. Selene closed her eyes again and nestled against him. Tomorrow they would have to make a police report and address what happened, but for tonight, she was safe, and all she wanted was to remain in Loki's arms.

Chapter 13

The rogue slayers didn't make a peep after their failed kidnapping attempt. At first, Loki had been overly protective, refusing to let her leave the house unless he was at her side. A week of that had been enough for Selene to put her foot down and protest the unofficial house arrest.

They'd compromised by agreeing to remain at his home while Loki and Ēostre added further protections to hers.

After a night of napping on and off for a few minutes at a time, Selene shook her mate awake. She envied the dragon for passing out after she'd paced the halls most of the night, wandering from one end of his enormous compound to the next. She'd walked to the stables where he kept a pair of fine horses, discovered he had a new pair of young zebras from Astrid's growing herd, and also dipped her feet into the pool.

"Loki. Loki, wake up."

The groggy dragon stirred and swept long hair from his face. "What's wrong?"

"I want to go to the bakery."

"It's Saturday. Are you not the same Selene who badgered me to sacrifice weekend work?"

"This is different. I can't sleep."

His brows raised. "Shall we go for another walk?" When he sat up, the sheets fell away to his waist. Selene's eyes lowered to follow the dark treasure trail leading to his cock.

"No, but…" She crawled onto his lap and straddled him. "I have a better idea."

Catching on, he removed her nightshirt and tossed it aside. Her breasts filled his palms. "This is the best part of your pregnancy by far."

"Which? The sex or playing with my breasts?"

The doctor had advised nipple stimulation to induce labor, which Loki had dutifully performed for three days without complaint.

"Both. But your breasts are stunning."

"They're heavy, and they ache."

"They're wonderful, and I'll be gentle."

True to Loki's word, his touch never caused discomfort. His thumb circled around one tender tip until it beaded tight and stiff. Then he soothed the dull throb by closing his lips around it, teasing with the warmth of his tongue. Selene sighed and tilted her head back.

He alternated back and forth between each breast until her core clenched with a desire only his cock could fulfill. Fingers alone weren't enough—she needed the thick girth of him, hard and throbbing between her thighs.

Two rounds of vigorous sex later, their stubborn baby hadn't budged an inch. The subtle Braxton-Hicks contractions continued. And she was ready for her endless pregnancy to be over.

Running water thundered against the porcelain clawfoot tub in the adjacent bathroom before Loki emerged from it, bare and glistening. "Perhaps a bath?"

Gods, I am so lucky. Miserable but lucky. Hand in hand, he led her to the tub and climbed in first. He helped her lower to join him with her back against his chest while one of her favorite bath bombs fizzed by her feet. For an hour, they soaked, saying little. Somehow she and Loki had transcended the need for words and idle chitchat.

"How do you feel?"

Selene twisted around as much as her belly would allow, propping her cheek against Loki's shoulder. "I feel like I've been pregnant forever."

He chuckled and kissed the top of her head. "Forever is indeed a long time, but not quite the duration of your pregnancy. I wish I could take away your discomfort, Selene. I would give you anything in this world if I could."

"I know."

After helping her from the tub, he initiated a head-to-toe pampering session. By the time Loki had buffed her dry and applied lotion to every inch of Selene's skin, she didn't want to return to the bed.

Reinvigorated by the bath, she tugged on one of her favorite spring dresses from the closet and let the flowy material dance around her knees. "I want to pop into the bakery for a few."

His brows drew together. "To work?"

"A little, but mostly I want to talk with Jacob for a while without a telephone line between us. And I need a break before I skin you."

"Skin *me?* What have I done?"

"Everything," she replied in a chipper voice. "And too much. You haven't taken care of yourself at all because you're far too busy doting over me. Do something fun. Scare an employee or two."

"Haven't taken care of myself? I think three days of sex disagree with you."

Selene sighed, exasperated. "Men."

After delivering her to the bakery office, he kissed her brow and vanished, startling her with his abrupt departure.

"Selene? That you?" Jacob called from the front counter.

"No, it's the boogeyman out to steal your delicious pastries," she called back.

She started in her office, tidying up her desk and organizing her files. Jacob poked his head in while she ran the vacuum across the carpet.

"Selene, honey, what are you doing?"

"Cleaning."

"I can see that, but why? I vacuumed in here yesterday."

"There was a spot on the floor."

Jacob regarded her with one brow raised and his arms crossed over his chest. "A spot."

"Yeah. A dust spot."

"Sweetie, there's no spot. If you're hallucinating spots, maybe you need to go lie down."

She didn't. Her cleaning whirlwind traveled beyond the office and onto the main floor. Armed with a squirt bottle of sanitizer and a cloth, Selene began with the glass surfaces.

Jacob's disapproving gaze followed her around the bakery. "Sweetheart. You should be at home resting."

Selene sprayed the counter with cleaning solution and swiped a few brisk wipes with a cloth. "I can't rest. I've been up all night. I can't sleep, and Loki is irritating me with the usual."

"What's he doing?"

"Follows me everywhere. Treats me like a fragile piece of china."

"Sweetheart, you have another person inside you. Like, a whole other being is in there. Growing. That's kind of a big deal. Can you blame him for wanting to make sure you're okay?"

"I'm not going to fall apart because I wipe a few counters down."

"Okay, okay, but can you stop punishing them? You're going to scrub through the varnish as hard as you're wiping."

She paused to blink at the spotless surface, then slumped her tense shoulders and laughed. "You're right. Sorry."

Jacob grinned and rubbed her back. "You're scary when you're nesting. How clean is your house?"

"Spotless. And not because Loki brought in his servants, either. I'm pretty sure I hurt Anura's feelings when I went back in after her and redid everything."

"That's the bunny, right?"

"One of 'em, yeah." It was a relief to talk with Jacob and not worry about watching her words. Her mom knew Loki was a dragon, true, but any time she brought up shifters or magic, her mother's eyes widened a little bit more.

He took her by the shoulders. "How about this? I'll make you a warm drink and you sit down with a snack or something, and we can chitchat since it's a slow day."

"Was lunch good at least?"

"Totally met our daily quota," he told her. "So relax."

Selene removed a muffin from behind the glass and studied it, unable to decide if she was starved for sugar or sick of eating. The last time Loki had referred to pregnancy and birth as one of nature's marvels, she'd wanted to kick him in the ass.

At one moment, she loathed the experience, and in the next, she wondered if they'd give their little one a sibling one day when she felt the little seamonkey twisting and turning inside her womb or felt hiccups jostling the unborn child.

Jacob joined her with an oversized cookie and two mugs of herbal tea. "My mentor makes this for pregnant ladies. So when I told her my boss was about to blow, she gave me a tin. Try it."

"Mentor?"

He rolled his eyes. "Yeah, I have a mentor now, and all it took was going behind the eastern coven mistress's back and contacting the head witch in charge by e-mail. River lost her shit and showed up at the next meeting two nights later. Took me as her pupil herself."

Before sipping it, she inhaled the steam of the suspiciously dark brew in the cup. "What's in it?"

"Red raspberry leaf and other witchy components guaranteed to do good things. I dunno. Brewing isn't my forte. Give me a cauldron and you're asking for a black sludge mess."

"Yet you bake bread like a dream."

"I know, right? I also mix a mean margarita. Oh well, at least the rest is coming together. River is some sort of super witch or something and seems to be trying to reorganize how everything works. She gave me access to the full library."

"Good. I'm glad things are working out for you finally. So…" Selene sipped her tea. Flavors of fruit and citrus danced over her taste buds. She inhaled the steam again and sighed, content. "How are things with Apollo?"

An uncharacteristic blush flushed Jacob's cheeks and he ducked his head, fiddling with the edge of the tablecloth. "I like him. I mean, I *really* like him."

"Any sparks from his end of things?"

"Yeah, I think so. I thought Loki was pulling my chain at first when he offered to introduce me to him. All the dragons you see in the news are with these gorgeous women, you know? Who'd expect one to be into a relationship outside the norm?"

"A guy who likes guys?"

He crumpled a napkin and threw it at her. "You know what I mean."

"Sure I do. But no one wants a gorgeous woman if that isn't their thing, especially when they can have a smokin' mage instead."

"I'm not that good looking."

"*Loki* was threatened by you, and he's like..." A dreamy sigh interrupted her.

Jacob snickered. "Yeah, I told him, out of the two of you, I'd rather rock his world."

Tea spewed across the table. Her friend grinned wider and passed over more napkins. "Did you seriously?"

"Totally did. You should have seen his face. Priceless."

"I'm glad you two are getting along now."

"Me too, which is why I know he doesn't mean to drive you crazy. He's just... He's so in love with you that I am pretty sure he would rampage the entire world if something happened to you or the baby. But hey, at least he hasn't locked you away in his hoard to protect you."

"I wouldn't be surprised if he considered it," she muttered. "Fine, you win. I'll go home."

"If you're really that restless, take the dogs for a walk. Get out of the house but in a relaxing way, not a working way."

"Yes, sir, bossman."

"Heh, bossman. You're the boss, woman."

"Nope, you're in charge while I'm out on maternity, so get used to it." She stood and headed to the back office. Instead of calling Loki, she dialed Astrid instead.

"Let me guess, sick of your man?" Astrid asked the moment she picked up.

"Yes. Please come save me from murdering him for his good, albeit bothersome, intentions."

Astrid laughed. "I'll be right there. Work or home?"

"I'm at work, but I'm being kicked out."

"Be right there."

Golden motes appeared in the air seconds before the portal opened in Selene's office. Jacob watched from the doorway with envy and awe.

"I wish witches could do that as easily," he said. "Drawing out those complicated circles is a bitch."

Astrid popped through, bright and cheery as always, with Arthur secured to her chest in a wrap. He laughed and waved, as happy as his mother with an equally personable temperament. The portal closed with a soft whoosh behind them.

"Hey, Astrid," Selene greeted. "Hello, Arthur."

"So what's the plan?" Astrid asked. She glanced over her shoulder, smiled at Jacob, and waved. "Hey there."

"Astrid, Jacob. Jacob, this is Astrid and her son, Arthur."

"Oooh, so you're the one Uncle Loki hooked up with Apollo."

"And you're mom to King-frikkin-Arthur."

Astrid laughed and tickled her son's bare feet. He squealed and kicked. "Not very kingly, is he?"

"I dunno, he gets carried around everywhere, people stop whatever they're doing if he's upset, and when he cries, a boob gets shoved in his mouth. I'd call that royal treatment." Jacob winked.

Selene stared at him. "You don't even like boobs."

"Hey, I can still appreciate them. They're like stress balls, but on a person."

"Right, and on that note, we're leaving," Selene said.

Jacob beamed at them, his mission accomplished. "You two ladies have fun. Nice meeting you, Astrid."

Her friend opened a new portal that led into Selene's living room. Baron and Dusty lifted their furred heads on the other side and barked in greeting as they stepped through, accustomed to the magical rifts.

Once the two were done sniffing the new visitor to their home, Selene attached their leashes. Together, the two friends made their way down the residential street. Flowers swayed on the gentle spring breeze and birdsong reached them from verdant branches.

Although Loki would be happiest if she surrendered her little home, Selene adored the neighborhood and had dreams of raising their child in a humble house instead of a sprawling manor fit for western royalty. She wanted their child to play at the bus stop on the corner and ride his bike down to the cul-de-sac at the end of the street. It was especially important to her for the baby to live among other humans and develop empathy some of the pureblood dragons lacked.

Contrary to his massive size, Dusty ambled along at a sedate pace. Her smaller pup, Baron, tugged the lead and tried to charge ahead to sniff everyone and everything.

"Wow. He really is a high-energy dog. Nate and I have a German shepherd at home. If I was thinking, I would have brought Echo along to make friends."

Selene chuckled. "Next time. We'll plan a doggy play date and let them all romp together in the yard. How'd the house buying go, by the way?"

"Slow. I'm going to miss my condo, but it's not really a good place for a dog or a growing kid. Grandma is helping me find a few suitable properties."

"Good, good. That sounds… good." A contraction rippled across her belly. Selene paused, leaned forward, and took in slow, even breaths.

"Selene?"

"I'm okay. Guess all that walking stirred the baby up."

Astrid rubbed her back. "I'll call Uncle Loki. C'mon, we should head back to the house."

When they reached the edge of the driveway, a sensation, like a snapping rubber band, popped within Selene's belly. A wet trickle followed, and then Dusty whined before nosing her thigh.

"I think my water just broke," she whispered.

A portal opened before them, the golden glitter-trimmed circle created by Astrid, and then the dragoness was pulling them all through to the other side. They arrived in Loki's office where he sat behind the desk with the phone to his ear.

"Pass along my message verbatim to those incompetent worms," her mate growled into the speaker, "and let them know I'll see them in court if—" His green eyes grew large. "Selene?"

"Her water broke," Astrid said. "I brought her directly to you."

"I'll pass along your message, sir, and initiate your absence procedures as directed. Congratulations," a woman's voice spoke into the room through the intercom.

Loki abandoned his desk and swept Selene into his arms, one beneath her knees and the other supporting her back. Another contraction ripped through her body, a hundred times more painful without the cushioning of amniotic fluid.

Oh sweet gods. And it had just started. How was she going to endure hours of this? Possibly days if her mother's terrifying stories of a thirty-one hour labor were to be her future. For the first few minutes, she was barely aware of anything around her or that their surroundings had changed until Loki tried to put her in bed. *His* bed. He'd whisked her to his mansion, and she hadn't even noticed.

"No! No bed," she cried out. "I… I need to walk. I need to move."

"Whatever you wish, *skatten min*, but allow me to peel these pants from you first."

"Oh, okay."

With Loki's help, she changed into a loose, oversized shirt. Each time a contraction struck, he paused and guided her through her breathing exercises. When the pain subsided, she stood on her shaky legs and paced across the floor. Loki moved up beside her and took her hand.

"You don't have to walk with me," she said.

He raised her hand to his lips and kissed each of her fingers. "I want to."

They walked together, taking their time on the stairs. Selene counted her lucky stars that they were going down and not up. The wide flight may as well have been a mountain, but Loki was with her every step of the way.

Astrid met them in the living room, child and dog free. "I hope you don't mind, Selene, but I figured it'd be okay with you if I took the dogs to our place to play with Nate, Echo, and Arthur for a while."

"That's perfect. They'd fuss otherwise."

"Is there anything else I can do? Fetch your mom maybe?"

Another contraction rippled across her belly. "Yes! My mom, please."

Whether fate or something to do with dragon magic, Selene didn't have to suffer hours of labor. Astrid fetched her mother and the doctor arrived through one of Ēostre's portals minutes later. And through it all, Loki stayed by her side, not muttering a single complaint, even when she squeezed down on his fingers hard enough to break bones.

"Honey, it's almost time. Do you wanna lie down or try something else?" Dr. Rourke asked.

"I'm so tired," Selene whispered. "I think… I think I want the bed."

Her mother smoothed her hand up and down Selene's back and guided her to the downstairs bedroom set up for the birth.

Loki settled on the bed first while Selene's mother helped her undress. Then he supported her from behind, his cheek against her temple and his hands on her swollen belly.

"You can do this," Loki whispered in her ear, his low, husky voice raising goose bumps across her skin.

"All right, Selene, we're going to push when you're ready. Listen to your body and trust it," the doctor said.

"We're all right here for you, baby," her mother said. Both she and Astrid took up a place at her sides.

Each contraction sapped her of her strength, but the encouragement of her loved ones kept her going. Loki whispered in her ear, beautiful words in his native language.

"You're almost there, Selene. I can see the baby's crown," the doctor said. "One more push."

"I can't, I can't."

Astrid squeezed Selene's hand in encouragement. "Yes, you can. You've got this down to one last push, girl. Just one more."

Despite all their confidence in her, Selene teetered on the brink of wishing she'd accepted an epidural instead. As she bore down one final time, her fists clenched around her mate's fingers and she squeezed her eyes shut. She didn't realize she was screaming until a second cry joined hers.

"It's a girl," Dr. Rourke announced.

"A girl, Selene," Loki whispered against her ear. "We have a daughter."

Selene cradled the infant against her bare breast and stared down in wonder. Thick black hair covered her head and both tiny fists grasped at her. Their daughter rooted against her and latched onto Selene's breast without assistance.

The rest of the room faded from Selene's attention, and in that moment, she only had eyes for Loki and their child.

Their nameless daughter. Selene pursed her lips and studied the tiny child greedily swallowing her first meal. "We didn't pick a name for a girl."

"Might I make a suggestion?"

Selene tilted her head back and looked at him, secure in his embrace. "Of course."

"Aslaug," Loki said. "After the wise queen."

Selene tested the name, whispering it to herself then louder for Loki to hear. "Aslaug. It's… actually pretty." Unique and different, a name no other child would have. "Aslaug Agnarhorn."

She ran her fingers through Aslaug's hair and sighed in contentment, the whole ordeal of labor forgotten.

"All right, Selene, you're looking good down here," Dr. Rourke said. She looked between them and smiled. "Loki, do you want the honors of cutting the cord?"

Loki tore his gaze away from Selene and blinked at the pair of scissors offered to him. "Cutting what?"

"Would you like to cut the cord, Dad?" Dr. Rourke offered again.

Appearing mystified all the while, Loki reached around her body and cut the cord where directed. Then he leaned down and kissed her damp brow again. "I love you."

"I love you, too."

Dr. Rourke smiled at them and spoke in a gentle whisper. "In my experience, dragon cubs are as hands-off as it comes and require little care. So if you'll excuse me, once you pass the placenta, I'll bugger off to handle some business on my phone. If you like, when I return in an hour, I'll assist with her first bath and also answer any additional concerns. Congratulations."

Anita kissed her brow and hugged Loki. Her mother and Astrid left the room together just after the doctor finished.

"Wait until you see his kitchen, Miss Anita. It's amazing," was the last thing Selene heard. Her mother shut the door behind them, leaving the family in total peace.

Loki drew a light blanket over them all.

Selene sighed. Sooner or later, she'd have to move. But not now. For the moment, all she wanted was to enjoy the comfort of her mate and bask in the glow of their newborn. "Everyone will be waiting to see her."

"Let them wait," he said before burying his face against her throat. "As I have no intentions of sharing my family with anyone for some time."

***

Aslaug appeared so tiny in his hands. Tiny and delicate and precious. He cradled her carefully in the crook of his arm, his daughter wrapped in a cheerful yellow blanket trimmed in white, and headed downstairs where he could hear the voices of his family.

Selene had bestowed the honor of introducing their daughter to everyone on him, while she enjoyed uninterrupted sleep.

"Allow me to present Aslaug Agnarhorn," he said as he stepped into the living room. Silence fell and all eyes turned on him. "My daughter."

Max approached first, a wide grin across his face. He stroked his finger down Aslaug's cheek. "She's beautiful, Loki. Congratulations."

"Go on. Say it."

"Say what?" Max asked.

"I told you so, or some variant thereof."

His cousin chuckled. "There's no need for that, Loki. I'm only glad that, for once, you listened to some of my advice. You deserve this happiness." Max smoothed a finger over Aslaug's curly hair. "Truly."

Ēostre, Astrid, and Chloe were next. They all cooed over the sleeping infant, clustering around Loki.

"She's so lovely."

"I can't wait to see her scales."

"Treasure this time, Loki," Chloe said.

Aslaug wriggled and blinked open her eyes, the baby blue color already tinged with green. Uncertain what to do next, Loki glanced about wildly until his gaze settled on Anita. Selene's mother smiled from an armchair and set aside the blanket she was knitting in soft shades of lavender, peach, and cream. Loki carried Aslaug over and gently set his daughter in her grandmother's arms.

"She's so lovely," Anita murmured. "She has your nose, I think, but her curls remind me of Selene when she was born."

"Should I go wake her?"

Anita readjusted Aslaug and rocked the little girl. "No, you don't have to do that. See? She's going back to sleep. Let her mama do the same."

"Loki?" Ēostre called over. "I know you have Anura to help, but Chloe and I prepared some meals for you. Everything is labeled and put away in the fridge."

"Thank you, that is much appreciated."

"We'll get out of your hair now, unless you need any of us to stay," Chloe said. "Don't hesitate to call if you or Selene need anything."

"I won't, believe me, but I believe we'll be fine. Anita has kindly offered to stay with us a few days."

"I get to fuss over my baby and her baby," the woman said, a twinkle in her eye. "Wouldn't miss it for the world."

His family said their goodbyes and left together through Ēostre's glittering silver portal, and silence fell again over the house. Loki dropped down onto the couch and leaned his head back against the cushions.

"I haven't done anything, but I'm exhausted."

Anita chuckled at him. "Go on and get yourself some rest with Selene. Little girl and I will be just fine down here. I'll bring her up when she gets hungry."

"Are you certain?"

"Of course I am. You gotta get sleep when you can now. You'll learn that right quick."

"Thank you, Anita."

"Of course."

Heading upstairs to join his mate, Loki knew he was leaving his daughter in good hands.

Chapter 14

The weeks passed by in a haze of familial bliss. The first few days, Selene did little more than feed Aslaug and sleep, only leaving the bed to use the restroom. Then her strength and energy gradually returned and she took great delight in carrying Aslaug around the house while she helped Anura with chores and cooking.

Anita stayed the first full week, and Selene had never been so grateful for her mother's unwavering support. After she went back home, various friends and family dropped in for visits and to deliver gifts. Even Jacob and Apollo. His first trip via dragon portal had left him wide eyed with wonder and full of questions.

Selene had been certain Loki was going to gobble him up at one point only to shut him up.

For now, she welcomed the blissful silence her home in Virginia provided. With Loki at work for a meeting, she had wanted to do something to keep herself occupied. Going through her things and deciding what to keep here and what to move to Loki's manor—their manor—seemed an appropriate chore.

With Aslaug strapped to her chest in a wrap, she started in the bedroom and worked her way through the house into the kitchen. Did he have a cast iron pan? She had no idea, so she added one of hers to the box.

Once Selene settled her daughter down for a nap, she followed the number one rule of new parenthood and crawled into bed. Sleeping whenever Aslaug slept had become an integral part of her daily routine. For once, she appreciated Loki's pampering methods, able to rest in a clean home without dishes to wash, laundry to fold, and all other random chores.

Instead of cleaning, she flopped onto her bed, turned on a movie, and settled back with the baby monitor beside her pillow.

It seemed her eyes had barely shut when a crash awakened her. Groggy, she reached for the remote and flicked the action movie off. The next thud jerked her into a sitting position. Dusty and Baron barked up a storm in the backyard.

Chills raced down her spine and goose bumps rose on her arms. Her dogs never barked during the day.

"Loki?" she called.

Selene tossed the blanket from over her legs and stood. When she reached the bedroom doorway to investigate the noise, a man clad in black tactical gear stepped into the hallway from the kitchen.

In the seconds that it took for her mind to digest what was happening, the man advanced on her. Shit. She stumbled back into her room and grabbed a shotgun from the closet shelf as the stranger stepped through. While her heart tried to leap from her chest, Selene twisted around, pointed the weapon at him, and fired.

At close range, the horrifying result sprayed against the cream-colored walls. She couldn't look and didn't dare to survey her handiwork as Aslaug shrieked from the nursery.

Selene fumbled to load another shell into the shotgun. Red cartridges tumbled to the floor around her feet after the box tipped over, a casualty of her shaking hands. A second masked figure rushed into the room and crashed into her before she had a chance to raise the gun.

They struggled, the shotgun trapped between them. Selene yelled and kicked. Her assailant shoved her up against the wall, but she pushed out with all her strength and cracked the butt of the shotgun against his face. His head rocked back.

"Goddammit!" As blood streamed down his temple, the man shoved her in the chest with both hands. Selene's head hit the wall and stars swam into her vision. The shotgun fell from her numb fingers. "Grab the damn target."

"Target acquired," a voice called from the hallway. Aslaug's cries sounded closer and Selene snapped her eyes open in time to see one of the men holding her daughter out in the hallway.

"No!"

Fury surged up and burned away the dizziness. Selene pushed away from the wall and struck out with every ounce of strength she possessed. Fear for her child sparked something within her and her magic swelled, manifesting in a glowing corona around her fist as it slammed against her attacker's face.

Between his hard jaw and the force behind her punch, her hand exploded into a landmine of pain. The home invader flew into the dresser and bounced off the wood furnishing before collapsing to the ground.

"Fuck! I thought you said the human didn't have powers?" another man said from the hall. "Retreat!"

Selene charged from her bedroom and crashed into the intruder between her and the figure retreating with her child. One shove was all it took to hurl him backward. He hit the door to the utility closet and smashed through it into her water heater. She tore past him into the front room and out the door onto her porch.

Barefoot, Selene sprinted outside over the grassy yard to see the kidnapper hurrying into the rear of a white van.

"Go, go, go!"

The door slammed shut.

Panic turned her frigid and cold. "No!"

She dashed behind the vehicle speeding down the road, desperate to recover her child. Her bare feet pounded against the scalding asphalt, but she pushed through the pain and strained to keep up, gaining on them with each desperate step.

In their frantic rush to escape her, they shot through the stop sign at the end of the residential road and turned into traffic on the busy highway. Brakes squealed and cars swerved to avoid striking the van, causing a multi-car collision. Then the van traveled beyond her line of sight. Her baby was gone.

Choked with anguish, Selene sank to her knees in the middle of the street and wailed.

***

Since Astrid deserved a few hours of peace and quiet, Nate gifted her with an appointment at her favorite spa and the promise of a child-free afternoon. She sat beside him in the passenger seat in a vibrant turquoise sundress. Her golden hair fell around her bare shoulders and glittered in the sunlight streaming through the open windows.

"You're the best husband."

"Of course. Happy wives give better blowjobs."

"Nate!" She swatted his arm. "Language."

He grinned. "He doesn't understand me yet." He paused to consider their child's odd growth rate and the tales his in-laws told him about his wife. "Does he?"

"We won't know until he's jabbering about BJs at his next play date," she grumbled.

Despite her fussing, she leaned across the center console and kissed the corner of his mouth. He turned his head and captured her lips in a longer kiss.

"Have fun. Give us a call when you're ready."

"You boys be good. And no more stuffed animals. He's drowning in them already."

"Shh. Go get your claws done."

Astrid rolled her eyes at him, stepped down from the car, and crawled into the back seat to kiss Arthur's chubby cheek. After she disappeared into the spa, Nate pulled into traffic and made his way toward the mall.

A short drive later, he passed through two levels of protection guarding the premises. The Anti-Mag Field always buzzed whenever Nate passed through it even if it didn't completely negate his gifts. It raised the hairs on his arms and made his fingertips tingle, but it made the normies feel safe, and the government was all about guaranteeing happiness for supernatural and mundane citizens across the United States.

After parking the car in the mall's garage, he unfolded the patriotic blue and white baby stroller they'd received as a gift from a pair of his friends in the navy. "You ready to do some extreme shopping, kid?"

Arthur gurgled up at him from the infant seat.

The walk up the ramp to the top level brought them out into the California sunshine. Nate adjusted the canopy on the stroller to shade Arthur's face then headed across the upper walkway into the mall. Like any weekend, Fashion Valley was crowded, but the open-air design minimized the oppressive volume.

Nate glanced beneath the canopy. "Where to first, huh?"

The plan was an afternoon of window-shopping, but the reality became a stroller with purchases packed into the basket underneath. Nate frowned down at the teddy bear tucked in beside his son.

"Your mom is going to kill me for getting another one, isn't she?" Arthur had a room full of stuffed animals. His own colorful, fuzzy menagerie.

Arthur babbled and slobbered on the red satin ear.

Despite the evening hour, the sun remained high in the sky. Nate adjusted the stroller shade and pulled his ballcap down lower over his forehead. They passed people coming in, young couples and old likely heading for the theater. Several of them smiled and peered down at Arthur.

He slowed as they headed down the ramp to the second level. The buzz from the Anti-Mag Field continued at the edge of his hearing, but there was something else. Something in the air had changed, almost imperceptible to his senses but increasingly apparent when he focused. Animosity.

Nate tightened his grip on the stroller bar. His gaze darted left and right.

All appeared normal, but he couldn't shake the sensation of eyes following him. Astrid would have called him paranoid.

The rapid slap of shoe soles against cement echoed across the garage. On the defensive in an instant, Nate spun in time to see two men hopping out of a black Tahoe parked a few vehicles away, another pair on the ground rushing toward him.

Before he could react, pain exploded across the middle of his back. He arched as the zap contracted his muscles and locked his joints. And if he was a normal man, he would have crumpled on the ground.

But Nate wasn't a normal man. He was a Knight of the Round Table. Adrenaline and magical endorphins flooded his body. He pivoted on a foot, grabbed his attacker by the back of the neck, and dragged the guy's head down to meet his rising knee.

Arthur began to cry and call out for him.

Nate summoned his armor, and in a flash of ivory light, the celestial steel formed around him. He slammed a gauntleted fist into the closest attacker's gut then followed it with a right hook to the face.

"Holy shit!" one of them cried.

"Yeah," Nate said. "Didn't expect that, did you?"

Further down the parking lot, more men in similar attire to the first attackers appeared from behind a parked SUV. Nate unhooked the car seat from the stroller and charged down the lane toward his car, with two pursuers chasing him. He made it as far as the Jeep before a third assailant stepped out, blocking his path. Nate skidded to a halt and twisted his body, raising his sword to block the baton coming down at him. The electrical discharge fizzled out.

At least he'd learned something new. Wizard-forged metal did not conduct electricity.

"The hell do you people want?" he demanded.

No one answered. They circled around him in search of the chink to his defenses. Outnumbered, he tried to keep them all within his field of vision as well as the spectators at the distant edges of the garage. No one rushed to his aid.

He couldn't fight like this. Not with Arthur in the danger zone. With no other recourse, he set the carrier down at his feet. Another Taser swung in for his face, but he grabbed the man's wrist, reversed his arm, and slammed it into the guy's stomach. Two more popped around the corner as Nate cracked the butt of his sword into the man's brow.

The attacker slumped to the ground, but another grabbed Arthur's carrier and took off with the squalling infant. Cold fury and terror lanced through Nate.

"Hey, wait, stop! That's my kid!"

Nate went down to a knee as they struck him again. A baton cracked him in the face, breaking his jaw in an explosion of blood and spittle. He raised one arm to fend off the next blow, then several more bashed against his armored back. The gleaming otherworldly metal resisted their attacks, but the body inside had been weathered and compromised by the first attacks.

They seemed endless, dedicated to fighting him but unprepared for his abilities. When Nate slammed one man face first into the cement, two more took his place. They weren't defeating him with skills; they overcame him with sheer numbers.

He pushed past the agony and the overwhelming sense of dizziness, and thrust his sword through a man's Kevlar-guarded midsection. The knight burst from beneath the pile of men attempting to hold him down. In a dead sprint, he overtook the escaping kidnapper and grabbed him by the back of the shirt.

"Give me back my son!" he roared.

They fought for control of the carrier, but the handle slipped from the abductor's hand and the carrier skipped across the cement, shaking the toddler strapped within it.

Arthur shrieked for him. A mosquito bite, only a brief flash of pain, stung his unprotected throat. Nate snatched the tranquilizer dart out of his flesh and staggered forward.

Can't lose it now. Have to keep fighting. Arthur depended on him.

He made it two steps before his knees turned to jelly. He crashed to the ground and watched, helpless, as one of the dark-clad figures lifted Arthur's seat.

"Let's go!" a gruff voice yelled. "All of you, fall back now."

"What about the guys he took out?" one asked.

"Leave them. They weren't strong enough to make the cut."

Van doors opened and shut, then the vehicle peeled down the parking lane and twisted around a corner to reach the next level. Seconds later, it was out of sight as Nate groaned from where he lay on the ground.

"Hey, dude? Dude, are you okay?"

"Someone call 9-1-1!" a woman screamed.

"Already did. Jesus, did you see that? Those people took his kid."

"Arthur," Nate slurred. He tried to push up to his hands and knees, but his limbs gave out and he slumped back to the pavement. The voices around him blurred and his vision went in and out of focus, until everything went black.

Chapter 15

After an hour-long business luncheon to discuss the future of an independent software company, Loki pushed away from the seat and rose to shake his lunch companion's hand. He had a soft spot for junior businessmen, especially software developers, and with Selene's encouragement had created a scholarship program to help bankroll underfunded companies.

"Excellent, Benjamin. I look forward to this new arrangement between our companies."

"Thank you for considering the proposition, Mr. Agnar—"

"Loki will suffice."

The young man standing on the opposite side of the table flushed with pleasure. "Either way, thank you, sir. I'll have an extended business plan to you by this evening."

Loki's phone rang, chirping gentle music. He'd programmed it to ignore all calls that didn't come from Selene or Anura, especially during business meetings. "A moment please," he murmured before accepting the call. He raised it to his ear, and almost indistinguishable sobs flooded through the line.

"Selene? What's wrong?"

Through her indecipherable wails, he heard something that sounded like, "She's gone! My baby's gone."

Benjamin glanced at him with concern.

Caught between maintaining his secrecy and rushing to his mate's side, Loki had only one option. He tore open a portal in the middle of the restaurant, but instead of finding himself in Selene's home, he landed further down the road by a stop sign.

"What in the name of the ancients…?"

A police circus awaited him, and the subtle buzz of a magical nullifying charm throbbed from the direction of Selene's home. Too weak to deter the great Loki, but powerful enough to deflect him by fifty yards.

In his business suit and Italian loafers, he sprinted toward the house only for a uniformed police officer to block his path to the front porch. "Excuse me, sir, but you can't—"

"That is my mate inside, and my child! I *live* here."

"I'll need to verify—"

Humans and their rules. Loki had no time for their nonsense. He tried to move around, but the lanky man side-stepped with him. "Please, sir, if you'll give me a moment, I just need to call this in."

Loki stepped forward, ending the obstruction by knocking the officer aside.

"Let him in," a senior officer called from the doorway. "Trust me on this one. Just let him in."

Inside the living room, Selene sat on the couch, between a female officer and an older man in plain clothes. Tears gleamed against her face, but when she saw him, she sprang from the couch and rushed into his arms.

"Where's Aslaug?"

The man rose from the couch and stepped around the coffee table. Gray streaks threaded his brown hair at each temple. "I am sorry to report that Ms. Richards's child has been abducted. I'm Chief Wallace, and I'll be organizing the search."

He'd known the answer, but his mind wanted to deny what he'd felt in his heart from the moment he received her call. "Why are you not searching for her now?"

"We are doing everything we can. I've already initiated an Amber Alert and notified police in the neighboring towns and all local sheriff departments to begin their searches for the vehicle Ms. Richards described to us. But before we can do more, we need information from both of you."

Loki tilted his head back and sighed, closing his eyes. On the next inhalation, he dragged in the scent of blood and gunpowder. Unfamiliar mortal men. He committed each smell to his memory and vowed to rip the flesh from their bones if they ever crossed paths. "I'll tell you whatever you need to know." After a pause, he leaned back to look at his mate's tear-streaked face and red eyes. "Was she injured? Are *you* injured?"

Selene shook her head. "No. I shot one of them."

Chief Wallace cleared his throat. "I don't want to rush you, but time is crucial at the moment, Mr. Agnarhorn. Your, ah, Ms. Richards provided as much information as she could. At this moment, we need to determine why these men may have taken your child."

"Money. Leverage." Loki shook his head and frowned, a deep furrow creasing his brow. "There are many in the world who believe our kind should not mix."

"Your kind?" the man asked.

"I am a dragon."

Surprise flitted across the chief's face. "Ms. Richards didn't mention that."

"I am also a very rich man with many enemies. Any of them could have taken her."

"All right. If you receive any ransom calls, we'll need to know right away. I can put in a call with the FBI."

Selene made a quiet, tiny sob. He squeezed her tighter then coaxed her to the couch. "What if it's those... those people?"

Wallace jerked his attention back to her. "What people?"

"I am certain you are aware of dragonslayers and their ilk."

"We've had some briefings," Wallace said. "They officially went down as the culprit behind the attack on President Emberthorn."

"Maximilian Emberthorn is my cousin. Nearly two years ago, dragons and slayers came to an understanding. All but two. They broke away from the knighthood and chose to continue hunting our kind."

"We've been briefed on that. And you think these people may be responsible for the infant's abduction."

Loki glanced at Selene. Her emotional state during the attack left echoes in her home, dancing across his mind as brief and fleeting memories of what she'd endured. "I don't think so. I know they are behind it. Weeks ago, one of them tried to abduct Selene. There will be a police report about it."

"I'm going to tell you what I'd tell any parents in this situation. The first hour following a child abduction is the most critical. After the golden hour passes, it becomes more difficult, but not impossible to recover your little girl. Since you're not the typical family, I need to know if you have any… unconventional methods to aid our search."

"Like magic?" Selene asked. She wiped her face.

The chief nodded. "Magic or other methods."

"I'm an accomplished sorcerer, but I need free reign of the house if I'm going to try to search for her with spells."

Chief Wallace's brows jumped up, mouth pursed into an impressed line. "Officer Miller will accompany you and assist with your needs. Ms. Richards can provide any more answers if we need them."

While Selene filled the officers in on the rest of their supernatural history, Loki made his way into the hallway, followed by a young woman in a black uniform, her blonde hair drawn into a tail.

The closet door concealing Selene's water heater had been shattered and dark, rust-colored splatters of drying blood stood out against it.

"What happened here?" He froze and stared into the master bedroom. Gore splattered the white door, and a man crouched beside a zipped body bag beneath it.

"She shot one of them," Officer Miller explained in a quiet voice. "Please watch your step. Normally we'd try to contain any contamination to the crime scene, but you have a special gift."

He had to navigate around the evidence markers and blood splatters in the carpet as he made his way into the nursery. Aslaug's room looked exactly as it had when he left, except for the empty crib.

"Is there anything you need to, uh, do what you're going to do?"

"I need silence," Loki said to the officer.

"Yes, sir."

With Aslaug in his thoughts and Selene in his mind's eye, he picked up the girl's favorite stuffed animal and searched for the thread connecting mother and child. A quiet gasp came from Officer Miller, the awestruck sound of a person who never witnessed magic in person. His hands and the ivory teddy bear glowed, surrounded by a nimbus of dark silver energy.

He searched deeper, finding a tenuous connection. Somewhere at its end, his daughter waited for them both. It frayed and split, extending beyond his magical sight.

Desperate to reconnect, Loki searched again, but a desolate void met him. He growled. Nothing but empty space where their baby belonged, her whereabouts cloaked.

Two hours, one dead lead, and three false sightings later, no officer could account for Aslaug's whereabouts. Pain radiated through Loki's chest with the force of a hammer and chisel, each passing moment chipping away more of his faith in human law enforcement.

After another recounting of the event, promises by the police to find the perpetrators, and the offer of a trauma specialist, the authorities allowed Selene to leave. Loki whisked her away to the one place he felt she would be safe as gaping officers witnessed their departure.

"Loki? What's wrong?" Max asked the moment they stepped through the portal into the living room. The pair were on the sofa with a pile of brochures spread over the coffee table. The magazine on the top highlighted the world's most popular vacation spots.

"Slayers," Loki spit out. "They've taken Aslaug and attacked Selene."

Ēostre rose from the seat and drew her robe around her. She wore only a swimsuit with her hair damp around her shoulders. "Bring her to the bedroom."

Unlike Ēostre with her white magic, Loki wasn't a healer. He only knew destructive spells, curses, and enchantments intended to cause grievous harm or trouble.

Setting his despondent mate down on the bed and leaving her in another's care rent his heart in two, but Ēostre insisted he step out and talk to Max while she tended to Selene. Max steered him to the couch and pushed a glass of brandy into his hand.

"Tell me everything."

Loki relayed everything the police had discovered, and what he'd been able to learn from Selene before she broke down into incoherent sobs. Her relentless, hysterical tears had dwindled after the first hours, only to transition into a terrifying, numbed silence.

The humans had suggested medical care and a visit to the hospital, but as far as Loki was concerned, Ēostre was a better healer than any emergency room doctor.

"They weren't expecting Selene to have a shotgun," Loki said in a quiet, hollow voice. "She killed one of them. The second is in critical condition at the hospital."

Max's expression tensed, jaw clenched. "And Aslaug?"

"No leads. They found an abandoned van fitting the make and model of the one Selene described. No prints and no witnesses. Less than a mile away."

"They had another car waiting. They planned everything out."

Loki knocked back his drink and set the glass aside. "Everything, down to a crude Anti-Mag Field surrounding her home. I suspect it was to prevent my unexpected return."

"I'll get in touch with Andrew."

Loki shook his head. "The FBI have already been called in. Whether or not they can help where I failed is another story entirely."

His cousin gazed at him through compassionate, amber eyes. "Loki, you cannot blame yourself for this. We'll do everything we can to find your daughter."

"I wasn't there when they needed me, Max. I *failed* my family—"

Max took him by the shoulders. "No. You were gone for only an hour, Loki. It could have happened to any of us. It was an organized assault in the middle of broad daylight by men who waited for you to leave the home. You had no reason to believe it would happen."

Ēostre stepped from the bedroom and closed the door behind her. "She's resting for now. Loki, I won't pretend that I know what you're both going through, but I can promise to do whatever is necessary to help you bring Aslaug home. If someone came for our twins…" She gazed toward the twins' bedroom door and hugged herself.

"Thank you, Ēostre."

"I assume you've tried all the usual methods to locate her with magic?"

He nodded. "Every single one."

Max frowned. "Then we'll have to do it the old-fashioned mortal way. I'll still make a call to the FBI and contact some people."

As much as their offers touched Loki, the guilt threatened to swallow him whole, a palpable force applying pressure on his chest each time he tried to breathe. "We should have tried harder to track down the remaining slayers." His hand tightened into a fist. He hadn't done enough to remove the threat, nor had he pushed the wizard enough to do his part in routing out the two remaining traitors to his faction.

Ēostre's phone chimed. "It's Astrid. Shall I tell her what's happened?"

"Please do. We must all be vigilant." Loki sank back in his seat, tipped his head back, and sighed. "I need to do *something*, Max. But I don't know where to even begin. I thought perhaps I could trace them with magic, or even track with a smell, but they've covered their tracks so well this time."

"We'll speak with Nate and Percivale. Perhaps we can come up with some leads," Max said.

Moments after stepping from the room to speak with Astrid, Ēostre returned with the phone clutched tightly in her white-knuckled grip. Her ever-present, magical glow had faded, leaving a tired woman with tight, drawn features in place of an elegant dragoness.

She and Max made eye contact at the same time. He tensed. "Tell me it wasn't more bad news, Ēostre. What happened?"

Her hands shook as she set the phone on the table. "Slayers put Nate in the hospital and took Arthur. She just found out. Mahasti can't get a read on his location."

"What?" Max stood.

"The same people who attacked Selene, from the description she gave me. They drugged Nate and took Arthur despite a dozen witnesses. Someone livestreamed the entire attack."

Max snatched his iPad from the adjacent table, reclaimed his seat, and searched for the video. Together, the three of them watched Nate's stand against the slayers as muttering humans commented in low voices in the background.

When Nate summoned his armor, the cameraman jumped back a step, shaking the phone. *"Holy shit! He's using magic in the Anti-Mag Field!"*

A woman spoke up. *"Should we do something?"*

"What the hell can we do? They have weapons."

"They all just stood there." Loki's hands clenched. "Sheep. Useless mortal sheep."

"What would you expect them to do?" Ēostre set her hand on his arm and gave a gentle squeeze. "Those men were armed. Dangerous."

Max tapped the power button and dimmed the screen. "Now we understand the reason for their silence. They've had us all under surveillance, waiting for an opportunity like this. Not to kill us, but to take from us."

Ēostre took her husband's hand between both her palms. "We couldn't have known, Max. Couldn't have guessed this would be the endgame."

Loki swore under his breath and stood. Too restless to remain still, he began to pace back and forth in front of the sofa. "Is Brandt safe?"

"She didn't say anything, but I'll call Chloe now to be certain." Ēostre turned away and put her phone up to her ear.

Unable to swallow the rage bubbling in his chest, Loki slammed his hand against the wall. The plaster cracked and bent inward, but neither Max nor Ēostre chastised him. "Why did they do this? What do they hope to gain?"

Max raked his fingers through his auburn hair and leaned forward, resting his elbows against his thighs. "It could be any number of reasons, but a few come to mind. We have to think as they would. These men are tacticians, and they've had nothing but time."

"They're cowards," Loki disagreed.

Max shook his head. "Brilliant cowards who planned in the shadows while we waited for their next move. *This.* As far as Arthur is concerned, they're recovering their reborn leader to raise as they see fit. Arthur is one of them, and so is Nate."

"And my daughter?"

"Leverage," Max replied. "They have the child of one of the greatest dragon sorcerers alive."

"I will kill them for this," Loki vowed. "I will flay them alive, drag them across hot coals, and make their last moments on this earth as torturous and miserable as I am able."

Max set a hand on Loki's arm. "But first, we have to find them. It's time to call the wizard."

***

Deciding there was safety in numbers, they all agreed to meet at Drakenstone Manor to consolidate their strength. With four dragons on the premises, as well as a bear shifter, a djinn, and a knight, the slayers would have to be fools to mount an attack.

Although Selene had resisted the offer at first—fearing for her family's safety—she allowed Ēostre to retrieve her mother from Virginia. Within the hour, the Drakenstone household bustled with activity. While Anita comforted his wife, Loki met with Merlin and the other dragons. He didn't like excluding her from their meeting, but he'd noticed a change in her. Not knowing how to console her, he trusted her mother would be up to the task.

Damn Pelleas and Bedivere for sinking to a new low by involving defenseless children. Had Aslaug been a dragon cub, she would have been born with claws and capable of tearing a human to pieces.

But his daughter was only half-dragon, and while he loved her endlessly with every fiber of his soul, he recognized her weaknesses. She'd be a defenseless infant for many months, unlike Gwydion and Branwen Emberthorn. The twins had learned to shift sometime before their first birthday.

What the hell was he supposed to do?

One by one, Mahasti arrived with the rest of their close dragon friends, one among them a protesting teenage half-dragon who yanked his arm away once the teleportation swept him into the living room.

"Damn, I'm not a child," Javier argued.

Teotihuacan, a powerful black dragon from the Yucatán Peninsula, shot his son a dark look. Javier shrank back a step, silencing before he turned to scurry away to parts unknown. With the child gone, he stepped up to Loki and took him by the shoulders.

"I am sorry, my friend. Until the day they are found, I will hold Aslaug and Arthur both in my prayers. Now we will do whatever we must to find both cubs. Have faith."

"Thank you."

Merlin arrived last, his robes rumpled and disorganized, hair mussed. "I've checked all the old haunts and hideaways used by the Order over the years. Nothing but tricks and traps."

Hopes dashed, Loki's shoulders slumped. "We knew it was a longshot. Bedivere is too crafty to use any place known to the knights, but I wanted to believe there was a chance…"

Merlin sighed. "They could be anywhere. There was a time when I could locate any member of the brotherhood, but they've perverted their connection to me and twisted it with the titan's magic."

"What about Arthur?" Chloe asked.

The wizard shook his head. "No. I tried to find the boy, and I suspect the children have been concealed behind a special barrier or taken to a protected, well-warded place."

"There can't be too many places that are strong enough to keep you out," Percivale protested. "Perhaps that's where we can start. We'll search the places where you've been blinded."

The wizard shook his head and spread his hands. "If only that were a plausible plan, Percivale, I may have already attempted such an undertaking. With these new procedures in place to curve magical intrusion, there are many—hundreds, if not thousands—of places across the United States where my sight is prohibited. The children could be anywhere."

Loki growled. "The very system designed to protect the people from us has been used to hide *our* children. Max, surely you can speak with the new president."

"And tell him what?"

"Tell him to take down the shields! To give us the right to use our full power in finding our children."

Saul shook his head and took Loki by the shoulders. "I know you're hurting and angry, but what you're suggesting will get us nowhere and only make the mortals fear us. You'll send them running to the Anti-Dragon Movement in droves."

"Perhaps that's what they want," Max said. "Not that it matters. I don't have that power and neither does President Miller. It would take an act of Congress, and nothing guarantees we'd find the children."

"Then what do you suggest for me to do?"

Max removed his cellphone and began to dial. "Call every dragon, every psychic, witch, immortal, and paranormal being we know. We'll work together in teams, but I give my word to you, no one here will rest until we've found those kids."

Loki looked from one face to the next, humbled by their willingness to help him after all he had done in the past. He knew without a doubt that they would all stand beside him, no matter what happened, as they tried to bring Aslaug and Arthur home.

But would it be enough?

Chapter 16

Through bribes, threats, and extortion, Loki kept story-hungry journalists out of their personal business and provided incentive to any news network willing to focus their attention on Aslaug instead. His company, relationship with Selene, and all other aspects of their lives didn't matter and weren't up for discussion.

Aslaug's photograph ran in every major newspaper, and news anchors spoke at length about her and Arthur's disappearances.

After all, what he wanted was for their child to be found safe from harm, not a media frenzy staked outside his private property or their phones ringing off the hook for Selene's story. Silencing the press wasn't nearly as difficult as he expected it to be.

Selene's pain was his pain, intensified and shared through their link, and if one more person phoned him asking for a statement, he couldn't be held responsible for what he said. Or did.

His mate's voice reached him from the master bedroom. "Loki?"

He'd been in and out throughout the day, leaving to take phone calls from police detectives, private eyes, and mages across the world. Stepping back inside, he approached the bed where she hadn't moved since the morning.

Helpless and miserable, he settled on the edge of the mattress and lowered a hand to her arm.

Officers had given them information three days ago about the crucial so-called "golden hour"—the stretch of time immediately after an abduction when law enforcement had the most favorable chance of recovering a stolen child. That had passed seventy hours ago.

And with each hour afterward, Selene grew more despondent. He stroked her arm and searched for words to give her comfort. None came.

"What can I do for you, Selene?"

"I want to go home to get my things. To get... I want her blanket. Something that smells like her. Would you open a portal?"

Loki shook his head. "I'll bring them to you."

"Loki—"

"I will do it. I don't want you to see."

Selene relented and rolled onto her side. He stayed with her until she fell asleep, waiting until her breaths smoothed to an even, deep rhythm, and then he opened a portal to her home.

The police tape had been taken down and the whole place stank of chemical solvents. Loki strode toward the master bedroom first. No sign of blood remained, but the sharp odor left behind from the cleaning service burned his sensitive nose. He wondered whether to have Anura and the others come through again or if they should simply burn the house down and build it up from scratch. While he fancied the idea, he had a good feeling Selene would argue.

She loved this house. And once they rescued their child, he'd do whatever was necessary to make her feel safe inside it again.

Loathe to enter the nursery, he busied himself with selecting clothes for Selene first. He gathered up a few outfits as well as her toiletries. A chew toy squeaked beneath his shoes as he roamed around the room, so he added the rubber bone to the growing pile.

Baron and Dusty would want their things as well.

With nothing else to distract from his true purpose in coming, Loki stepped into the nursery. Less than four days ago, he had stood over the crib and kissed his little girl goodbye before taking a portal to Sacramento for a necessary meeting. He grasped onto the memory of her rosy cheeks, her dimpled smile, and her drowsy eyes.

An hour. He had only been away for a little over an hour.

As he approached the crib to fetch Aslaug's extra blanket for Selene, blue light spilled from the carpeted floor beneath it. The glow intensified with each step until Loki crouched alongside the bed and reached underneath. His fingers wrapped around a smooth, glossy ball as large as a jumbo marble.

A memory stone.

Within seconds of closing his fist around the polished stone, a vision played across his mind and became part of his memory. He saw Bedivere the dishonored knight holding the same piece of rock.

"If you wish to see your daughter again, come alone to the Neptune statue on the Virginia Beach boardwalk at sunset. Warn your fellow wyrms, and both children will die."

The image faded, leaving only nausea churning in the pit of Loki's stomach.

In all his life, he'd never felt helpless, never felt trapped, but the loss of one child had changed everything. He swallowed the stony lump forming in his throat and crushed the memory stone to dust in his palm.

For Aslaug, he'd kiss the ground beneath Bedivere's feet if it returned her safely to Selene's arms.

Using a portal to travel brought him to the famed beach in seconds. Bedivere had chosen a good spot. The summer crowds meant lots of witnesses and plenty of cover. Any one of the many beach goers could be an attacker ready to strike, and they all smelled the same, nothing identifying them as mercenaries or dragon-hating bigots in disguise.

Loki made his way down the wide cement pathway, hands in his pockets, shoulders hunched, and eyes alert. Several pedestrians gave him a wide berth.

The sun hadn't begun its descent to the horizon, but he discovered Bedivere had arrived equally as early. The slayer occupied a bench near the statue. They stared at one another in silence before Loki closed the short distance between them.

"I wondered how many days might pass before you found it," Bedivere said.

"Give me one good reason I shouldn't roast you on the spot."

He could do it. He *wanted* to do it. All Loki needed to do was transform and gobble the slayer down, and no one would be able to stop him.

"I told my men to expect my return in thirty minutes. If I fail to arrive, they'll drown your beastling."

Heat flashed over Loki's skin in a molten rush. Rage turned his vision red, and the tenuous control he held over his human body faltered, a split second from adopting his draconic form. "If you hurt her—"

"No harm will come to her for as long as you remain obedient. Dial it back, son. We both know killing me right now will accomplish nothing. I'll be back in a few years, and you'll never see her again. We know how it works for your kind. All that power in one finite shell."

He wanted nothing more than to rip Bedivere's head from his body, but concern for his daughter's safety trumped his desire for retribution. Loki brought his turbulent emotions under control and steadied his hands by clenching both fists against his thighs.

"Excellent. I knew we could count on you, Loki. You were always the smartest of your scaly brethren."

Loki clenched his jaw. "Cut the shit, Bedivere. What do I have to do for you to return my daughter?"

"Stand with us. Of all the dragons, we find you the most tolerable. After all, you've killed your own kind before, haven't you? More than any other." The slayer steepled his fingers and smiled at him.

Bedivere gestured to the space on the seat beside him. Reluctant but unwilling to cause a scene and jeopardize his daughter's safety, Loki sat on command.

"What do you want? Let's not play games. You obviously have something in mind, so spit it out."

"We want the death of the dragon known as Zeus… or would that be Odin to you?"

Loki blinked. "To what purpose? He's been asleep for the past two centuries. Perhaps longer."

"Then it shouldn't be hard for you to do as I ask. Bring me his head as proof of your deed and your daughter lives to see another day. Perhaps I'll send a photo to you."

"No. If I kill Zeus for you, I need to know she'll be returned to her mother."

Bedivere chuckled and glanced at his watch. "You don't get to make the demands, sorcerer. We have all the cards, and releasing your little… what did you name her? Aslaug? It isn't part of our plans. Not yet."

"All right."

"Excellent. I knew you'd see things our way. Standby until you receive our next commands."

Loki remained sitting on the bench long after Bedivere was gone, rubbing his face and staring at the crashing waves against the shore.

How the hell could he even hope to pull off murdering Zeus? Whether the ancient behemoth remained asleep or not, Loki had a challenge to undertake.

Aslaug was worth it.

For a while, he tried to find peace in watching the foamy water spill over the sand. It receded and splashed over the beach anew, the tranquil rhythm holding him captive until a notification chirp in his pocket drew his memories back to Selene.

Selene: Where are you?

His finger hesitated over the virtual keyboard.

Loki: The baby's room. I'll be there shortly.

He returned to the house, grabbed everything he had packed, and was by her side within the minute. She was where he'd left her in his bedroom, curled up on the mattress with both her dogs. A mountain of fur raised his head to greet Loki, and a soft cotton ball yipped in greeting as if to welcome him home. He drifted closer and ran his fingers over the top of Baron's head, petted Dusty, then passed the blanket into Selene's possession.

His mate buried her face against the fleece square. After a few quiet moments, her shoulders quaked.

"I've never felt... never felt so afraid. Never thought I could hurt so much." Selene moaned into the blanket and hugged it tighter than a life preserver. "I feel so helpless. I let them *take* her."

Red-rimmed eyes filled with despair and gazed up at him, puffy from continuous crying but dry. Loki crawled into the bed beside Selene and took her into his arms. "No, no. What happened was *no* fault of yours."

"If I was a real witch, I could have done more. I could have stopped all of them!"

After days of morose silence, he was glad to hear her speaking again. Relief flooded him. For days, he'd wondered if she blamed him, if she'd resent and hate him for failing to protect their family. Loki ran his fingers over her disheveled hair and kissed the top of her head.

"You did everything you could. If anyone is to blame, it should be me. I should have been there. Set better wards and protections around your house. They never should have been able to breach the doorway."

"I killed one of them," she whispered, bringing up the incident for the first time. According to Nate, humans reacted differently to taking lives than dragons.

He hesitated and set his hand on her back. Did he want to tell her?

Yes, she deserved to know. "Two, Selene."

Her face rose, violet-gray gaze lifting to his face. "What? No, I only shot the one."

Despite everything he knew about his mate's humanity, she'd pulled off a feat of Herculean strength. He'd seen the shattered utility closet door and the dented water heater. He also saw the bruised face of the surviving assailant left behind by his squad, although it had taken every ounce of his willpower not to tear the man off the stretcher and finish what Selene ended. Consoling her had taken precedence.

"The one you knocked into the closet died this morning. You were asleep when the call came from the police, and I didn't want to awaken you."

Selene curled into a tighter ball and closed her eyes. For a moment, he regretted giving her the news, fearing she would crumble beneath the implication. Then her eyes opened, dry and hard.

"He deserved it. They all did," she said in a low voice.

"And when we find the others, they will meet the same fate."

"I love you." The words escaped her in a fierce whisper. She buried her fingers into his shirt and seized him by two handfuls. "Promise me we'll get her back."

"We will. I'll do everything within my power to find our child, *skatten min*. I swear it to you."

He'd just have to kill the oldest known living dragon among them to do it.

Chapter 17

The next day dawned bright and beautiful with clear skies full of birdsong. Loki wanted to eat them all for being so cheerful. He did the next best thing and cast a muffling spell on the window, drowning them out to allow Selene to sleep undisturbed.

Fresh brewed coffee lured him downstairs through the quiet house to the kitchen, where he discovered Ēostre sitting at the breakfast counter. She had the news open on her tablet.

"Anything interesting?" He moved to the coffee pot and filled a mug for himself.

"Nothing new," Ēostre replied. "They're circulating the pictures Nathaniel provided of the two knights and also posted the reward we offered. I imagine we'll receive plenty of false sightings, but it's better than nothing."

"Appearances can be disguised," Loki muttered. In some cases, they weren't required at all. Bedivere had gone overlooked at the beach, unnoticed by all he encountered. "Anyway, how is Nate? Has he recovered?"

Ēostre's fragile smile faltered. "His doctor plans to release him today. On top of the other injuries inflicted during the fight, he had a skull fracture and a broken jaw. I mended the bones, but they kept him anyway for observation."

"I imagine so. Humans are slow to trust when it comes to magical intervention."

"To be honest, circulating YouTube clips of the assault in the garage has returned attention to the paranormal again. I believe they're more interested in studying him, but Astrid's been at his side to protect him from unnecessary poking and prodding."

"She's strong," Loki murmured. And so was Selene during her lucid moments when she wasn't in an apparent trance and staring with vacant eyes out the window. "I wondered something, Ēostre. How long has passed since you spoke with Zeus? Perhaps he would take interest in the circumstances."

"Father?" Ēostre gave a low, bitter laugh. Her eyes flashed, and for a moment, Loki saw the resemblance between her and the sleeping god of the skies. "The great Zeus wouldn't be moved for Fafnir's death, he certainly wouldn't stir for a half-breed. He sleeps as he always has, useless and hateful. Why?"

He shrugged and gave a dismissive wave with his hand. "He's killed more dragonslayers than any of us, is all. I thought he might have some insights."

"Perhaps, but he would be the last wyrm we should ask to stand beside us. Aside from the thousands of human casualties and collateral damage, he'd be as likely to harm your daughter as save her. She is a half-dragon after all." Ēostre sighed. "How I wish we could depend on him, but Father is... There's never been a time when he's cared about anyone but himself."

"I suppose you're right. He should remain in Mount Olympus. Asleep."

"He should, yes," she agreed.

Without losing his composure, Loki sipped his coffee and stole a glance at Ēostre. He'd gleaned the information he needed, confirming Zeus had yet to leave Greece.

If anyone knew of his whereabouts, it would be the favorite of his many daughters.

***

For some reason Nate couldn't understand, Astrid remained by his side each day of his hospital stay. He'd awakened hating himself, ready to accept the complete blame for losing their child, but instead of resentment, she'd only bathed him in unconditional love and limitless concern.

Because she couldn't bear to lose both of them in the same day.

Because despite his fuckup, she still loved him deeply and knew they'd recover Arthur safe and sound.

Coming home to Drakenstone Manor, he expected his in-laws to loathe him. Instead, Chloe had rushed over and hugged him the moment Astrid brought him through the portal. "Thank God you're okay."

Last to welcome him home with an embrace after Saul and Ēostre, Max held him by both shoulders and leaned back to look at his face. "How are you feeling, son?"

Like he let everybody down. Even his own mother, when she'd visited in the hospital, hadn't wanted to place any blame on him, but it didn't change the truth of what resonated in his heart. Somehow a knight who had taken down dragons singlehandedly in the past had been insufficient when it came to protecting his own child.

Nate didn't try to force a smile anymore. "Like I tried to stop a bus with my face." And like he lay on the ground like a bitch while a dude ran off with his child.

Saul frowned, alarmed. "Didn't my mother—"

"She healed me."

Before Nate could excuse himself from the entrance hall, Ēostre drifted over. Astrid's grandmother acted as the family's principal healer, more experienced than her son and granddaughter. She touched his cheek gently, tilting her head and studying his face. "The pain should subside by tonight, but if it doesn't, I expect you to come to me right away."

"I will."

In no mood for socializing, even with the family who loved him, he retreated to the steps. "I'm going to go lie down for a few."

Astrid's eyes followed him to the stairs, and he paused on the low step, divided between wanting to comfort his wife and wallow in self-pity. How the hell was she taking it better than him?

Before he could utter a word, the others dispersed and she took his hand. "Come on. We need to talk."

Unable to argue with a woman who had just lost her child, he nodded. "All right."

Astrid led him upstairs to her childhood bedroom, though it was still decked out in pink and white, outfitted in lace with cosmic stars on the ceilings and stuffed animals on the bed. She seated him on the mattress first then straddled his lap.

"I love you, and I'm not blaming you. Not even for one moment, one second."

"I let them—"

"You fought with everything you had, and that's all anybody could ask for. Even if I hadn't seen the video, I'd know that."

"I just wish I'd done more, baby."

"Wherever he is, he's safe, and he's warm. I can make it through each day without losing my shit because I know our son is alive. Here." She placed one hand over her heart. "They're not going to hurt him because they need him."

Nate sighed. "That's what worries me. What the hell do they need a toddler for? Arthur can barely walk on his own yet. He's not going to be picking up a sword any time soon or summoning his armor."

"I don't know. I guess they want to raise him the way Kay raised you. Or tried to, at least. But we won't give them that chance. We're going to get our son back. We're going to get Aslaug and we'll crush any of them who get in our way."

"I know we will." But at what cost? He sighed, lifted Astrid from his lap, and lay back against the comforter. "I really am going to take a nap, though."

"You want me to get you anything?"

"Nah, I'm good. Go be with your family. Do some clever dragon plotting."

A faint line creased her brow. "You're my family too, Nate."

"I know, and you've been at my side this whole time. Go see the rest of them now, too. Your mom's been waiting to fuss over you for days. Let her do her thing."

"All the more reason to hide up here."

He chuckled and rolled onto his side. "Go on. I'll be down a little later."

Astrid closed the door behind her as she left. Nate waited until he heard her steps retreat down the hallway, then pulled a round stone from his pocket.

The memory marker had arrived with a balloon bouquet during one of Astrid's brief absences from his hospital bedside. Nate knew the message by heart, but it didn't stop him from activating the magic again.

Clear as a daydream, he saw Pelleas holding the same stone. "We have the boy, and if you want to see him again, you'll heed this message well. Go with Loki to kill Zeus, and once he's weakened from battle, slay him as well. Turning your back on the dragons is the only way to reunite the order as we once were. Once the deed is done, use the teleportation enchantment bound to this stone to bring us proof of his demise. We'll be waiting."

Released from the magical imprint, Nate sighed and turned the stone over. A spell had been etched into the smooth rock with expert precision. All he needed was to apply some of his own blood and magic to be whisked away to the rebel knights.

But where the hell would it take him once he'd used it?

Of all the things Nate had been prepared to do to rescue his son, killing the most powerful dragon wizard in the world hadn't been on the top of his list. Leaning his head back against the headboard, he sighed and wondered how the hell he'd pull it off.

And if he could bear to commit the treacherous deed at all.

True to his word to Astrid, he surrendered to the pull of the pain medication. He napped less than an hour, roused and washed his face, then made his way downstairs. A dragon occupied every damned room in the opulent manor.

Chloe, Astrid, and Brandt's voices echoed from the den. To avoid them, he ducked past the door and made his way into the kitchen instead to tiptoe out onto the patio. He found Selene at the round table beneath the fanned umbrella, her vacant stare trained on the distant pasture.

"Hey, Selene."

She looked up at him with haunted eyes smudged with dark circles beneath. "Hey."

He sat beside her, at first uncertain of what to say. Of all the people in the estate at that moment, she was the only one who knew remotely how he felt to have a child snatched from her arms, even if it wasn't in the literal sense.

Stumbling upon her felt like providence, and as a believer in fate, Nate decided to take a chance. "Do you think we did everything we could?"

"Yeah…" She drew up her knees and hugged them to her chest. "I keep thinking maybe there was more I could do, but… we fought. Gods, we fought."

"We did." The words held more value—had a deeper impact coming from her than the others. "I'm glad you're all ri— that you didn't end up in the hospital like me. I heard you really gave them hell."

Selene nodded, barely dipping her chin. "I killed someone. *Two* someones, and… it didn't bother me. I don't even care." She added in a quiet whisper, "I think something's wrong with me."

"Why do you say that?"

Her shoulders lifted and dropped. "I did something to one of them. Magic or something, but I didn't cast a spell. I've never cast a spell in all my life, Nate. Not one, no matter how hard I tried or who tried to teach me."

"You were fighting for your daughter. Stress and high emotion have a way of bringing out magic at the worst of times."

"Maybe…" Her gaze drifted away again. "I hear her. At least, I think I do. I don't even know." She muffled a quiet, humorless laugh with both hands and rubbed her face. "I feel like I'm losing it."

The sliding door opened and shut again. Nate glanced up to see Loki on the steps, lingering with his hand on the frame. "Is there room for one more?"

Nate stood. "I was just on my way ou—"

Selene stood and shook her head. "I'm going back inside. Thanks for the talk, Nate."

"Anytime. We're going to get them back, Selene, I swear it."

Once she was gone, Loki leaned against the door and ran his fingers through his hair. The disheveled dragon wore rumpled, unironed clothes, his exhausted appearance at odds with the suave businessman Nate knew from previous encounters.

And Pelleas wanted him dead. With the memory charm searing a figurative hole in his pocket, Nate jumped up from his seat. "Hey, you have a moment? I was hoping to talk with you."

Loki nodded. "Of course."

They moved to the edge of the patio, putting distance between them and the house where numerous supernatural ears put their privacy in jeopardy. Dropping his voice to a whisper, Nate murmured, "I know where you're going. What you're supposed to do. They want me to go with you to make sure it's done."

"Do they now?" Loki's dry, bitter laugh made Nate's skin crawl and a chill trickle down his spine. Afterward, the dragon stared at him, eyes boring with painful intensity.

Nate rubbed his damp palms against his jeans. *Can he read my thoughts? No. We'd know by now if Loki was a mind reader.*

"Two is better than one I suppose. Are you prepared for what they intend to have you do?"

"To kill in cold blood? No. To do whatever it takes to get my kid back? Fuck yeah."

The dragon pressed his lips into a thin line and glanced away. "You may not survive the encounter, and I don't trust Bedivere to return Arthur to Astrid if you're not alive to press them. If you're to accompany me, I expect you to accept my orders and follow instructions."

As soon as Nate opened his mouth to complain, Loki stared at him. "These are my rules. Take it or leave it, knight."

"Fine," Nate gritted out between his teeth.

"I want your word and sworn promise. On your sword."

"Christ."

"Your sworn promise."

A quick glance to the left and right determined no one was within dragon's ear shot to eavesdrop on their conservation or feel the mild fluctuation in magic when Loki held him to his word. He sighed and tipped his head forward. "On my honor and on my sword, I vow to follow your instructions *within reason.*"

"Excellent. We can depart now."

Nate blinked at him. "Wait, now?"

"Are you not eager to have your son returned to you?"

"Of course I want him back."

"Are you perhaps too injured to lift your little toothpick?"

Nate glowered. "If we just up and disappear, the others are going to freak out."

"Then we will make a suitable excuse. You and I have decided to investigate the parking garage together, as well as other locations recently surfaced in your memory where the knighthood may have taken their operations."

"And how do you expect to keep Astrid from coming along?"

"Put your foot down and tell her to remain," Loki answered in a huff.

As much as he wanted to snap at the dragon sorcerer for his dismissive and abrupt manner, Nate understood his frustration. He shared it.

"I'll ask her to stay with Selene."

It took less convincing than he expected. Whether she thought he needed space or that the time with Loki would be good for him, his wife took up his offer to speak with Selene, kissed his cheek, and wished him luck in his search.

Lying to her made him nauseous.

To keep up appearances, Loki's portal took them to the mall parking lot first at the fringe of the Anti-Mag Field. Then he opened a doorway into an unfamiliar expanse of rock and craggy stones.

Nate hesitated to step through. "Where are we going?"

"Mount Olympus."

"Seriously?"

Loki's face hardened, expression cold and harsh. Terrifying. "Do I appear to be joking?"

The dragon's intimidating and cruel countenance should have made facing his task easier, but all Nate could see was a father in pain willing to do anything to get his child back. A father like him.

Nate shook his head and summoned his soul sword and armor for protection. "No."

Cool weather greeted the knight when he stepped through, leaving the muggy San Diego summer for the breezy Balkan Mountains. Aside from photos in National Geographic, he'd never seen Mount Olympus before. His dragon sense burned, the area rife with the presence of an unfamiliar draconic being. He'd long ago grown used to Saul, Ēostre, and the rest of the Drakenstone family, but Zeus's nearby lair petrified him.

"Don't tourists swarm this area?" Nate asked.

"The peaks, yes. The gorges, less so." Loki led the way down a narrow track into the forested zone below them. He adopted his draconic form midstride, becoming an immense black dragon with ruby-edged scales.

Fire and earth magic. Dark sorcery that can make my blood boil in my veins. They want me to kill this guy? The hysterical urge to laugh came over him, tasked with an impossible goal he couldn't hope to meet.

For a time, Nate was happy to let there be silence between them. He didn't have anything to say as it was, and he had a feeling questions would be met with the same cold and snide attitude as before. But after half an hour wandering over the rocky terrain, he couldn't keep it up.

"You know where we're going, right?"

"I haven't traveled here in many years," Loki admitted. "Once, centuries ago, Zeus was a leader among our kind, and then he eventually withdrew to his mountain. Perhaps out of sheer laziness."

"Right. The whole Greek gods thing. So, if you don't mind me asking, who were you? I mean, did you have any role in Greek myth?"

"Don't be absurd," Loki scoffed. "I couldn't care less about these islands or their tangled stories. Odin, on the other hand, as a leader had to make his appearances here as well as Scandinavia. So he has taken multiple names. Zeus is merely one of several guises he has worn over the years to pull the wool over the mortals' eyes."

The closer they came to Zeus's lair, the harder Nate's heart slammed in his chest, beating a frenetic tempo worthy of a rave. Pressure surrounded his ribs, each breath tighter than the last.

Loki stopped when they reached a stretch of polished rock, worn smooth by the elements. "Here we are."

When he exhaled over the uneven surface, the stone shimmered and faded away into smoke, leaving a hole large enough for a dragon to pass through.

"Wait, so an illusion is all that's keeping people out?"

"An illusion so real they actually feel the rock beneath their hands, yes. There are some repelling charms as well to prevent most humans from reaching this point. There was once a time when we'd merely eat any mortal who stumbled into our domain, but many of us have taken to kinder, gentler methods to discourage intrusion." He gestured to the stone.

"Zeus left illusions to be kind to humans?"

"No. Ēostre made those. It pained her each time her father devoured an innocent mortal. She came at the start of his last hibernation to lay those charms. Thor and myself are among the few who know how to reach Zeus if necessary."

"Which is why Pelleas and Bedivere needed you. They'd never stumble on this entrance if they were alone."

"Precisely. And now we go to do their work for them."

Nate tightened his grip on the sword and considered the peril ahead of them. He'd never fought a dragon in all his recent life, although he had memories of slaying evil wyrms in the past, beasts who were as much a danger to their own kind as they were to humans.

Could he kill Loki in cold blood, knowing he'd be depriving a child of a father and widowing a good woman?

Loki glanced back at him. "Are you coming or not?"

His hands trembled inside his gauntlets. How could he possibly raise Arthur to be a good man, when he'd committed murder? The more he puzzled over the commands from Pelleas, the more troubled he became.

Before Loki could enter the cave, Nate reached out and grabbed him by one of the bony, black spurs jutting from his elbow. "Wait. We can't do it."

Loki dragged Nate forward a step, pulling him off balance before he glanced back over his shoulder. He hissed out a frustrated breath. "Do you think I want to do this? I don't, mortal, but if we don't... We have to do this for our children."

"Loki, no. You don't get it, man. Zeus isn't my target. *You* are."

"I know."

"I—wait, what?" An icy jolt rushed through Nate's veins.

"Did you think me to be too stupid to realize what they intended to do? Zeus is the most powerful of all living dragons, and with Watatsumi gone, Ēostre and I are next. But it seemed a worthy sacrifice."

"You came here to die."

"Did you believe me to be so daft I wouldn't realize? I knew their intentions the moment you told me they ordered you to accompany me. It is a calculated and cunning plan. Deceptive. It's what I would expect of them, but I promised Selene our daughter would be in her arms again."

"Then don't throw your life away fighting Zeus. I'm not going to kill you."

"You have to. It is the only way to recover our children."

Nate tossed his sword to the ground. "No. Screw this, man. I'm not doing it. Do you really think they're going to give our kids back? This is just their sick and twisted way of getting rid of anyone strong enough to oppose them. I kill you and they're just going to dangle another target out for me to kill in exchange for a chance to get my son."

"And then another target until they've squeezed you like a sponge."

"Right, man. I just can't do it. I love Arthur, but I remember the man he used to be before he was my son, and he'd be sick if I went through with this."

"Then we're back to square one."

"You're the greatest trickster of all time. If you can't outsmart an idiot like Bedivere, what good are you? We need to think."

The deep furrows returned to the dragon's brow beneath both his ebony horns. "What did they demand for proof of my death?"

"They didn't specify. Only that I was to kill you after you slew Zeus and bring them something."

A sly smile came over Loki's draconic face, revealing all of his front teeth. "Then we'll have to give them proof."

Chapter 18

The teleportation spell brought Nate to a deactivated freezer. Lines of gray paint beneath his feet created a matching magical circle, still shimmering from the enchantment he'd activated. If not for the afterglow, it would have blended seamlessly with the cement floor. A single red light glowed in the corner of the room, and the shelves held empty trays. The only door wouldn't budge when he twisted the knob. They'd locked him inside until they wanted to come for him.

Nate tested the door with his shoulder. Solid steel. Checking his cell phone proved fruitless too. No signal.

His watch still worked, and over an hour passed before the door flew open, yanked by an overweight man with a chest-length beard. Another fellow beside him with an athletic build and broad shoulders held a shotgun in his hands.

Nate stepped forward. "Where's my son?"

The muzzle landed square on his chest and nudged against his armor.

Didn't these guys know a shotgun shell wouldn't blast through it? He bit his tongue and stared them down.

The one with the gun laughed. "Figured that would calm you down."

Amused by Nate's hesitation, the bearded man grinned. "Just so you know, we got permission to shoot you if you misbehave. You be quiet and come with us."

The fat one tugged a black hood over Nate's head then pulled him along by the arm, but didn't seem concerned with whether or not Nate made it unscathed. His elbow struck the doorway and a few yards farther on he stumbled over an obstacle on the ground. A few quick steps and a vicious yank from his handler kept him from sprawling face first.

"Frisk him and check his bag."

Nate released the canvas sack into their possession and waited as rough hands searched his body with practiced ease. Blind to the world around him, he tried to rely on his other senses, but nothing was giving him any clue as to where he was. All he smelled was wet dirt.

"What the hell is this?"

"The proof I was asked to bring," Nate replied. "What? Haven't you ever seen a dragon claw before?"

"Fuck. This thing is still oozing blood."

Nate snorted. "Yeah, that's kinda what happens when it's cut off a fresh body."

"Put it in the back and get him in the car. Boss wants him."

The big guy pushed his head down to get him in the vehicle at least. Taking no chances, the guy crawled in beside him and a quiet ride began. Nate tried to count turns and seconds in between while listening for identifying noises and sounds, but they cranked the music loud.

He lost track of the turns and the time on the long ride. By the time they reached their destination, Nate was no closer to figuring out where he was. They dragged him from the car and walked him inside where the savory scents of tomato sauce and spicy sausage surrounded him.

"Ah, good, you're here. I think you boys can uncuff him now." Bedivere spoke up from Nate's left. They freed his hands and pulled the hood off.

Nate stood in a kitchen. A look out the window above the sink revealed a sprawling yard with a tall stone wall and lots of trees. The kitchen appeared spotless and tidy with pristine granite countertops and stainless steel appliances. A pot of sauce bubbled on the stove.

"Where's my kid?"

"Unharmed.

"You keep saying that, but I want to see him."

Bedivere clucked his tongue. "Let's see the sword."

Nate summoned his sword. Resisting temptation, he reversed his grip on it and passed it hilt first to Bedivere. The blood had dried on the mystical weapon, staining the silver blade dark red along one edge and its tip.

Bedivere's shotgun-wielding crony passed over the sack. "He brought this, boss."

Nate smirked. "A little something to hang over your mantle. You understand why I didn't bring back more than that."

"This is more than sufficient. Tell me, did he go down easily?"

"He kept me out of the fight with Zeus until the end. After that, it wasn't difficult to take him out," Nate said. Lying always hurt him, sending pain lancing through his chest like a stab wound to the heart. He hated it. Of all the knights, he'd always struggled the most with dishonesty. But he needed to play into their game if he wanted to save Arthur and Aslaug.

How the hell had Bedivere and Pelleas fallen so far from Merlin's original intentions for them? With a phony smile on his face, he glanced around again.

Beyond the doorway, the next room appeared as sophisticated and luxurious as the kitchen. The slate-blue tile floor transitioned to golden hardwood.

"You really did spill Loki's blood," Bedivere muttered. His hands moved over the bloodied blade, a dark green nimbus glowing around his fingers. Loki's draconic reflection flashed across the Celestial steel.

Nate grunted. "He was a prick anyway, so it wasn't much of a hardship."

Hilt first, Bedivere returned the weapon to Nate. "We're pleased to have you back with us, Galahad."

While it wasn't necessary for him to have the sword in his physical possession again to dismiss it, it was a matter of respect. Bedivere returning it to him meant something. He exhaled, bottling the rest of his relief before he spoke. "I held up my end. Now it's your turn."

Bedivere gestured to a tablet sitting on the nearby breakfast table. The older knight activated it with his thumbprint and initiated a live video feed. "Show the boy, Pelleas."

The room on the other end of the live chat struck Nate as familiar. He searched the soft blue, yellow, and sage green walls, and recognized the print of a baby nursery. Tiny pale gray elephants decorated the wallpaper. Pelleas sat in a chair with the unhappy toddler in his lap.

Arthur's tears stopped when Nate's face filled the corner window of the screen, but he appeared unbruised and unharmed. Seeing his son's red-rimmed eyes and snot encrusted nose tightened a vice around Nate's heart.

"See? Didn't Uncle Pelleas tell you Daddy would be on the screen soon?" the other knight asked the child he bounced on his lap.

"Dada!"

"Hey, buddy," Nate greeted him without false enthusiasm. Swallowing the emotion in his throat, he forced a smile to his face. "Daddy is going to see you real soon. I promise."

"Dada! Dada!" Arthur raised his chubby fists and reached out for him.

"I miss you so much, kiddo."

Arthur reached for him again.

"I think it's time to eat," Pelleas said. He passed Arthur to someone off-screen, much to the toddler's displeasure. A piercing shriek traveled over the chat, followed by a series of wails.

Helpless to soothe his distressed child, Nate blinked back tears. "Now show me the girl is safe."

Bedivere eyed him. "Why do you care what happens to her?"

"I care because I met the human woman you devastated by ripping a child away from her."

Bedivere scoffed. "Human? That's what she told you?"

Nate's brows drew together. *The cold, unfeeling bastard.* He couldn't remember the last time he'd yearned with as much intensity to put his fist through someone's face. "*Witch* then. Whatever. We've never had a problem with witches before, so why should it matter? Just, please, show me the girl. She's only a baby, and we're not baby killers."

"Show him."

Pelleas moved the camera on his end and angled it down at a crib in the room. Aslaug slept, swaddled in a white blanket.

"As you can see, both children are being well taken care of. Like you said, we're not monsters," Bedivere said. "Unless you force us to be. Thank you, Pelleas. I'll check in on the hour, as discussed."

Unless I force you to be? Would they really hurt a child who had no control over their parentage? Nate didn't want to find out, but his gut instinct told him to take them at his word and to leave nothing up to chance.

"You can't keep him from me forever. He'll remember this, man. He may have King Arthur's soul inside him, but he has the body and mind of a dragon now. He's aging differently. And that girl needs her mother. You want me to help you, then you need to work with me too."

"With Loki out of the picture, arrangements can be made to acquire the mother. It would be better to have her under our watch, anyway. She's dangerous."

Dangerous? Nate raised a skeptical brow but kept his mouth shut. Selene had looked anything but dangerous.

"Besides." Bedivere smirked. "She's not bad looking. Maybe she'll make a better match for you than the creature you're leaving behind. Now, have a seat and tell me everything we need to know about Drakenstone Manor."

***

Limping into the tunnel beneath Mount Olympus, Loki made his way into the heart of Zeus's lair.

Most dragons preferred to burrow deep into the earth and to surround themselves with beautiful things. Loki's personal lair had all variety of treasures from gold and jewelry to historical portraits. Holding some humans in disdain didn't mean he couldn't appreciate their artistic talent.

The metallic and rich scent of cold metal wafted to him through the tunnel. In the distance, the musical chime of uncut gems created their own mystical harmony. He listened with his head tilted toward the melodious symphony.

Down another passage he scurried, pushing himself ahead despite the pain. He'd cauterized the wound with his own fire magic, mourning how much he'd miss that single digit.

Not nearly as much as he missed Aslaug. For her, he'd have sacrificed all five claws, but Nate had assured him only one was necessary, anything more was too large to conceal and easily carry back to the dragonslayers.

But it hurt. It burned, a dull throb reminding him of his minor sacrifice. With the blood imprint in the blade, they'd know he was struck by it, but not realize he'd survived. He hoped. Nate seemed confident their power wouldn't work that way.

Navigating the subterranean lair by memory, Loki crawled lower and slithered into the next area until the corridors widened and he emerged into a stone chamber larger than a football field. Columns of marble rose toward the ceiling, each one intricately carved by Zeus's many human followers during a time when dragons had been revered as gods.

A dozen enchanted torches glowed in subtle shades of blue and silver beside a large, subterranean spring carved into the polished stone. Curls of steam and smoke arose from the tranquil surface as he passed the basin into the next chamber. The treasure room awaited him, the soul of any dragon's lair where the owner guarded prized possessions valued above all other objects in their hoard.

Instead of a sleeping giant, he found an awake and alert Zeus. The largest and eldest living dragon lay upon piles of coins, pearls, and rubies. He'd surrounded himself with marble statues and busts, some of which bore his own likeness as the ruler of Mount Olympus.

Of the other dozen or so statues, one bore an incredible resemblance to Éostre. Hera, the one dragoness Zeus could never charm into obedience or intimidate with his power, had walked out of his life centuries ago. Wise dragons never mentioned her.

"Come to finally kill me, have you?" Zeus's dry chuckle rumbled through his chest.

"The idea was tempting, I'll admit. Of course, I also expected you to be asleep."

Zeus pushed up to all fours. His bones and joints creaked, protesting the first movements of the century. Loki's confidence took a direct hit as he tipped his head up to regard the thousands of pounds of muscle and enormous frame surpassing his build by at least six feet. "I sensed the moment of your arrival. If you thought to have the advantage of surprise, you've failed, trickster. Your cowardly desires will be denied."

"Splendid, since I decided I have a proposition for you instead—something far better than the two of us beating one another bloody."

"Whatever will your titan masters think of that? Do you truly think I would deal with you—trust you—when you reek of them?"

Loki drew up short, both brows shooting up high. "My what?"

"Heh. Even the master of tricks has been fooled." As Zeus ambled down from his bed, silver drachmas dripped from the spaces between his scales. They had always been his preferred currency.

"No one's fooled me, you old git. Have the years of solitude addled your brain?"

"Mind your words and do not forget to whom you speak." A thousand sparks danced across the elder dragon's silver scales.

"I speak to a dragon who once called himself friend to many and father of us all, yet you lurk here, hiding like some frightened rabbit. How far the mighty Zeus has fallen."

Lightning arced across the cavern in a blinding display. Loki narrowed his eyes to protect them from the brilliant flashes and waited out the tantrum. He held his ground even as the larger dragon charged him.

"I do not hide," he roared.

"Really? Where were you when Watatsumi died destroying a titan weapon? Where were you when your daughter's mate was raised from the dead? The mighty Zeus sees and knows all when he slumbers, and yet you've done nothing."

His words made Zeus pause and quiet. He settled back on his haunches and regarded Loki with solemn eyes. "I sensed his passing. It stirred me from my slumber."

"Then do something about it. Help us with the titans."

Zeus snorted. "Don't you know how to deal with them, little trickster?" The ancient dragon leaned in close and drew in a deep, scenting breath. "You're drowning in their scent, but it is muted. Dimmed by mortality and entangled with your very soul."

"That is ridiculous. The only essence joined with my soul is Selene." He paused. Clarity overwhelmed the rest of his thoughts, bringing understanding of Selene's mysterious parentage. She wasn't a witch; she was something more.

"All-Father," he said in a more respectful tone, scaling back the resentment and anger that had grown over the years. "Have the titans ever borne children with humans?"

Zeus flicked his tail, no less dismissive now than he'd been prior to his hibernation. "They have created many things. Such abominations would not be unheard of."

Loki's spine stiffened. Selene was no abomination. Not even close. From her loving nature to her indomitable spirit, every inch of her was profound perfection. "The world is changing. We've found salvation in the humans. They've taken us as Soulmates."

Zeus huffed. "Impossible."

"The truth. Saul and Teotihuacan have both fathered *strong* cubs with their human mates, and mine... mine has the blood of a titan in her veins, it would seem. It's the only logical reason for her unusual abilities and what you smell on me."

The great silver dragon leaned in close again and growled. "What. Do. You. Want?"

Time and time again, other dragons had appealed to Zeus and pleaded for his help, only for their requests to fall on deaf ears. Loki embraced another method and returned to his original idea. He shrugged one of his shoulders and turned away, even as his heart pounded fast in his chest.

"Perhaps I've come to the wrong person after all. Hera would take pity. After all, it was always she who loved us the most."

"She still lives?"

With his back to Zeus, Loki smiled. "Did you not realize?"

"I have searched to the ends of the earth for my Hera and found no sign of her. When last I spoke with Ēostre, she said her mother was beyond my reach. Why else would she say such a thing?"

When he turned to face Zeus again, he'd put on his solemn face. "I hold as much affection for Hera as I do my own mother, All-Father. Few of us know where she has chosen to lair, and out of respect for her privacy, I have held its location secret for these centuries. A thousand years you have sought her, have you not?"

The ancient silenced with unconcealed longing on his creased and weathered draconic face. "Yes. Tell me. Tell me where to find her."

"Why should I? You've offered me no reason to grant you such a valuable secret."

"I'll give you whatever you desire from my hoard."

"There is no object within this hoard or anywhere else on this green earth more valuable or precious than my cub. Help us, Zeus. If you're unable to fight any longer, grant me a portion of your power. Share part of your essence with me, and I'll fight them *for* you."

"Ah, is that it? I offer you an inch and you take a mile, little Loki?" The silver dragon scoffed and turned aside, pale gaze falling to the bust of Hera in her human form. "Yet another trick and play for power. I was a fool to believe you truly cared for this cub."

"I do!" Loki roared. He rose to his full height in challenge and flared his wings, but fell short of matching Zeus by nearly three yards. His elder, the first dragon in all the world, sneered down at him. "I came here to kill you and to die for her safety."

"The first honest thing to leave your mouth since your arrival."

"This is my final offer. The secret pathway to Hera's lair in exchange for help to defeat the slayers." Prepared to bluff his way into a deal, Loki raised his chin and met the gaze of his elder. Groveling at Zeus's feet had never impressed him, and it wouldn't now.

"You have always been my favorite nephew," Zeus muttered.

"Will you help?"

"You ask a great price for knowledge of Hera's home... but I long for her." Their mighty draconic king flicked his tail, sending coins scattering across the pile. He sighed. "And I long to see the titans put to rest one final time. I will grant what you seek, and you will take this cause in my name."

"I—"

Zeus exhaled a cool breath, releasing power instead of lethal lightning bolts from his enormous maw. The mist of life washed over Loki, and its electric tingle began at his snout and ended at the tip of his tail. Sensation flooded his mind and overwhelmed him, harder than a sledgehammer blow to the face. He staggered back, reeling from the indescribable strength bonding to his soul.

When the world came into focus again, Zeus had returned to his silver throne, and he sensed hours had passed. Loki blinked open his eyes to see a brighter cave, his vision sharp and hearing keener than ever. The thunder of raindrops reached his ears from the distance. He smelled the storm on the wind far beyond the cavern and counted innumerable heartbeats throughout the surrounding forest.

With only a fraction of Zeus's life essence, he felt undefeatable.

And also wondered how he'd ever been convinced he could kill the sleeping ancient.

"Go rescue your mate and cub with my blessing."

"Thailand," he told Zeus. "She made her lair in what is now the Huai Kha Khaeng Wildlife Sanctuary. I wish you luck in your reunion."

Regretting nothing about their deal, Loki hurried outside beneath the night sky and shrank to his human form. With his newfound power, he saw the threads of sorcery that had transported Nathaniel away. The foul, twisted magic hung in the air like a poisonous fog, unpalatable to his tastes.

He tore open the space between Olympus and Chicago and crossed the world. His daughter awaited him.

Chapter 19

Bedivere led Nate down a narrow, wooden staircase into the basement level. The steps creaked beneath their weight and shifted, damaged from age and dampness.

"Where are we going?" Nate asked.

After hours of captivity, he'd been able to discern little about their location, only that the weather was warm and sunny outside, ruling out anywhere in New England where a recent, last-minute spring blizzard had dumped a yard of snow on Massachusetts.

Despite furnishing proof of Loki's demise, Bedivere and his cronies kept him in their sight at all times. He hadn't even taken a piss without the big bearded guy lurking over his shoulder.

Those two didn't follow Nate and Bedivere into the basement.

"Look, dude, I did what you guys wanted, and now it's time for you to answer some of my questions. Where are we going?" Nate repeated.

Bedivere drew short and stared at him. "Finally got your balls back, eh, Galahad? All right then. Since you've rejoined us on the true path, Pelleas and I have decided it's time to introduce you to the boss calling the shots."

"You mean you're answering to someone else?"

"You'll see," Bedivere replied. "Caleb, it's time."

Only one other person stood in the large underground cellar, a thin man in ripped jeans and a black T-shirt. His midback-length brown hair hung loose around his shoulders, streaked with gray. He looked as though he belonged in a biker bar. Or death row for murdering a lot of people. A malevolent aura hung around him, like spiritual filth clinging to an unclean soul.

A warlock. Nate suppressed the urge to shudder.

The dark spellcrafter finished drawing out the final details on the magical circle spread across the cellar floor. He drew a dagger down his palm and dripped blood around the circumference. One by one the runes flared to life with an eldritch green glow. The air above shimmered and rippled as a tear split open. Heat rolled through, blasting waves carrying the scent of brimstone and molten metal.

Nate stared at the nightmare landscape beyond the portal, frozen in place by awe and terror. Everything within him screamed for him to run, to put as much space between himself and the otherworldly place only steps away. Creatures made of fire and ash moved across his field of vision.

"What the—? Where is that?"

"Tartarus." Bedivere stood proud beside him. "This is where the coward Zeus exiled them."

"Them?" Nate's voice cracked.

Bedivere chuckled. "The titans. There were once many of them, but they've fought this war with the dragons for millennia. Now they require our aid. They can't leave this plane without help—without working their gifts through us."

Pelleas appeared on the other side of the gateway. "Everything is ready."

"Good. Come along, Galahad, it's time for our true work to begin."

For his son, Nate would walk through hell itself. Energy crackled across his skin as he passed through, searing his flesh like a fiery brand. Then the pain vanished and left nothing in its place. The comforting, shining presence that had been with him since the moment he bonded with Astrid disappeared.

"Welcome back, brother." Pelleas grinned and clasped his arm.

"Thanks," Nate mumbled. His gaze darted behind the former dragonslayer to the brittle rock formations and occasional gout of flame soaring into the air. "So, uh, what's next?"

A sharp pain seared across Nate's skin, and when he tried to jerk back from Pelleas, he found himself held fast in place. Black tendrils of magic snaked from the fallen knight's fingers and twined around Nate's forearm. They burned on contact and sliced through flesh, digging into his veins.

What the hell?!

Alarmed by the touch of magic, Nate tugged again then slammed his other hand into Pelleas's wrist to break the hold. He struck the other knight, a futile attack doing nothing to dislodge him.

"Let go of me!"

Pelleas chuckled. "Not yet, my friend. Not yet."

The magical hooks sinking into his flesh seemed to attach to every nerve ending. Agony swept over Nate from head to toe, and he stumbled to one knee. As Pelleas grinned, the magical shell falsifying his handsome appearance fell away and revealed his true face. Like Bedivere and Kay, something had happened to him. Black veins crept across his discolored skin, his exterior as ugly as the rotted soul corrupted by the titan's influence.

"Wh-what are you doing?" Nate's voice slurred.

"Once the ritual is complete, you'll be one of us again, brother. After you've accepted the true gods into your heart, we'll do the same to Arthur," Bedivere said. "The brotherhood will be united. Once again, we'll stand strong, and we'll wipe the filth known as dragonkind from the world for good."

***

Selene awakened from a nap to the high-pitched wail of an infant crying. Positive it was Aslaug, she flew from the bed and hurried to the left to rush down the hallway, only for the realization to dawn when unfamiliar wallpaper greeted her. Memories flooded back. She slowed midstep and gazed around the bedroom in Drakenstone Manor.

Only a dream. For the second time since her arrival, she'd heard her little girl screaming for her. This time, Loki wasn't there to coax her back to bed or hold her tight.

Although her mate had taken an extended leave of absence from Ragnarok and informed his personal staff to look after his home, he hadn't remained by her side exclusively. If he wasn't holding her, he was alongside Maximilian or even Merlin visiting abandoned hideouts once favored by the Anti-Dragon Movement's extremist faction.

An endless procession of dragons, mages, and knights rotated in and out of Drakenstone Manor, each of them assigned some task or another. When Apollo led the search in the Mediterranean for Pelleas, Jacob offered to close the bakery and fly to her side for support. He took up another cause instead when she turned him down, calling with daily updates about the local scrying rituals he'd organized with the coven in Norfolk.

By evening, when neither man answered their mobile phones, Astrid and Selene made the best of it and cooked dinner together in the kitchen. Chloe had hurried away back to Texas to meet with a witch friend, and the others all had their own assignment.

After covering the leftover supper with foil and returning it to the oven for the others, Selene joined Astrid at the table. Then she picked at her meal.

Why did she have to be the useless one?

Selene cleared her throat. "You don't have to stay to babysit me."

"It's all right."

"No, it isn't. You have magic and things you can do, and now you're stuck here to look after me."

"It's not like that," Astrid said in halfhearted protest.

Silence returned while they both sat there and stared at their meal. Selene's breasts ached. After her dream about Aslaug, she had filled two bottles with pumped milk, but no relief came. Her body yearned for her daughter as much as her heart and soul did.

"I'm going to get cleaned up," Astrid mumbled. She pushed aside her neglected dinner and left the table.

Selene cleared both plates. The entire family had insisted she didn't need to do anything, but activity provided a necessary distraction for her troubled mind. With no one else in the house and Astrid occupied, she meandered upstairs to her bedroom and lay down. The final rays of the day's golden sunlight slanted in through the blinds over the window.

It should have been warm and comforting, but the cold, dark knot of worry in her chest kept her from enjoying the sunset. She hugged her pillow, closed her eyes, and wished Loki were back.

Where are you? she wondered.

His phone, one of the few items always within his reach, taunted her from the bedside table.

Loki never leaves his phone unattended. The longest she'd seen him away from it was his two-day mini-hibernation in the hoard months ago.

As her eyelids grew heavy, a silver sculpture filled her mind. Its strange and unusual shape gleamed beneath colored lights in dozens of vivid hues. The mirrored surface reflected a city skyline aglow with towering buildings beneath a dark sky. Above it, the moon shone bright and full.

A shriek shattered the manor's unbearable peace. The vision popped like a soap bubble, and Selene jerked upright in the bed, heart pounding. Another cry followed. She hurried from the room and paused in the hallway. Adrenaline pounded her pulse through her veins.

"Astrid?" she called.

No one replied.

Put on edge, she tiptoed down the carpeted corridor then nudged Astrid's door open and peeked inside.

"Astrid?"

Selene's gaze darted around the pink and lacy interior of a princess-themed room decorated with an abundance of animals, stars, and teddy bears. In the corner, Astrid huddled in a tight ball with one of her son's stuffed bears clutched to her chest.

"Are you all right? What happened?" Selene slowly approached her friend.

"He's gone. I can't feel him," Astrid whispered.

"Honey, no, don't think like that. Your son is going to be fine."

"Not Arthur. Nate. I can't feel Nate." Astrid looked up, her eyes wild and rimmed in red.

"What? What do you mean you can't feel Nate? Doesn't your bond let you...?" Selene still hadn't adjusted to the relative newness of her bond with Loki. She always sensed when he entered the same room, knew his feelings even when he tried to hide them, and felt the warmth of his love like a small fire burning in her heart.

Astrid shook her head. The tears continued to fall, endless trails glistening against her cheeks. "It's like... like someone ripped out my heart."

"Should I call your mother?"

"No!" Astrid reached out for her and caught her hand in a vice grip. "Please don't leave. I... I..." She closed her eyes and shuddered. Tears leaked out from beneath her lashes and rolled down her pale cheeks.

"I'm right here." Selene inched closer. "Breathe, Astrid. Breathe and talk to me."

"I-I was in the shower and he was there, you know? Somewhere. He was alive and in my heart, and I knew wherever he was he was okay."

"But now he's not? Is he hurt?"

"He's gone!" Astrid wailed. Her head tipped back and knocked against the wall. "The link is gone."

"But that means..." Death, Loki had told her, was the only way to sever a bond between soul mates. She swallowed back the word, refusing to utter it aloud, and wrapped Astrid in her arms. Her friend wept, hard and bitter tears that soaked through Selene's shirt.

When Astrid finally cried herself out, she sat back and scrubbed at her blotchy face with the heels of her hands. "How do I go on without him?" Her voice didn't rise above a whisper.

"You get your son back and you make them pay."

Astrid's missing link and Loki's absence provided the clarity Selene had needed during her days of self-pity. Waiting and hoping wouldn't return their children, and neither would the police.

What if the police are involved? The thought crept through her mind, an insidious whisper of intuition.

After shifting to her knees, Selene leaned back and placed both hands on the dragoness's shoulders. "I can't stay in this house another day while other people look for my daughter."

"I know. I can't either. And if Nate's—if he's gone... I can't sit here."

"Loki's link isn't gone. That has to mean something. They're hurt, or they need our help, but I refuse to believe they're dead." And if the men were in trouble, if something had gone wrong during their investigation, it was up to Astrid and Selene to pick up where they left off.

Another hiccup hitched Astrid's breath; then she nodded, drew in a deep breath, and released it. "Sorry. I know I'm a mess. I couldn't stop it."

"Sweetie, no one would fault you for falling apart." Selene gave Astrid's shoulders a gentle squeeze. "I envied you at first. I didn't know how the hell you were keeping it all together. I thought I was lost without her. And I am. But I think it was something else." Her body tingled with unrecognizable energy, power flooding down to her fingertips. "I think I was recharging. I don't know what's happening to me, but I won't figure it out while hiding here."

"Where do we even start?"

Selene helped Astrid up from the floor. "We follow our mates. My guess is that we should start at the garage, unless you have a GPS tracking app on Nate's phone."

"It must be off because every call went to his voicemail, and his last known GPS location was in Greece. What about Loki?"

"He left his phone here. He's *never* without it."

Astrid's eyes grew large and round. "You're right. Uncle Loki always has his phone. Dad always jokes about him being glued to it. Should we look at it?"

After retrieving the cell phone from the bedside table, Selene entered Loki's passcode. The device opened to a photograph of Selene swaddling Aslaug in a blanket. Nothing out of the ordinary popped out at her while she navigated the phone through a stinging haze of tears.

A recent text from Anura asking about their health and if they had any leads.

A text from his executive assistant, wishing them the best of luck during their trying time of need.

Redialing his most recent calls didn't help. He'd made only two since the morning, one to his lawyer and another to a private detective seeking information for them about the Anti-Dragon Movement.

Disgruntled with her failure, Selene tossed the slim phone onto the table. "Ugh. I wish Sif could tell me what the hell Loki is doing."

"Loki has created a recent entry into his personal documents for Selene Richards," the phone's virtual interface replied. "Would you like to hear it?"

Astrid and Selene exchanged glances before she snatched the phone from the table. "Yes!" Selene cried. "Yes, Sif. Please read Loki's most recent personal document."

"Hello, Selene," the recording began in Loki's accent. "I want to begin this by telling you how much... There are no words in any language worthy of describing the happiness you've brought to my life. You've completed me."

Selene bowed her head and listened. "I love you too."

"If you are listening to this message, it is probable I have met my demise while attempting to recover our daughter. Two days earlier, I received orders from Bedivere in exchange for her safety. If I do their bidding, she and Arthur will be free, and naturally I now go into this knowing it may mean my death."

She sank into the chair beside the table, clutching his phone tighter.

"I have bequeathed all of my personal belongings and financial assets to Aslaug, to be held in trust by you until such a time that she is able to bear the responsibility on her own. My lawyer knows my wishes, and the necessary arrangements have been made in advance of this recording. If... in the event Aslaug is never returned to you, all properties will be deeded in your name. Take my holdings, my businesses, and make someone happy. Move forward one day and know I did all I could to bring her home. Goodbye, *skatten min.*"

A beep concluded the message. "End of recording," Sif announced.

Selene blinked away the tears gathering beneath her lashes. "This can't happen. I can't let him go without a fight."

"Then we need to figure out where the hell he and Nate have gone. What would the slayers ask them to do that required them visiting Gree...ce... Oh no."

"Oh no what?" Selene demanded.

"Nate's GPS told me he was last seen at Mount Olympus. There's only one reason both of them would show up there after leaving on an errand for the slayers. They're going to kill Zeus!"

"Isn't Zeus the oldest—"

"And the most powerful of them all. We have to stop them before they get killed."

Selene glanced at the forty caliber handgun she had shoved into the waist of her jeans. A lot of good it would do against a dragon. "Open the portal. I'm ready."

In the span of seconds, they traded the California's darkening, pre-dusk for the pitch-black night of Greece. The moon shone above them, a great silver orb in the sky.

"I have no idea where we go," Astrid whispered. "Grandmother brought me here once a few years ago in case I ever need to know how to find him, but it's all a jumble of rocks in the dark now." She opened her phone and activated the flashlight application.

"I feel Loki. We can follow that."

Astrid stared at her. "You're also *glowing*."

"What?"

"You're glowing like a Tolkien elf!"

One look down at her arms and hands confirmed Astrid's astonished observation. Selene twisted her wrist back and forth, staring awestruck at the subtle, pearly gleam radiating from her skin.

"I guess you really were charging up," Astrid continued. "I've never seen anything like it."

"A mystery for another time I guess," Selene murmured. "For now we need to find Zeus, then our men and kids."

Their night time descent into the gorge was slow and careful, footing made treacherous in their poor lighting. Selene hit a patch of loose pebbles and skidded down a few feet before she caught herself against a boulder.

"I suppose taking a portal straight to the entrance would have been too easy, huh?"

Astrid shook her head. "Dragons are pretty territorial, especially when it comes to their horde. Opening a portal would have set off all sorts of nastiness and spells. Silver dragons are almost always sorcerers."

"Good point."

With Astrid leading the way, they continued forward, reaching trees and shrubs and a gentler slope. Twice, Selene paused to touch her hand against a tree where the bark had been scraped away. "He was here…"

As they approached the opening in the mountain, the ground trembled beneath their feet.

Selene hesitated and reached for Astrid's hand. "What's that?"

The other woman frowned and glanced around. "I'm not sure. It could be—"

An enormous silver beast burst from the mouth of the cavern with enough force to send shudders through the ground. His mouth opened to reveal a thousand teeth, each dripping with saliva, and when he roared, the hot wind ripped through Selene's hair. Static exploded against her skin.

Astrid and Selene stumbled back, clutching each other and shrieking into the night air. She lost her footing, but found it again when Astrid transformed to her draconic form and put herself between them. She bounced off the golden dragon's flank instead and clutched a handful of her hide.

The force and volume of the roar taxed Selene's eardrums and brought tears of pain to her eyes.

"Who dares to trespass within my domain?" he demanded.

"Astrid Drakenstone, your great-granddaughter."

After an extraordinary feat of maintaining bladder control, Selene stepped forward to Astrid's side. "Selene Richards."

Zeus huffed. Twin jets of smoke curled up from his nostrils. "Yes. Your mate came to my lair with nefarious intentions, as is typical of him. He is fortunate I allowed him to leave in one piece, but I cannot say I may do the same for you, half-breed."

Before Selene could correct him, Astrid blurted out, "Loki isn't my mate."

Zeus chuckled, the deep bass of it booming across the mountain. "Not you, half-whelp. Her. That half-breed." Extending a claw toward Selene, he pointed at her. "The one born of titans."

"Excuse me? What the hell are you talking about?" Within seconds of opening her mouth, Selene realized she should speak with a more respectful tone to the oldest known dragon in the world. She also wasn't convinced she was still awake and conscious. Maybe she'd tumbled down the mountain and cracked her head. *I have to be dreaming.*

"So the god of mischief spoke the truth after all. You truly know nothing of your birth."

"I've always been told I'm a human. A witch. My mother didn't remain in contact with my father for long."

"Such is the way of the titans. Short-sighted and childish creatures. Their tantrums nearly destroyed the world once."

The two girls exchanged uncertain glances. "Well, then we need to make sure they don't do it again," Astrid said.

"Come into my lair." Zeus turned away from them and descended into the hole. His wide tail trailed behind him, dragging grooves into the packed mountain soil.

After twenty or thirty yards, the uneven ground became polished rock beneath Selene's feet. Before they ventured far, Astrid transformed to her human body and linked their hands together.

Despite the turmoil churning in her gut, Selene spoke up. "Will you tell us what happened to our mates? If Loki's gone, where did he go?"

"Only one dared to venture within my hoard. The knight traveled by way of a black enchantment while Loki came to seek my aid."

"Will you give it?" Astrid asked.

"What are you to me that I should?"

"I'm family," Astrid replied. "And even if I wasn't, aren't you the king of all dragons? Shouldn't you be helping and protecting your own kind?"

"Do good things not come to those who help themselves?" He chuckled, amused at his own joke. "I have always enjoyed that line."

His dismissive behavior set something off inside her, raising a tidal wave of fury. Words tumbled from her mouth in a rush before Selene could stop. "So you'd rather see the slayers raise two dragons to become mindless, murderous slave beasts. What kind of a leader *are* you?"

Her words gave the old dragon pause. He swung around, agile and nimble for a creature so large. "As brash and disrespectful as your sire. I smell the stink of your father in your veins, little one."

The Selene of two years earlier would have shrunk back, petrified. She stood taller and raised her chin instead. *And now I'm smarting off to the king of dragons. What more do I have to lose? He already knows if he wants to help or not.*

"That's funny because I've never met him. I guess it runs in the family. Who is he?"

"A coward who takes neither side, straddling the fence of neutrality until a battle is won."

She crossed her arms over her chest. "That's not exactly an answer."

"There are few dragons alive today who remember the days of old, and fewer among the rest who would believe it. The young prefer fairy tales to reality." He spat in disgust.

"Then tell us what happened," Astrid said in a pleading voice. "Teach us the truth, but don't dismiss us."

"Would I be correct to assume Watatsumi never shared the true origins of the dragons?"

Astrid regarded the ancient dragon with wariness. Her teeth skated across her lower lip and she shot Selene an uncertain glance. "I'm not sure I understand. Dragons have always been here, though my father says we once lived in another plane."

Zeus snorted. "That is correct in some regards, though vital pieces of the story are missing."

"I'm guessing the titans are involved," Selene said.

"We were once their pets—trifles for their amusement, no different than a human's common mongrel. Regardless of what the ancient Greek's scribbled in their books, this was no war for power to rule over Mount Olympus. I led the war for our *freedom* and liberated each dragon beneath Cronus and Gaia's thumbs."

"And earned your title as leader of the dragons."

The elder nodded. "Watatsumi took no interest in ruling, and Hel desired dominion over the gateway to the afterlife. Such was her call—"

"Hel?"

"Our sister, though you may know of her as Hades."

Selene's head hurt. She held up her hand for him to pause. "Excuse me. Are you implying Watatsumi was Poseidon?"

"I imply nothing, little cub. He was. And he took great joy in taunting Caligula and driving that fool emperor into declaring war against the beaches and seas." He sighed. "Of all the dragons lost over the years, it is Watatsumi I will miss the most. My dear brother."

Everything she grew up learning had been twisted from the truth, because the real story was too damn terrifying to consider—dragons and gods, titans and other planes of existence.

"I'm gonna sit down a second," she muttered before lowering to a golden bench covered with a red velvet cushion.

Zeus shifted, becoming a broad-shouldered human man with a majestic ivory beard. His hair fell as radiant as liquid silver past his shoulders to the small of his back.

Whether created by magic or something worn in his old days as Zeus, the Olympian god of the sky, he wore dated garments trailing to his sandal-clad ankles. He wore a deep blue cloak secured beneath his left arm and over the right shoulder, bright as the dawn sky with glittering embellishments sparkling against the fabric like starlight.

And if her thoughts were anywhere but on her mate and child, she might have been able to appreciate him as a dangerous silver fox.

"Well, the titans are back," Astrid said after an uncertain moment.

"I am old, and I've grown tired. This fight belongs to another generation of dragons. I have gifted sufficient help to Loki and shall give no more. This is now his battle and yours."

Stress made Selene crotchety, also obliterating her verbal filter. She stared at him. "That's it? You're just going to give up and pass the torch after you kept these valuable secrets all these years?"

Zeus rose tall above them without transforming from his human body. "If you wish to fight the titans, go to Tartarus and do it yourself," he rumbled back at her. "Better yet, find your father, if the coward still lives. I've bled for this cause and spent my energy. What have *you* done?" With each word, his voice boomed louder, echoing over the gilded walls and marble columns of his opulent lair.

Selene shrank back, properly cowed. Was this it? Had they made their visit to Olympus all for naught?

No. They'd gained valuable information and had armed themselves in knowledge, even if the greatest wyrm who ever lived refused to help beyond telling a few stories.

"I don't know how to find him." The words left her in a hoarse whisper.

"Magic calls to magic."

Astrid deflated. Her shoulders drooped and the shining hope in her blue eyes dimmed. "Grandmother told me you care for no one but yourself."

"I beg your pardon?" In a single step, he closed the distance between himself and Astrid, leaning in close. "Explain yourself, cub. My daughter would never say such a thing."

"She did." Astrid lifted her chin and stared him in the eye. "She said you only get involved in anything if it affects *you*. You couldn't be bothered to awaken when Fafnir returned as an undead abomination. You didn't wake up for my birth or even for the twins, and they're pure-blooded dragons. You weren't there when Watatsumi sacrificed himself to destroy the knight possessed by the titans through their weapon. You were here. Sleeping. Ignoring us."

"Did you and Loki practice your tirades together?" He huffed and turned away. "I have already done my part, now go do yours. You already know where to go."

"If we knew where to go, do you think we'd be here?"

Zeus pointed his finger toward Selene. "Ask her. She's seen. She can follow her mate if she makes the effort. Now be gone and leave me be."

Selene opened her mouth to speak, but Astrid grabbed her arm and shook her head. It was probably for the best. Selene would help no one if she was incinerated for pissing the elder off.

"C'mon, Selene, let's leave."

Astrid remained silent until they left the cavern and the entrance wards sealed behind them. Selene couldn't even admire the way the illusionary mountain face shimmered back into place, too nauseated by their failure.

"What do we do?" she asked.

"I don't know, but Zeus is known for seeing things the rest of us couldn't even comprehend. Can you think of any reason he'd say you knew where they all are?"

"No!"

"Breathe, Selene, and help me think this through. We learned something, at least, that you're part titan. It would explain your strange powers, so focus on that. What gifts do you have besides kicking ass and glowing?"

"I... I have weird dreams sometimes. Like déjà vu, I'll dream about something inconsequential and then see it happen a few days later."

"Have you had any recently?"

"Before I heard you crying, when you lost sense of Nate, I was dreaming about a sculpture. I don't know how that helps us."

Astrid's blonde brows drew together. "Okay, um, describe it. Maybe it's nothing, but maybe it's something we can use."

"Big. Metal, I think. It was really shiny and reflected everything around it like a mirror, but the shape was weird. Sorta oblong and curved, like a—"

"Bean?"

Selene blinked. "Yeah, like a jelly bean sorta. It was night and there was a city reflected in it."

"Chicago."

Bright golden light washed through the dark forest. Astrid's portal shimmered between them, the sculpture from Selene's dream visible on the other side. The connection between her and Loki tugged, drawing her forward, and she knew without a doubt he was somewhere on the other side.

And their daughter.

"They're over there somewhere," she whispered.

"Then let's go get them." Astrid took her hand, and they stepped through together.

Chapter 20

The unspoken law between knights and dragons had always encouraged Loki to play nice when it came to humans. With his daughter at stake, all bets were off.

Following Nate's trail delivered him to the cold, unforgiving walls of a warehouse storage freezer, the door half ajar and a deactivated teleportation glyph beneath him.

Loki peered through the doorway into a long, multi-level warehouse. Flickering fluorescent lights buzzed overhead and revealed a cache of weapons stockpiled on the shelves. The slayers had recruited their wicked cronies for years and accumulated enough weapons to wage war.

Outside, the heartbeats of a half dozen humans drummed in wild disharmony—tainted humans with corruption lingering on the edges of their souls.

Six of them, one of him, and while they were no match for the great Loki, he treaded with caution. Part of him expected some kind of Anti-Magical Field to erupt and alert them to his arrival, but when nothing happened, he grinned.

Zeus had really given him one hell of a gift.

With new electrical power coursing through him, Loki focused his sorcery on the dim surroundings. Three feet of concrete floor beneath his feet disintegrated into a fine powder; then he grounded his senses to the dirt beneath. It sang back to him as he took hold of the energies called from the earth.

He released the pent-up magic in a single, powerful pulse. The deep, resonant bass thumped and flooded out from him in a tremendous arc, rocketing through every technological device on the premises. Startled cries and alarm rang through the building as the lights flickered and power died.

Voices approached from beyond the other side of high shelves.

"What the hell is that? Think it's the circuit breaker?"

"Fuck no, my phone won't even turn on. I just paid five hundred dollars for this thing."

"Maybe a transformer blew somewhere."

"That wouldn't kill my phone. Look."

Loki crouched down and listened. As the great god of mischief, he could have taken any number of actions to acquire the knowledge he needed. With a few illusions, he could coerce the foul hunters and trick them without bloodshed.

Or he could torture them and have the info in two minutes.

Reminded of Selene's terror, the raw soles of her feet, and the suffering his mate had endured, he made up his mind and strode out of hiding to confront them.

Two unarmed men turned the corner and came down the lane between the industrial shelves. "What's the big deal?"

"Just shut up and check it out. I—oh, shit!"

They both saw him at once, seconds too late to save their lives after they reached Loki's field of vision. Once he saw them, their lives belonged to him. He reached out with magic and his conscious mind to grab both in his favorite spell.

Their blood boiled in their veins, faces reddening from the sharp, sudden stabs of agony he inflicted over their bodies with his sorcery. Unable to breathe, the first of them collapsed to the ground and convulsed.

No remorse touched Loki's heart for the two hunters. The second clutched his chest and lay gasping on the floor.

His enhanced senses picked up four other humans in the vicinity, but he only needed one to give him answers.

Desire to rescue his child drove him forward in his dragon body. His widening bulk and long tail knocked aside the shelves in his path, and in an act of savagery that would have made his mother and father proud, Loki became death incarnate.

Of the four, only one had a firearm. Its useless bullets bounced off his scaled hide before he bit off the offending hand. He chased down another and slammed him into the concrete and caught the fourth attempting to flee out the door.

In all his life, he'd never delighted in killing humans as much as he did shredding the foolish bound to Bedivere and Pelleas's service.

"Not so brave now, are you, humans. Is this not what you wanted? You have your war with my kind now, and you won't even battle me like men! All of your weapons and you're reduced to prey in a box."

By the time he had dispatched the five, he found the final mortal cowering beneath an overturned shelf and stinking of fear. He fought when Loki dragged him out and slammed him into the floor.

Reaching with his magical senses, Loki placed his open claw above the man's ribs and searched for his essence, the spark of life inside every living creature. It was the same source of power Ēostre found whenever she healed with her white gift. "Tell me where to find the children."

"I ain't telling you sh—" Loki adjusted the spell, scrambling the human's insides. "Ahhh!"

"My friend came here less than three hours ago. Tell me where to find him."

"I ain't telling you! Fuck you, dude."

"Such tough words for a man who smells of his own piss." Loki chuckled dryly and thrust his magical power against the human's soul, burning through it with undiluted energy. The human arched against the floor and shrieked as the sensation of being burned alive sizzled through his nerves. His physical body remained unharmed, but the pain throbbed without mercy.

"I want you to know something, human. This is as easy for me as breathing."

His victim blubbered and writhed on the floor, but wriggling ignited a fresh wave of agony.

"I want you to know your masters care nothing for what happens to you. Whether it ends five minutes from now or goes on all night, they will do *nothing* to help you."

"Please. No more, no more."

Loki smiled, divorced from all rage and emotion. "Tell me where to find the children and I will stop the pain."

"They have a house in the suburbs. The address is programmed into the car. It's something like Chestnut or Elm. Please, that's all I know, I swear."

Merlin's words came back to him. Once corrupted, a human couldn't be cured. He would always be under titan control. "Thank you," Loki murmured appreciatively, but not without regret. One twitch of his fingers snuffed out the unfortunate human's life.

***

In their rush to leave Drakenstone Manor, neither woman had a purse, credit card, or wallet. Without the cash for a cab to ferry them around the city, Selene devised another alternative for tracking down Loki.

Astrid took her dragon form, and they flew from the iconic Cloud Gate over downtown Chicago, soaring toward the west. Selene followed her bond with Loki, letting it lead her toward him. Like a melody on the edge of her hearing, it guided them to an industrial area outside the main city limits. People took pictures of them in action, both with cell phones and the occasional camera.

"Keep going!" Selene called over the sound of the wind cutting through Astrid's feathers. "Just up ahead, I think! Down there!"

"Hold on tight."

Flying by dragon surpassed Uber and any taxi she'd ever taken. The descent brought them to a small parking lot on the corner of a sluggish intersection. A man standing across the street stared at them, and his cigarette fell from his mouth.

Selene slid down and glanced around the small lot occupied by two cars and a pickup. "Power seems to be down in this area. Weird."

"Not weird. I smell magic," Astrid said. She took her human shape and drew the magical sword Ascalon. The blade's edge gleamed with a muted ruby light.

At this point, nothing startled Selene anymore, and it amazed her how quickly she'd adjusted to the strange and abnormal. Enchanted blades, Knights of the Round Table, and sleeping gods beneath historic mountains.

An awful stench wafted from the burnt-out building on the street corner, like seared meat and rotting flesh. They passed through a chain-link fence and approached the darkened warehouse. Through the doorway, a large figure moved beyond the smoke pouring outside.

Astrid scrunched her nose and hung back a few steps, coughing. "It's black dragon's breath. I can't go in there."

It bothered Selene no more than a little chlorine in pool water. As her eyes adjusted to the darkness, the vague shape of her mate gained clarity. She sprinted through the miasma and threw herself into his arms. "Loki!"

He squeezed her tight and buried his face against her wavy hair. "I thought I'd never see you again. What are you doing here? *How* did you get here?"

Astrid lingered near the doorway and waved a hand in front of her face. "Great-grandpa Zeus gave us a clue."

Loki ushered them all away from the building until they were clear of the eye-stinging fumes. "The old asshole helped?"

"More or less. He told us how to find you," Selene clarified. Then she punched him in his shoulder. He stumbled back a step and grimaced. "You're one to speak of assholes after the stunt you pulled."

"Ow. I thought I was doing what was best for our little girl. Trust me when I tell you that excluding both of you was the furthest thought from our minds. I feared for our children and what would happen if I failed to obey their orders to the letter."

"You should have said something to us."

"Impossible under the circumstances. I've been hiding ever since Nate and I parted ways to make the slayers believe Nate killed me."

Astrid inhaled a sharp breath. "What?"

"I received orders to kill Zeus, and Nate was tasked with killing me. He couldn't do it."

"Couldn't or wouldn't?" Selene asked.

"Wouldn't."

"Of course he wouldn't!" Astrid said. "Nate isn't a cold-blooded killer, not even for our son, Uncle Loki. So where is he?"

"He is with the slayers. After spilling my blood with his sword, they should be convinced he is truly giving in to their demands in exchange for Arthur's freedom."

"Spilling your blood?" No longer distracted by her relief, Selene's gaze swept over Loki for injuries and paused when she reached the pinky finger of his left hand. Or where his pinky finger belonged. "Your hand!"

"It is fine," he murmured. "A small sacrifice."

Selene cradled his hand to her chest. The wound still appeared red and angry, in need of medical care. "But why?"

"Because a dragonslayer's sword has a blood memory," Astrid answered. "It absorbs a small amount of their opponent's power and can reveal each kill they've ever made. Nate once told me it's how they're able to stand against supernatural threats. And because the sword is part of the slayer himself, and burned into his soul, it makes him stronger."

"Your mate has a little of me inside him now," Loki informed her.

"I... did not want to think of that. Not creepy at all, Uncle Loki."

He beamed. "Anyway, it wasn't necessary for Nate to slay me after all to mark his sword with a portion of my essence. And now that he's fulfilled his part of our bargain, they believe me to be dead and Nate on their side. I'm now following his tracks and trying to unravel what's happened without tipping them off."

"What have you discovered so far? Have you found the babies?"

"No. According to one of the lackeys I killed, there are GPS coordinates programmed into his vehicle. That was my next destination." He dangled a set of keys.

Astrid drove the SUV and followed the navigation to the suburbs north of Chicago. The city streets gave way to nicer neighborhoods filled with trees and large yards behind fences.

"Well, they sure went for the fancy places," Astrid muttered. They turned onto a private drive and parked outside a three-car garage tucked away to the side of the property.

"I don't feel her," Selene whispered once they were out of the vehicle. "Not here, at least. Finding you was easier."

"Then we'll make them tell us where they took her," Loki promised.

A door at the side of the house opened and two men stepped out. Their expectant expressions transitioned to alarm when they realized it wasn't their cohorts who had arrived.

Selene lunged forward to test her newfound gift. Her powers flared and launched her with the speed of a meteor. Before either henchman could draw his gun, the collision bowled them over and into the wall where they slumped.

She turned and found the dragons staring at her with wide, astonished eyes.

"What?" she asked. "I handled it."

Loki recovered his wits first and moved to her side. "So you did, and I think we're safe to go in. I hear no more heartbeats, but I do sense a strong, magical source below us."

No one else stirred in the house and no wards activated upon their entrance. Loki led them down a steep flight of stairs into the cellar. The deeper she descended, the brighter the world around her became until it was a room of pale blue light and glittering stardust floating in the air.

"Uncle Loki? Are you doing that?"

Selene glanced over her shoulder to find her mate staring at her in wonder.

"No," he murmured. "It's Selene."

All of Selene's life, she'd wished her abilities would develop into more than the occasional prophetic dream, and when it finally happened, she was too queasy with desire to see her child again to truly enjoy it.

Potent waves of magic rolled upward in sickening pulses. At the foot of the stairs, she found a typical basement with a cement floor, filled with cardboard boxes and plastic storage bins.

And in its center lay an open portal with a shimmering, semi-translucent image of another world. Fire-blasted rock and a sandy hellscape awaited them on the opposite side.

"You're too late," a voice rasped from the corner.

Selene jumped. Her eyes darted toward the sound to find a lanky man slumped beside a stack of cardboard boxes. Blood pooled beneath him, and a thin trail of it led to the grisly drawing beneath the portal.

"It's him," Astrid said. "He's the source of the black magic creating this portal."

Before she reached the injured man, Loki jerked Selene back by her hand. "He's a warlock. Don't bother. One of them."

"If he's one of them, why is he bleeding?"

Astrid crouched beside him and flashed her cell phone light over the dark bloodstain spreading over the back of his shirt. "She's right. This doesn't look like a self-inflicted wound."

"Bingo to the smart lady. Fucking Bedivere stabbed me in the back the moment he had what he wanted from me. Took that knight through then came back for me."

"Did you expect any less?" Loki glared balefully down at the man. "The slayers have no love for anyone in the supernatural community. You are tools to be used and discarded, nothing more."

"You think I don't get that now."

"Our children," Selene said. "Where are they? Why keep their secrets when they screwed you over, right?"

The warlock's breaths wheezed in and out of his chest, and he was still long enough for Selene to think he'd already died. "South of the city. Neighborhood called Country Club Hills."

"I know that area," Astrid said. "A little, at least. The knights owned some property there, but Nate and Percivale donated it for some program they founded. Homes for military and law enforcement families basically."

"There's an address written... written on the fridge. That's where they took your kids." His labored breaths quickened. "He has a weakness... he needed... he needed power from me. For... his sword. They're feeding..."

"Who's feeding?"

Another rasping breath rattled in the man's chest. Then it didn't move at all. Astrid shook her head. "He's gone now. Shit. I should have tried to heal him. We could have gotten more out of him."

"He wasn't worth your energy, girl. We have everything we need anyway."

"You two go and retrieve our children," Loki told them. He glanced at Astrid and forced a fragile smile. "I'll rescue your mate."

"You don't even know where that leads. It could go anywhere," Selene protested. But she had a feeling, a gut-wrenching intuition born from the whispering voices calling to her from the other side. The titans wept for freedom, driven mad from years of solitude and incarceration.

"No matter where it goes, it's where I need to be. Save our daughter, Selene."

"There are one, possibly two dragonslayers there," Astrid said. "They'll tear you to ribbons."

Loki growled. "I've fought dragonslayers before." He stalked to the portal, but upon reaching it, a static blast blew him away like a leaf caught in the wind. He struck the wall and tumbled to the floor, groaning. "I did not anticipate that."

The whispers continued, beckoning her toward the portal. Selene followed the sound, inching closer, straining to understand what they were saying. Stars sparkled around the portal in soft silver hues.

"Selene!" Loki cried in alarm. He scrambled up from the floor and lunged for her, his hand closing around her wrist.

The portal didn't repel her. Or Loki this time.

"I have to go with you," she whispered. "Or I have to go alone."

"There is no way I am allowing you to face two slayers alone." Loki peered back over his shoulder. "Astrid, go. Trust us to save your mate as I am trusting you to save our daughter. I will not fail you. You have my solemn vow."

"All right. Good luck." Astrid darted up the stairs, her pounding footsteps fading fast.

With her hand twined with his, Selene stepped through to Tartarus.

Chapter 21

Astrid's portal landed outside a small community in the Chicago suburbs. She'd only visited the area once with Nate because there'd been a meeting house nearby he wanted to place on the market. Now that he and Percivale handled all financial matters concerning the brotherhood, it made sense to sell and donate their unused assets.

In the end, they'd given the home to a police officer with a family of four.

Please don't let it be them.

The officer's wife had smiled at her and gushed about how happy she was to make a new home for their family. Sick to her stomach with disgust, Astrid approached the same green yard. A dozen stairs flanked by verdant shrubbery led to the two-story residence at the top of the low hill. A police cruiser was parked in the drive beside a white minivan.

She glanced down at the address written on her palm, compared it to the mailbox number, and felt her heart sink. This was the place.

Her son and baby cousin were inside waiting for her to rescue them.

And heaven help anyone who stood in her way.

I need a plan. I need to know what the hell to do. Do I just stalk inside? Tear the roof off the house?

The tall and imposing house loomed before her. Neighborhood children played basketball in the driveway across the street beneath a spotlight angled from the garage. Not only were there innocents around, but a cop lived there—a cop who would take offense to her throwing around baseless accusations.

What if Arthur's not here and I'm wrong? the insidious voice of reason whispered through her thoughts. Cool logic paused her ascent up the porch steps.

Divided, Astrid crouched low and moved off the stairway to the side of the house until she found a window. Four men played pool in a lower-level room. One wore a Chicago police uniform, the others jeans and casual clothes. With as much patience as she could muster, she reached out with her arcane talent, aware of the subtle ebb and flow of magical defenses intended to keep her from opening a portal inside.

Nothing unusual. Most households and even some communities had magical protection and commercialized wards.

It didn't mean this house had her son.

But her heart told her it did. Pressing close against the brick home, she strained to listen through the open window.

The cop glanced at his watch. "We haven't heard from anyone at Alpha Point in hours. Think we need to check in?"

One of the men, a bearded dude with the build of a motorcycle gang member, shook his head. "Nah, Greg. Pelleas said to sit tight, so we sit tight. Anyway, how's your wife handling the brats? Haven't heard the boy scream in a while now."

The cop chuckled. "Eh, she's gotten attached to the girl, and it's going to kill her if Pelleas decides to off it. They haven't decided yet. So far, they want the boy raised in a nice human family."

"What about the knight we caught in the trap at the warehouse? Didn't Bedivere promise the traitor they'd let him do it?"

"That idiot? Nah, they have something special in mind for him, and once they're done, he won't give a fuck about raising the kid."

It was all she needed to know as fury swelled inside her chest. Her heart hammered fast, and sweat dampened her palms. She had one chance to maintain the element of surprise, one chance to get ahead of them.

She shifted in a flash of gold scales and feathered wings. A woman mowing her yard across the road screamed, and two kids on bicycles stopped in the middle of the road to gawk. Astrid thrust her clawed hand through the window and curled her talons around the wall. She tore it outward and made enough room to crawl inside.

"Holy shit!" The cop drew his gun and fired. Two years ago, Astrid had been shot multiple times while escaping dragon hunters carrying armor-piercing rounds. She had the softer, baby hide of a juvenile dragon then, and still did now, but the two shots felt like mosquito stings in comparison.

Then, she'd been a child. Now, she was a furious mother, a whirlwind capable of anything to rescue her baby.

Astrid exhaled her breath weapon, releasing an inferno aimed at the officer. Lightning arced across the room as he dove behind the billiard table; then he and one of the men shoved it over on its side. A storm of dragonbreath lapped against it.

"Don't just stand there!" the officer screamed. Despite his orders, one of the non-combatants fled the room.

Astrid noticed one of the remaining guys hid behind an arcane shield. He held a talisman in his hand and the air around him throbbed with a field of magic. More bullets pelted her hide, but she struck out with her tail and batted the pool table aside.

No pain was too great for her son.

She smashed into the warlock's shield and gnashed her teeth against the magical force protecting him. He spoke in an unfamiliar tongue, holding his amulet of defense in one hand and a grisly token made from dragon's claw in the other. Her blood boiled in her veins.

Astrid stumbled and cried out.

If she'd been thinking, she would have brought her father, grandmother, or even Merlin with her. One phone call would have brought a flock of dragons down upon the entire suburb.

And that was precisely why she hadn't called. Because terrorizing an innocent, unsuspecting suburb wasn't her intention. The fear she'd stirred up with her appearance had been enough.

If Uncle Teo, Grandpa Max, Dad, and others arrived, there'd be avoidable human casualties. No matter how much her grandfather tried to minimize the damage and control them, it'd be wholesale fire and acid raining from the sky. They were already worked up into a frenzy and ready to kill anyone in their way.

"Looks like we got one of the weak ones! Hurry up and finish it off."

When the officer ejected the magazine from his gun, Astrid whirled and shrank to her human size. She drew Ascalon from its sheath and opened a portal—now within the ward boundaries and able to travel freely.

In one step, she appeared behind the warlock and impaled him through the back. He gurgled as she ripped the blade free and kicked him forward into the flames crackling above the ruined pool table.

The next wave of gunshots began before she could return the sword to its scabbard. A bullet clipped her in the shoulder, and pain lanced down her torso in white-hot waves. Small caliber bullets as a dragon had been annoyances, as a human, it introduced her to agony.

With the most dangerous player off the field, Astrid returned to her dragon form and lunged through the flames. Her teeth closed around the officer's arm, and the vile taste of human flesh filled her mouth.

Unable to stomach it, she clamped down then raced from the room without looking back. He wouldn't be following her any time soon.

She spat out his severed limb and shifted back to her human shape as she reached the stairs. A pounding, staccato beat pulsed in her head with each step, adrenaline rushing through her veins. Arthur's familiar cry led her down the upstairs hallway to the bedroom door at the end. The flimsy barrier stood no chance against her. She ripped the door from its frame and stepped inside the room.

A woman with a gun huddled at the back of the nursery. She had both children with her, Arthur clutched against her right side and Aslaug held to her chest in a black baby carrier.

"Stay away, monster."

"That's. My. Son." Astrid stepped forward with each clipped word. Her fingers tingled with magic waiting to be released.

The gun wavered in the woman's hand, but she didn't lower her aim.

Arthur waved his chubby hands. "Mama!"

In the split second her son's captor glanced down, it was enough time for Astrid to lunge forward and snatch the gun. Their fight for control of the firearm lasted mere seconds. One press from Astrid's thumb broke a bone in the human's wrist.

She didn't resist after that and surrendered the children without further struggle.

Astrid took both kids into her arms and held them close. Arthur snuggled his face into her throat and her heart swelled, threatening to burst from her chest. Aslaug whimpered and grasped at Astrid's chest.

"I'll get you back to your mommy, sweet girl, just you wait."

Although the worst was behind them, their ordeal was far from over. As sirens wailed in the distance, Astrid wondered what the hell she was going to tell the police. What guaranteed they would take her side over the humans?

Chapter 22

Tartarus, the most distant of the nine realms, had never interested Loki in all his many years of traveling across the planes. What point was there in visiting the scalding landscape when it was a dead world composed of molten rock and ash? He had never guessed at its true purpose, that it truly was the prison from legend.

Smoke and dust swirled around them on a hot wind. Selene's fingers tightened around his, and a tremor ran through her, fear tingling across their link.

"I hear them," she whispered. "They're louder now, shouting in my head."

"Then you must block them out." He turned to face her and set his free hand against her cheek. "Picture a wall in your mind. A wall constructed of your own thoughts, each brick a memory held close to you."

Selene closed her eyes, breathing in and out in a slow, measured pattern Loki had her do many times whenever she needed to focus. Little by little, her pinched features relaxed, the line creasing her brow smoothing out. "Do you think she—"

"Astrid will recover the children, but we must do our part to keep the slayers away from her. If they return to the other realm…"

He had no doubt in his mind they were capable of slaying Astrid, though she had her sword and would be an even match for one of them. Not two.

Damn. He should have called Max or Ēostre, and his niece had been so filled with righteous vengeance, he doubted she'd given it any thought before rushing into battle.

Selene gazed into the distance and tightened her grip on his hand. "We won't let them return for her. I'm ready."

A subtle sheen encompassed her, a pearlescent glow like soft moonlight. When Selene opened her eyes, Loki's breath caught in his throat. The gray eyes he had come to love shone like liquid silver.

"This way," she said. "It isn't far."

She led the way, keeping her hand in his. They strode through a bleak and dreary landscape, maneuvering around charred boulders and towering obsidian pillars. The ground sloped downward, rough pumice stones clattering beneath their feet.

"What's that?" Selene whispered.

A dark shape hovered in the hazy air ahead. Loki drew Selene behind him and took over the lead. He hadn't seen any sign of Bedivere or Pelleas, and that very lack of presence set him on edge. Were they even here?

Selene gasped, drawing his attention back to their surroundings, and the dark shape they had been approaching became clear.

Nathaniel floated within a necrotic sphere above a black pool. Two tethers composed of swirling energy fed from the mystical prison, each leading deeper into the gloom, down into the fiery depths below.

"I should have known he didn't have the stomach to kill you."

Loki spun around and tucked Selene behind him. Bedivere stood only a few yards away, clad in his armor. While it had once been silver and gold, the spiritual platemail had taken on a black, oily sheen.

"I am here for the children, Bedivere. Give them to me now, and you can walk away with your life."

Bedivere's cold, rumbling laugh raised the hairs on Loki's arms. Selene's hold on his hand tightened.

"Did you hear that, Pelleas? The wyrm is trying to grant us mercy."

The second knight appeared over the low ridge behind them. Loki swiveled around and swore under his breath. They'd come at him from different sides, maintaining distance that wouldn't allow for him to battle them both at once, not if he wanted to keep Selene out of harm's way.

"Selene, run back for the portal."

"No, I'm not going to leave you."

He wanted to argue with her, to put his foot down and order her away, but one look into her determined eyes and glimpse at her feelings through their bond told him everything he needed to know. Selene would do whatever it took to save their daughter, exactly as he would. Rather than insist again that she leave, he nodded, squeezed her hand, then released her.

"Then trust your magic, *skatten min*, and let it guide you. I didn't come this far to lose you."

He moved away and transformed in a single step, taking on his draconic form. Bright green flames jetted from his toothsome maw, burning bright in the stygian gloom. Everything the liquid fire touched ignited, the caustic fluid clinging to the rocks and Bedivere's shield. The blackened vines covering the Celestial steel shrank away from the flames.

Bedivere rushed at him in a fury with his shield raised. His broadsword sliced through the air and drew sparks across Loki's scales. He leapt back and exhaled an acidic fog at the knight, but

Bedivere sank into the dirt and vanished, only to burst out several feet to the side and lunge forward again.

Dammit! He'd forgotten about the jewel Bedivere had used to escape during the last encounter between the knights and the dragons, a remnant of Gaia with the power to move through the earth. It didn't matter the plane, dirt was dirt.

Loki spun about and swung his tail at the knight, while also trying to get a look at Selene. She and Pelleas circled one another, the knight armed with his massive warhammer and Selene alight with magic. It swirled around her, vivid and bright.

Pelleas swung his mighty weapon at her head, and in that moment, Loki's heart stopped. His breath caught in his chest, and he saw his whole world begin to crumble away. Selene was far away, too far for him to leap in and save her.

Time sped up again, and before the warhammer could connect, Selene tore the weapon from Pelleas's hands in an awe-inspiring feat of strength. She grew in size, doubling in height, a giantess towering above her opponent. Before she could bring the hammer down on the knight, it vanished into a cloud of celestial matter and reappeared in his grip. She ducked aside and Loki lost track of her, having to avoid his own opponent.

Selene would be fine, he told himself. She had to be. He had to trust her and fight his own battle.

Bedivere continued his cat and mouse game, taking to the volcanic soil each time Loki struck out with fire or acid.

"Are you a coward or a knight?" Loki roared. "Face me!"

Bedivere popped up from the earth and jammed his sword into Loki's hindquarter. Pain exploded through the limb and blood flowed freely from the deep puncture, but Loki pushed through the agony and struck out with an ebony claw. He cleaved the shield in two and exhaled another chartreuse inferno. Then he struck with all his fury, slashing with his claws and gnashing with his teeth, always close but never striking, forcing Bedivere backward on the defensive until he had the knight exactly where he wanted him.

He exhaled a caustic fog, filling the air with the noxious green fumes. Bedivere charged through the cloud. His blade cleaved through the air, and in a stroke of luck, met Loki's chest. Effortless as gliding through softened butter, it penetrated his ebony scales and bit into the muscle beneath. As the trickster roared and collapsed to the ground, his blood spilled against the heat-blasted rocks.

Bedivere stalked forward with a triumphant, manic gleam in his eyes.

"The great Loki, brought down at last. Your death will honor my masters and raise me up in their eyes. I will live fore—"

The knight choked on his words. Blood bubbled from his mouth, and his eyes flew open wide. He stared down at the claw embedded in his chest and coughed another spray of his life fluid. The illusion of Loki vanished and left only the true dragon behind him.

"Did you forget I am the god of mischief?"

"Im...possible..." The tainted slayer's final breaths rattled in his chest and the light dimmed from his eyes. His lax body slid from Loki's polished talon and crumpled onto the ground.

Loki flicked the knight's blood from his claws then wiped the remaining digits on the ground.

Selene.

One powerful wing beat brought him into the air. He swung his frantic gaze around until he found his mate. She stood out, bright as a star—more brilliant than the sun—with Pelleas's broken body at her feet. The bulk of the knight's armor had been blasted away, only charred remnants remaining.

"How dare you take my daughter?" The words escaped in a roar, and Selene's voice rang with power equal to the dragons.

An azure and silver halo blazed around her fist, growing with intensity as it drove down into Pelleas's chest. The force of the strike buried him into the ground, where he remained.

"Selene!"

She didn't stop. Her next blow crushed Pelleas's armor. The third reduced it to dull fragments of crumbling metal. The next pulverized him until nothing recognizable remained.

Loki soared to her side and took ahold of Selene's wrist with his claws, avoiding her flesh with the tips of each talon. At her current height, he had no need to bend his serpentine neck to press their cheeks together and hold her close.

Selene must have been at least thirty feet tall.

"It's over," he told her. "They're defeated."

A roar echoed from the deep chasms and rocked the ground beneath their feet. The magic holding Nate in suspension flickered and sparked as the tendrils linking Bedivere and Pelleas to the dark spell were broken.

Loki lunged for the knight and caught Nate inches from falling to his doom in the acid below. He moved him a safe distance away and laid him down on the stone ground.

Selene knelt beside them, silver eyes ablaze with worry. "What did they do to him?"

"This magic is beyond the scope of my ability, Selene." Loki returned to his human shape and ran his hands over Nate's supine body. "He's uninjured, but the titans were draining him, feeding off his spiritual life force. I suspect the same is what happened to Kay, Pelleas, and Bedivere."

"Can you help him?"

"No, but I think you can. This is their brand of magic, Selene. *Your* magic."

Selene shrank down to her normal size, but the silver luminescence radiating from within her remained. "I don't know what to do."

"Do exactly as you did before. Trust your magic and yourself. Surrender to intuition and allow it to guide you. Look for anything linked to him or his soul and break it."

Starting at his feet and working her way up, Selene held her hands a few inches above Nate's body and swept them upward. Her examination stopped over his heart and her hands wrapped around something Loki couldn't see. She pulled, and Nate's body arched upward, a groan leaving his lips.

"I can't. It's hurting him," she said.

"It will hurt him more to remain. You can do it."

Selene strained, pulling on the magical tether binding Nate to the titans. The knight spasmed and jerked beneath her grasping hands. Loki strained to see what she did, catching glimpses of pulsating threads in crimson and black in a tangled knot.

The moment the bond snapped, the parasitic leads recoiled into the darkness and Nate's features went slack. He relaxed and lay sprawled across the uneven, heat-blasted terrain.

"Did I kill him?" Selene whispered.

Loki leaned closer. As he did, Nate's lashes fluttered, and he gazed up at them with unfocused eyes.

"You better not be about to kiss me," he uttered in a raspy, dry voice.

"And risk Astrid skinning my hide? Never." Loki offered him a hand up from the ground then steadied the knight when he stumbled.

"My head is killing me more than it did after that dude cracked it open. Shit."

A low rumble shook the ground. Selene drifted away toward the nearest chasm. Kneeling at the edge, she leaned forward to gaze into the abyss below the cliff. "They're down there. In the pits."

"And they're awake and angry. This won't hold them forever. According to Zeus's tale, Theia and the other titans fighting on our side helped to put their brethren under a magical sleep. Without them, we can't do it again."

"Can't you do it?" Selene asked.

"I'm touched that you have so much faith in me, *skatten min*, but ensorcelling titans lies beyond my ability. Perhaps even yours."

"What do we do?"

"For now? Nothing. We leave this place and seal it behind us, and we hope it buys us time."

Another enraged bellow made the ground tremble and the stone at the chasm edge crumble. Loki grasped Selene and pulled her back.

"Take Nathaniel through the same portal we arrived in. Call the others and assist Astrid."

"What are you going to do?"

"These portals must be closed simultaneously, and to do that, I must remain here to unravel the magic."

"Then how will you come home?"

Loki gazed at the pair of twin portals projecting from two different slayer lairs. "I'll find another way. Zeus once spoke of many different pathways and hidden loopholes between the nine worlds."

Nate gazed at the edge of the chasm. The ground trembled and an ear-splitting wail arose from edge of the abyss. "Dude, that's crazy. You don't even know if you'll find one. What if *they* come after you before you can get away."

"They will not, because *I* will close them."

Zeus's unexpected arrival made Loki spin about on his heels. The ancient wyrm towered over them, his silver scales dulled in the muted red light. Beneath them, the ancient titans stirred. Their jailer's presence whipped them into a frenzy. Lava spewed up in a geyser from the nearest gorge and the wind quickened, howling across the blasted mountainside. Loki flinched from the heat.

"Go, you don't have much time," Zeus told them.

"But you'll be trapped here."

"Better an old, selfish man than one with a family. Now go."

Zeus batted him aside.

Selene ran up to his side and tugged on his arm. "Loki, please, we have to get our daughter."

The thought of Aslaug stirred him into action. Loki shifted to his dragon shape, grabbed Selene and Nate, and took to the air without any further prompting. He touched down at the portal, shifted again, and rushed them through.

He didn't glance back.

***

The portal shut behind them with a snap, leaving them in the silence of the cellar. Loki stared at the space where the rift had been, struggling to accept the sacrifice that had been made. For him. For his family. For everyone.

"Arthur," Nate said. "Where's Arthur and Aslaug?"

"Astrid went after them."

"Then we have to help her."

With the information he'd gleaned from the anti-dragon bigots, Loki retraced Astrid's steps and opened a new portal. They arrived on a suburban street corner in Chicago amidst a flurry of activity. Several police cruisers and two firetrucks flashed their lights in front of a house across the street. Dozens of humans stood on their lawns and porches, watching the spectacle as it occurred.

Part of the house had been decimated, the side gaping open to reveal a blackened, water-logged interior. EMS sirens screamed, and the ambulance roared down the road at top speed.

"Nate!" Astrid called from the back seat of a cruiser where she sat with the door open and both children in her arms.

Selene cried out and made a mad dash toward the car. An officer moved to intercept her, but she blew past him. He tumbled aside like a weightless leaf the moment her shoulder struck him.

"That's our daughter," Loki told the man, quick on his mate's heels.

Astrid held out Aslaug and Selene cradled her daughter in her arms, stepping back from the car to allow Nate past. Tears streamed down her cheeks, but her smile was brilliant to behold, her eyes bright with joy and life. Loki moved in beside her and wrapped both of his girls in his arms.

"Hey buddy. Didn't I tell you I'd get you soon?" Nate knelt down next to the cruiser door and hugged his mate and son. "What happened? Are you under arrest? Are you all right?"

"I'm okay. They haven't arrested me. They tried to take me to the hospital, but I just wanted to wait here for you guys."

Nate gazed at the two-story home and furrowed his brows. "I know this house. What the hell? I donated it to a family in need last year."

"What?" Loki looked over.

"You did," Astrid said. "I recognized the couple. The husband is a cop. An armless cop, now."

Loki's esteem for Astrid went up another notch. He'd always known her to be fierce. He admired her restraint in what had likely been a heated situation. If it had been him, he didn't know if he would have stopped with an arm.

His mind wandered to the warehouse, and he decided his niece had the restraint he lacked.

"But they aren't arresting you?" Nate asked again, his worry hanging heavy in his voice.

"No. No. The other officers here have been great. They recognized me right away from the interview we gave after the kids were taken. And… they knew this cop was an asshole about paranormal types. Then his wife confessed to everything before they took her away."

Wary of leaving the other adults to worry and continue a fruitless search for the children, Astrid sent a text to her mother, notifying them that both kids had been found. And then she promptly ignored all following texts demanding to know where they were and what had happened, promising they'd return to Drakenstone Manor soon with the full story.

"It's already a circus without adding a half dozen dragons and a wizard to the scene," Loki muttered under his breath. "Let me assuage their worries while you speak with the police."

While Loki took over communications with the family, Astrid and Nate gave their statements to the department. Hours later, the station released them despite Astrid's rampage. The only casualty had been a warlock. The officer was mauled but alive, and for once, no one had to convince Astrid to use her ties to the former President of the United States.

Hours later, the police released the happy quartet of parents and their young. After all, they'd be easy to find, and the arrival of Loki's lawyer knitted up any further complications.

Nate glanced at his watch and scowled. "Man, it's time to get everyone home. The others must be going crazy by now."

When Loki opened a portal to Drakenstone Manor, Saul's startled voice spilled through the arcane window. "Loki is returning at last. Perhaps he can explain why no one will answer their damned phone. They tell us they've found the cubs then not another word." He growled.

"Prepare yourselves," Loki muttered, gesturing Astrid and Selene through first.

"Oh my God, Astrid! The babies! You really found the babies!" Chloe dashed across the room to greet them. "We've been waiting forever to know what's going on. Tell us everything."

"It's a long story, but the short and quick of it is Loki and Selene went into Tartarus to kill the slayers, then Great-grandpa Zeus sealed it up behind them while I rescued the cubs."

For a moment, there was complete silence. Everyone stared, wearing matching expressions of shock and awe. Then a thousand questions spilled from the other dragons, a combination of outraged criticism and shock interspersed with the occasional impressed remark.

"You went into Tartarus without us?"

"You fought the slayers alone?"

"Zeus showed up?"

Loki held up his hands and waited until the din died down enough for him to speak.

"What matters is it's over. There was no time to rally the forces and gather you all while the children were in danger. We had Pelleas and Bedivere where we wanted them. They're dead, but now there's a greater danger. The titans are free from their prisons in Tartarus, and it's only a matter of time before they find their way back to this world."

"And Zeus?" Ēostre asked.

"Your father closed the portals himself," Loki replied.

"Zeus helped you?" Ēostre's fair brows rose.

"Indeed he did, much to my surprise," Loki replied.

Max curved his arm around his wife and hugged her close. "Then we will certainly hear from him again when he is ready. What matters now is the children are safe and you are all home in one piece."

A flash of radiant silver light forced Loki backward a step. With the baby cradled to her breasts, Selene placed her back to the threat and Astrid mimicked her, both women tensed to run.

Loki growled low and crouched on the defensive; then the light waned and understanding dawned over him.

Zeus stood in the center of the room, alive and as haughty as ever even with a bruised cheek and blood staining his disheveled hair. "And the titans, for now at least, are contained in Tartarus," his voice boomed across the living room.

Saul's eyes widened as large as saucers. "Grandfather?"

"Is this what you've taught the boy, Ēostre? To gawk at his elders? Offer me a drink and prepare to celebrate. We have won a victory today."

Max recovered first and shook out of his stunned stupor. He moved to the sideboard then poured a healthy portion of amber liquid from a crystal decanter. Zeus accepted the drink and tossed it back in a single gulp.

As startled to see the ancient dragon as anyone else, Ēostre stepped forward to regard him with a dip of her head and a flawless curtsy. "Father, your arrival is unexpected. What are you—"

"What am I doing here?" Zeus helped himself to the largest chair in the room, settling in it as he would a throne. "Should I have returned to my cave? After these inconsiderate youngsters invaded my territory to lay their disrespectful accusations, I've decided to see the world and explore this age."

"But I thought you were locked behind in Tartarus," Selene said.

"My child, there are ways in and out of Tartarus no one else knows or understands. It was once my hobby to explore the mysteries of the different worlds... alongside your father, Hyperion," he said to Selene.

"My father...?" Selene swayed on her feet, so Loki led her to the couch and helped her get settled with Aslaug at her breast. "You knew him?"

"Quite well," Zeus replied. "Of the titans, he, Theia, and Prometheus were the best of them."

"Where *are* the other titans?" Chloe asked. "The old myths say that you—"

Zeus gave a dismissive wave and frowned. "Mortals and their exaggerations. Prometheus perished long ago during the battle with the titans, and I took his body to the east to be interred in the mountains he loved. Theia left this world altogether, and I assume has never returned."

"Obviously Hyperion is still alive and kicking if he's boning mortal women," Nate commented. Astrid swatted him.

Stern, storm-gray eyes fixed on Nate as Zeus frowned. "As I said, Hyperion is a wanderer of many worlds. There is no way to determine where he is now."

Nate shrank back a step behind his wife.

"What if the titans discover those secret ways and hidden paths out of Tartarus?" Astrid asked. Arthur had fallen asleep, his chubby cheek against her shoulder. She kissed the top of his blond head and closed her eyes.

Zeus shrugged his massive shoulders. "Many of our ancestors"—he swept his hand from Astrid to Selene—"and yours perished during the last Titanomachy. I've only bought you time. The day *will* come when they escape Tartarus, and without Theia or Hyperion to assist you, dragonkind will need a new means of defeating them."

"Why imprison them at all? Why didn't you kill them before, Grandfather?" Saul asked.

"Killing a titan is no easy task. A suggestion to you all—discover first how the slayers breached their prison."

All eyes turned on Nate, who held up his hands. "I'll talk to Percivale, but I don't know anything about that stuff. I can look through Kay's things again, too."

"Then you have a plan. As for me, I have someone to find." Zeus moved away, only to pause and glance at Ēostre. "Not a day has passed without you or your siblings in my dreams, little one. I have always cared, and I am proud of the dragoness you have become, as well as the mate you've chosen."

He opened a gleaming portal and stepped through into a lush, emerald forest inhabited by a pair of green peafowl. The rift sealed behind him seconds later.

Chloe glanced out over the group. "I don't know about the rest of you, but I'm ready for some wine."

Saul grunted and left the couch. "I'll open a keg."

Max poured another tall glass from the decanter. "Any for you, cousin?"

"No." Loki smiled as he passed on the offer. He held Selene tighter and touched his cheek against the top of her head. Aslaug gurgled and made a gentle coo. "Not this time, Max."

Perhaps there was a time when Loki would have sought solace in alcohol, but the only comfort he required now was his family.

Epilogue

Loki relaxed against the grass while admiring the butterfly flitting across his daughter's bare toes. Aslaug giggled and reached for the delicate creature. Unlike the other dragon-hybrids, she appeared to develop faster than the typical human, and he wasn't sure whether he liked it or not. A month ago, she'd been tiny and helpless, and now she was practically sitting unassisted by her mother.

His mother-in-law had told him Selene took her first steps at seven months and met all her milestones months ahead of other children.

"Oh no, little one. Gentle," he coached her. "The butterflies are the spirits of our ancestors, and deserve our respect."

Colorful flowers in starter pots sat around them in a wild disarray, part of Selene's pet project to add more color to his manicured gardens. He'd offered to lend his magic, but she'd shaken her head and kissed him before declaring a desire to do it on her own.

"I'm glad to see your happiness at last," Ēostre said. She lounged in a nearby chair with an ice cold glass of lemonade in hand. "The Loki I knew would never walk around his yard barefoot, let alone sit on the grass in jeans."

He chuckled and ducked his head, considering her words. They were true enough, and he felt the changes were for the better. He had come to learn he could be both Loki the powerful business man, as well as a casual and fun father.

"Any word from your father?"

"Not yet, nor do I expect it. He'll do what he does, when he desires. He was gone before I had the chance to see where he'd spirited himself away to visit next. Do you have any clue?"

"Well…"

Ēostre's gaze narrowed. "What? What aren't you telling me?"

Shit. He'd forgotten Ēostre protected her mother as fiercely as she protected her son and the rest of the family. When he grimaced, Selene gazed up at him in concern, her brows wrinkling and knitting close. He kissed her temple and rose. "I'll be right back."

"Loki," Ēostre said in warning when he guided her away from the picnic.

"It's not as bad as you think. I believe he is seeking Hera, is all."

"Good luck to him with that," she said, scoffing. "Her hoard is better hidden than his."

Loki squirmed. "True. Unless he knows exactly where to look."

Startled, Ēostre stiffened and stared at him. "You told him where to find my mother's hoard? How could you? She trusted so few of us."

Loki raised both hands to ward her off. "Shhh."

"Don't you dare shush me, trickster. Whenever I begin to think highly of you, you do some foolish, absolutely selfish thing to—"

"Your mother isn't there."

"What? That's ridiculous. I checked on her twenty years ago. She was asleep."

"I went to visit Hera for advice some years ago, during…" He hesitated to continue, ashamed of what he'd done to Maximilian years ago in his petty vendetta. "I found her awakened, drowsy but awakened, and we talked for some time. She wanted to see the new world."

Understanding slowly dawned, and Ēostre's lips parted in surprise. "That ridiculous scheme of yours. It has my mother's handiwork all over it."

"No one surpasses Hera when it comes to vengeance and petty acts of jealousy," he admitted. "But no, I came up with it on my own and asked her if I should proceed with my plan. She gave me a few suggestions and sound advice, most of which I ignored to behave like a child. Honestly, when I first sought Mahuika, I wasn't convinced I would find her alive."

"And yet you worked alongside her."

"Wait. Hear me out, Eostre. I wanted to cause trouble, but I had nothing to do with her resurrecting your deceased mate with dark magic. When I discovered she'd overstepped our plan, I sent clues to Watatsumi."

"Ah. Now it all makes sense. All this time, we wondered who had warned us. Max will never forgive you if he finds out the part you played in that awful affair," she warned.

"Which is why I haven't said anything." He paused. "Yet. I will speak to him about it one day and apologize. It's… I've been ashamed. I know it was wrong. That involving Mahuika in your lives was an unforgivable transgression, but the truth is… I'm also afraid no amount of apology will mend our friendship."

Ēostre reached across the distance and squeezed his shoulder. "Then perhaps he will forgive you after all, though I suspect a large quantity of alcohol and gifts will be required."

Loki grinned. "Anyway, I wouldn't risk crossing your mother. Zeus perhaps, but not her, for the aforementioned reasons."

"I'm certain he's infuriated by her absence, and I'm surprised he hasn't come back to rage at you."

"He has no reason to. I lived up to my part of the bargain and supplied him the location of her hoard."

Chuckling, Ēostre rose and called forth a glimmering silver portal. "I should go home. Max and I have plans to take the twins climbing in the mountains. Enjoy the rest of the day with your family. For what it's worth, I'm proud of you. You deserve this happiness." She waved to Selene from across the distance.

Tears misted his eyes and Ēostre left before he could find his voice to thank her. Once he suppressed the emotion again, he rejoined his family. Aslaug cooed and waved her fists at him.

"Everything all right?" Selene asked.

"Everything is perfect," he replied.

Taking a seat beside his mate, he curved one arm around her waist and tickled his daughter's toes with his other hand. Ēostre had tried to regrow his finger with little success, but he had no regrets. With two arms to hold Selene and Aslaug, Loki the Trickster had everything he needed in the end.

A commotion from the house shattered the peaceful moment. He twisted at the waist to see what the fuss was about and froze. He blinked, certain he had to be seeing things.

His mother, a dragoness he hadn't seen in centuries, came through the double doors leading from his den. She hadn't changed, not that he'd expected her to—raven hair worn dark and long to her waist contrasting her fair skin. Loki had inherited his tanned skin from his father, Aries.

"Loki, who's that?" Selene asked. She drew Aslaug into her lap.

"My… mother?"

"Hello, my dear." Hel beamed at him from the double doors and descended the steps without a hitch to her stride despite her razor-thin stiletto heels. As always, when she chose to appear on the mortal plane, she wore the latest fashions.

The last time he had seen her it had been boned corsets and hoop skirts, though she had passed on the powdered wigs.

Loki stumbled to his feet and stepped forward across the lawn. "What are you doing here?"

A jubilant smile spread across her ruby lips. "Why, I've come to live with you of course."

Stunned, Loki glanced over his shoulder to his mate. If his mother's words unsettled her, she hid it behind a gracious mask. As flawless as ever, Selene rose and placed their baby on her hip. "Well… welcome to our home."

If learning to live with a dragon had been Selene's initiation to the supernatural world, handling his mother would be the final exam.

And somewhere out there, Loki had the feeling Zeus had gotten the last laugh by sending Hel to live with them.

About the Author

Vivienne Savage is a resident of a small town in rural Texas. While she isn't concocting sexy ways for shapeshifters and humans to find their match, she raises two children and works as a nurse in a rural retirement home.

29895051R00178

Printed in Great Britain
by Amazon